JOY WILLIAMS'
TAKING CARE

"Joy Williams is a writer no one should neglect. Her exactness of vision, unexpected nuances, and a prose both careful and serene combine with subject matter at once elliptical and disturbing."
— THE WASHINGTON POST

"*Taking Care* should be widely read... an elegant reverie from a writer of compassion and intelligence."
— THE BOSTON GLOBE

"Joy Williams is without question one of the masters of the contemporary short story."
— GEORGE PLIMPTON

"The world according to Williams is a world unlike any other in contemporary short fiction. *Taking Care* is a stunning collection of stories, and Joy Williams is simply a wonder."
— RAYMOND CARVER

"Precisely wrought fictions of contemporary, middle-class life. Williams is a writer with many more stories to tell."
— THE BALTIMORE SUN

Taking Care

TAKING CARE

SHORT STORIES by
Joy Williams

VINTAGE CONTEMPORARIES

VINTAGE BOOKS · A DIVISION OF RANDOM HOUSE · NEW YORK

Published in the United States by
Random House, Inc., New York, and
simultaneously in Canada by Random House
of Canada Limited, Toronto.
Originally published by Random House, Inc., in 1982.
"The Farm" was first published in *Antaeus*.
"Summer" was first published in *The New Yorker*.
"The Excursion" originally appeared in *Partisan Review*,
Vol. 43, no. 2, 1976.
Other stories in this work, some in different form,
have been previously published in *Audience*, the *Carolina
Quarterly, Esquire, Ms., Northern Ohio Live*,
the *Paris Review*, and *Viva*.
Library of Congress Cataloging in Publication Data
Williams, Joy.
Taking care.
(Vintage contemporaries)
I. Title.
[PS3573.I4496T3 1985]   813'.54   85-40150
ISBN 978-0-394-72912-1

146122990

For Caitlin and Rust

Contents

The Lover

*T*HE girl is twenty-five. It has not been very long since her divorce but she cannot remember the man who used to be her husband. He was probably nice. She will tell the child this, at any rate. Once he lost a fifty-dollar pair of sunglasses while surf casting off Gay Head and felt badly about it for days. He did like kidneys, that was one thing. He loved kidneys for weekend lunch. She would voyage through the supermarkets, her stomach sweetly sloped, her hair in a twist, searching for fresh kidneys for this young man, her husband. When he kissed her, his kisses, or so she imagined, would have the faint odor of urine. Understandably, she did not want to think about this. It hardly seemed that the same problem would arise again, that is, with another man. Nothing could possibly be gained from such an experience! The child cannot remember him, this man, this daddy, and she cannot remember him. He had been with her when she gave birth to the child. Not beside her, but close by, in the corridor. He had left his work and come to the hospital. As they wheeled her by, he said, "Now you are going to have to learn how to love something, you wicked woman." It is difficult for her to believe he said such a thing.

The girl does not sleep well and recently has acquired the habit of listening all night to the radio. It is an old, not very good radio and at night she can only get one station. From midnight until four she listens to *Action Line.* People call the station and make comments on the world and their community and they ask questions. Music is played and a brand of beef and beans is advertised. A woman calls up and says, "Could you tell me why the filling in my lemon meringue pie is runny?" These people have obscene materials in their mailboxes. They want to know where they can purchase small flags suitable for waving on Armed Forces Day. There is a man on the air who answers these questions right away. Another woman calls. She says, "Can you get us a report on the progress of the collection of Betty Crocker coupons for the lung machine?" The man can and does. He answers the woman's question. Astonishingly, he complies with her request. The girl thinks such a talent is bleak and wonderful. She thinks this man can help her.

The girl wants to be in love. Her face is thin with the thinness of a failed lover. It is so difficult! Love is concentration, she feels, but she can remember nothing. She tries to recollect two things a day. In the morning with her coffee, she tries to remember and in the evening, with her first bourbon and water, she tries to remember as well. She has been trying to remember the birth of her child now for several days. Nothing returns to her. Life is so intrusive! Everyone was talking. There was too much conversation! The doctor was above her, waiting for the pains. "No, I still can't play tennis," the doctor said. "I haven't been able to play for two months. I have spurs on both heels and it's just about wrecked our marriage. Air conditioning and concrete floors is what does it. Murder on your feet." A few minutes later, the nurse had said, "Isn't it wonderful to work with Teflon? I mean for those arterial repairs? I just love it." The girl wished that they would stop talking. She wished that they would turn the radio on instead and be still. The baby inside her was hard and glossy as an ear of corn. She wanted to say something witty or charming so that they would know she was fine and would stop talking. While she was thinking of something perfectly balanced and amusing to say, the baby was born. They fastened a plastic identification bracelet around her wrist and the baby's wrist. Three days later, after they had come home, her husband sawed off the bracelets with a grapefruit knife. The girl had wanted to make it an occasion. She yelled, "I have a lovely pair of tiny silver scissors that belonged to my grandmother and you have used a grapefruit knife!" Her husband was flushed and nervous but he smiled at her as he always did. "You are insecure," she said tearfully. "You are insecure because you had mumps when you were eight." Their divorce was one year and two months away. "It was not mumps," he said carefully. "Once I broke my arm while swimming is all."

The girl becomes a lover to a man she met at a dinner party. He calls her up in the morning. He drives over to her apartment. He drives a white convertible which is all rusted out along the rocker panels. They do not make convertibles anymore, the girl thinks with alarm. He asks her to go sailing. They drop the child off at a nursery school on the way to the pier. She is two years old now, almost three. Her hair is an odd color, almost grey. It is braided and pinned up under a big hat with mouse ears that she got on a visit to Disney World. She is wearing a striped jersey stuffed into striped shorts. She kisses the girl and she kisses the man and goes into the nursery carrying her lunch in a Wonder bread bag. In the afternoon, when they return, the girl has difficulty recognizing the child. There are so many children, after all, standing in the rooms, all the same size, all small, quizzical creatures, holding pieces of wooden puzzles in their hands.

It is late at night. A cat seems to be murdering a baby bird in a nest somewhere outside the girl's window. The girl is listening to the child sleep. The child lies in her varnished crib, clutching a bear. The bear has no tongue. Where there should be a small piece of red felt there is nothing. Apparently, the child had eaten it by accident. The crib sheet is in a design of tiny yellow circus animals. The girl enjoys looking at her child but cannot stand the sheet. There is so much going on in the crib, so many colors and patterns. It is so busy in there! The girl goes into the kitchen. On the counter, four palmetto bugs are exploring a pan of coffee cake. The girl goes back to her own bedroom and turns on the radio. There is a great deal of static. The Answer Man on *Action Line* sounds very annoyed.

An old gentleman is asking something but the transmission is terrible because the old man refuses to turn off his rock tumbler. He is polishing stones in his rock tumbler like all old men do and he refuses to turn it off while speaking. Finally, the Answer Man hangs up on him. "Good for you," the girl says. The Answer Man clears his throat and says in a singsong way, "The wine of this world has caused only satiety. Our homes suffer from female sadness, embarrassment and confusion. Absence, sterility, mourning, privation and separation abound throughout the land." The girl puts her arms around her knees and begins to rock back and forth on the bed. The child murmurs in sleep. More palmetto bugs skate across the Formica and into the cake. The girl can hear them. A woman's voice comes on the radio now. The girl is shocked. It seems to be her mother's voice. The girl leans toward the radio. There is a terrible weight on her chest. She can scarcely breathe. The voice says, "I put a little pan under the air-conditioner outside my window and it catches the condensation from the machine and I use that water to water my ivy. I think anything like that makes one a better person."

The girl has made love to nine men at one time or another. It does not seem like many but at the same time it seems more than necessary. She does not know what to think about them. They were all very nice. She thinks it is wonderful that a woman can make love to a man. When lovemaking, she feels she is behaving reasonably. She is well. The man often shares her bed now. He lies sleeping, on his stomach, his brown arm across her breasts. Sometimes, when the child is restless, the girl brings her into bed with them. The man shifts position, turns on his back. The child lies between them. The three lie, silent and rigid, earnestly conscious. On the radio, the Answer Man is conducting a quiz. He says, "The answer is: the time taken for the fall of the dashpot to clear the piston is four seconds, and what is the question? The answer is: when the end of the pin is five sixteenths of an inch below the face of the block, and what is the question?"

She and the man travel all over the South in his white

convertible. The girl brings dolls and sandals and sugar animals
back to the child. Sometimes the child travels with them. She
sits beside them, pretending to do something gruesome to her
eyes. She pretends to dig out her eyes. The girl ignores this.
The child is tanned and sturdy and affectionate although sometimes, when she is being kissed, she goes limp and even cold,
as though she has suddenly, foolishly died. In the restaurants
they stop at, the child is well-behaved although she takes only
butter and ice water. The girl and the man order carefully but
do not eat much either. They move the food around on their
plates. They take a bite now and then. In less than a month
the man has spent many hundreds of dollars on food that they
do not eat. *Action Line* says that an adult female consumes
seven hundred pounds of dry food in a single year. The girl
believes this of course but it has nothing to do with her.
Sometimes, she greedily shares a bag of Fig Newtons with the
child but she seldom eats with the man. Her stomach is hard,
flat, empty. She feels hungry always, dangerous to herself, and
in love. They leave large tips on the tables of restaurants and
then they reenter the car. The seats are hot from the sun. The
child sits on the girl's lap while they travel, while the leather
cools. She seems to want nothing. She makes clucking, sympathetic sounds when she sees animals smashed flat on the side
of the road. When the child is not with them, they travel with
the man's friends.

The man has many friends whom he is devoted to. They are
clever and well-off; good-natured, generous people, confident
in their prolonged affairs. They have known each other for
years. This is discomforting to the girl, who has known no one
for years. The girl fears that each has loved the other at one
time or another. These relationships are so complex, the girl
cannot understand them! There is such flux, such constancy
among them. They are so intimate and so calm. She tries to
imagine their embraces. She feels that theirs differ from her
own. One afternoon, just before dusk, the girl and man drive
a short way into the Everglades. It is very dull. There is no
scenery, no prospect. It is not a swamp at all. It is a river, only

inches deep! Another couple rides in the back of the car. They
have very dark tans and have pale yellow hair. They look almost
like brother and sister. He is a lawyer and she is a lawyer. They
are drinking gin and tonics, as are the girl and the man. The
girl has not met these people before. The woman leans over the
back seat and drops another ice cube from the cooler into the
girl's drink. She says, "I hear that you have a little daughter."
The girl nods. She feels funny, a little frightened. "The child
is very *sortable,*" the girl's lover says. He is driving the big car
very fast and well but there seems to be a knocking in the
engine. He wears a long-sleeved shirt buttoned at the wrists.
His thick hair needs cutting. The girl loves to look at him. They
drive, and on either side of them, across the slim canals or over
the damp saw grass, speed airboats. The sound of them is
deafening. The tourists aboard wear huge earmuffs. The man
turns his head toward her for a moment. "I love you," she says.
"Ditto," he says loudly, above the clatter of the airboats. "Dou-
ble-ditto." He grins at her and she begins to giggle. Then she
sobs. She has not cried for many months. Everyone is as-
tounded. The man drives a few more miles and then pulls into
a gas station. The girl feels desperate about this man. She
would do the unspeakable for him, the unforgivable, anything.
She is lost but not in him. She wants herself lost and never
found, in him. "I'll do anything for you," she cries. "Take an
aspirin," he says. "Put your head on my shoulder."

The girl is sleeping alone in her apartment. The man has
gone on a business trip. He assures her he will come back. He'll
always come back, he says. When the girl is alone she measures
her drink out carefully. Carefully, she drinks twelve ounces of
bourbon in two and a half hours. When she is not with the
man, she resumes her habit of listening to the radio. Frequently, she hears only the replies of *Action Line.* "Yes," the
Answer Man says, "in answer to your question, the difference
between rising every morning at six or at eight in the course
of forty years amounts to twenty-nine thousand two hundred
hours or three years, two hundred twenty-one days and sixteen
hours, which are equal to eight hours a day for ten years. So

that rising at six will be the equivalent of adding ten years to your life." The girl feels, by the Answer Man's tone, that he is a little repulsed by this. She washes her whiskey glass out in the sink. Balloons are drifting around the kitchen. They float out of the kitchen and drift onto the balcony. They float down the hall and bump against the closed door of the child's room. Some of the balloons don't float but slump in the corners of the kitchen like mounds of jelly. These are filled with water. The girl buys many balloons and is always blowing them up for the child. They play a great deal with the balloons; breaking them over the stove or smashing the water-filled ones against the walls of the bathroom. The girl turns off the radio and falls asleep.

The girl touches her lover's face. She runs her fingers across the bones. "Of course I love you," he says. "I want us to have a life together." She is so restless. She moves her hand across his mouth. There is something she doesn't understand, something she doesn't know how to do. She makes them a drink. She asks for a piece of gum. He hands her a small crumpled stick, still in the wrapper. She is sure that it is not the real thing. The Answer Man has said that Lewis Carroll once invented a substitute for gum. She fears that this is that. She doesn't want this! She swallows it without chewing. "Please," she says. "Please what?" the man replies, a bit impatiently.

Her former husband calls her up. It is autumn and the heat is unusually oppressive. He wants to see the child. He wants to take her away for a week to his lakeside house in the middle of the state. The girl agrees to this. He arrives at the apartment and picks up the child and nuzzles her. He is a little heavier than before. He makes a little more money. He has a different watch, wallet and key ring. "What are you doing these days?" the child's father asks. "I am in love," she says.

The man does not visit the girl for a week. She doesn't leave the apartment. She loses four pounds. She and the child make Jell-O and they eat it for days. The girl remembers that after the baby was born, the only food the hospital gave her was Jell-O. She thinks of all the water boiling in hospitals everywhere for new mothers' Jell-O. The girl sits on the floor and plays endlessly with the child. The child is bored. She dresses and undresses herself. She goes through everything in her small bureau drawer and tries everything on. The girl notices a birthmark on the child's thigh. It is very small and lovely, in the shape, the girl thinks, of a wineglass. A doll's wineglass. The girl thinks about the man constantly but without much exactitude. She does not even have a photograph of him! She looks through old magazines. He must resemble someone! Sometimes, late at night, when she thinks he might come to her, she feels that the Answer Man arrives instead. He is like a moving light, never still. He has the high temperature and metabolism of a bird. On *Action Line,* someone is saying, "And I live by the airport, what is this that hits my house, that showers my roof on takeoff? We can hear it. What is this, I demand to know! My lawn is healthy, my television reception is fine but something is going on without my consent and I am not well, my wife's had a stroke and someone stole my stamp collection and took the orchids off my trees." The girl sips her bourbon and shakes her head. The greediness and wickedness of people, she thinks, their rudeness and lust. "Well," the Answer Man says, "each piece of earth is bad for something. Something is going to get it on it and the land itself is no longer safe. It's weakening. If you dig deep enough to dip your seed, beneath the crust you'll find an emptiness like the sky. No, nothing's compatible to living in the long run. Next caller, please." The girl goes to the telephone and dials hurriedly. It is very late. She whispers, not wanting to wake the child. There is static and humming. "I can't make you out," the Answer Man shouts. The girl says more firmly, "I want to know my hour." "Your hour came, dear," he says. "It went when you were sleeping. It came and saw you dreaming and it went back to where it was."

The girl's lover comes to the apartment. She throws herself into his arms. He looks wonderful. She would do anything for him! The child grabs the pocket of his jacket and swings on it with her full weight. "My friend," the child says to him. "Why yes," the man says with surprise. They drive the child to the nursery and then go out for a wonderful lunch. The girl begins to cry and spills the roll basket on the floor.

"What is it?" he asks. "What's wrong?" He wearies of her, really. Her moods and palpitations. The girl's face is pale. Death is not so far, she thinks. It is easily arrived at. Love is further than death. She kisses him. She cannot stop. She clings to him, trying to kiss him. "Be calm," he says.

The girl no longer sees the man. She doesn't know anything about him. She is a gaunt, passive girl, living alone with her child. "I love you," she says to the child. "Mommy loves me," the child murmurs, "and Daddy loves me and Grandma loves me and Granddaddy loves me and my friend loves me." The girl corrects her, "Mommy loves you," she says. The child is growing. In not too long the child will be grown. When is this happening! She wakes the child in the middle of the night. She gives her a glass of juice and together they listen to the radio. A woman is speaking on the radio. She says, "I hope you will not think me vulgar." "Not at all," the Answer Man replies. "He is never at a loss," the girl whispers to the child. The woman says, "My husband can only become excited if he feels that some part of his body is missing" "Yes," the Answer Man says. The girl shakes the sleepy child. "Listen to this," she says. "I want you to know about these things." The unknown woman's voice continues, dimly. "A finger or an eye or a leg. I have to pretend it's not there."

"Yes," the Answer Man says.

Summer

CONSTANCE and Ben and their daughters by previous marriages, Charlotte and Jill, were sharing a summer house for a month with their friend Steven. There were five weekends that August, and for each one of them Steven invited a different woman up—Patsy, Teddy, Mercedes, Annie and Gloria. The women made a great deal of fuss over Charlotte and Jill, who were both ten. They made the girls nachos and root-beer floats, and bought them latch-hook sets and took them out to the moors to identify flowers. They took them to the cemeteries, from which the children would return with rubbings which Constance found depressing—

> This beautiful bud to us was given
> To unfold here but bloom in heaven

or worse!

> Here lies Aimira Rawson
> Daughter Wife Mother
> She has done what she could

The children affixed the rubbings to the side of the refrigerator with magnets in the shape of broccoli.

The women would arrange the children's hair in various elaborate ways that Constance hated. They knew no taboos;

they discussed everything with the children—love, death, Japa-
nese whaling methods. Each woman had habits and theories
and stories to tell, and each brought a house present and stayed
seventy-two hours. They all spent so much time with the children because they could not spend it with Steven, who appeared after five P.M. only. Steven was writing a book that
summer; he was, in his words, "writing an aesthetically complex response to hermetic currents in modern life." This took
time.

Ben was recovering from a heart attack he had suffered in
the spring. He and Constance had been in a restaurant, arguing, and he had had a heart attack. She remembered the look
of absolute attentiveness that had crossed his face. At the time,
she had thought he was looking at a beautiful woman behind
her and on the other side of the room. The memory, which she
recalled frequently, mortified her. What she couldn't remember was what they had been arguing about.

Ben was thin with dark hair. He was twelve years older than
Constance, yet they looked about the same age. He was the
love of Constance's life, but they quarreled a lot; it was a small
tragedy, really, how much they had quarreled before his heart
attack. Without their arguments they were a little shy with one
another. Things appeared different now to Constance: objects
seemed to have more presence, people seemed more vivid, the
sky seemed brighter. Her nightmares' messages were far less
veiled. Constance was embarrassed at having these feelings, for
it had been Ben's heart attack, after all, not hers. He had always
accused her of taking things too personally.

Constance and Ben had been married for five years. Charlotte was Constance's child from her marriage with David, and
Jill was Ben's from his marriage with Susan. The children
weren't crazy about one another, but they got along. It was all
right, really, with them. Here in the summer house they slept
in the attic; in Constance's opinion, the nicest room in the
house. It had two iron beds, white beaverboard walls and a
small window from which one could see three streets converg-
ing. Sometimes Constance would take a gin and tonic up to the

attic and lie on one of the beds and watch people place their postcards in the mailbox at the intersection. Constance didn't send postcards herself. She really didn't want to get in touch with anybody but Ben, and Ben lived in the same house with her, as he had in whatever house they'd been in ever since they'd gotten married. She couldn't very well send a postcard to Ben.

August was hot and splendid for the most part, but those who stayed for the entire season claimed it was not as nice as July. The gardens were blown. Pedestrians irritably swatted bicyclists who used the sidewalks. There was more weeping in bars, and more jellyfish in the sea.

On the afternoon of the first Friday in August, Constance was in the attic room observing an elderly couple place their postcards in the mailbox with great deliberation. She watched a woman about her own age drop a card in the box and go off with a mean, satisfied look upon her face. She watched an older woman throw in at least a dozen cards with no emotion whatever.

Charlotte came upstairs and told her mother, "A person drowning imagines there's a ladder rising vertically from the water, and he tries to climb that ladder. Did you know that? If he would only imagine that the ladder was horizontal he wouldn't drown."

Charlotte left. Constance sat on a bed and looked around the room. On the bureau mirror were photographs of two little boys, Charlotte's and Jill's boyfriends. Their names were Zack and Pete. They were just little boys but there they were. It worried Constance that the children should already have boyfriends. Another photograph, which Constance had not seen before, showed a large yellow dog grinning in front of a potted evergreen. Constance was not acquainted with either him or his name. She got up and began picking up candy wrappers that were scattered around the room and putting them in her empty glass. She was thirty-three years old. She thought of F. Scott Fitzgerald's line that American lives have no second act.

Constance went downstairs to the kitchen where Patsy was

drinking some champagne she had brought, and waiting for
Steven to appear at five o'clock.

"I just love it here," Patsy said. "I love it, love it, love it."

Her eyes were shining. She was a good sport but she had
rather bad skin. She was a vegetarian; for three days after she
left, the children demanded bean curd. She was Steven's typist
in the city, where she and her epileptic golden retriever Scooter
lived in the same apartment building as Jill's aunt.

"You were in my apartment a long, long time ago," Patsy
told Jill, "when you were a little tiny girl, and you pulled
Scooter's tail and he growled at you and you said, 'Stop that
at once,' and he did."

"I can't remember that," Jill said.

"It's a small world," Patsy said, pouring herself more champagne. She sighed. "Scooter's getting along now."

Charlotte and Jill were sitting on either side of Patsy at the
kitchen table, making lists of the names they wanted to call
their children. Charlotte had Victoria, Grover and Christo-
pher; Jill had Beatrice, Travis and Cone.

"Cone?" Patsy asked. "How can you name a child Cone?"

Constance looked at the ornately lettered names. The future
yawned ahead, filled with individuals, each expecting to be
found.

"Do you swim?" Constance asked Patsy.

"I do," Patsy said solemnly. "I just gave the girls a few
pointers about panic in the water."

"Would you like to go swimming?" Constance asked.

"It's almost five," Patsy said. "Steven will be coming down
any moment."

" 'Cone' is both a nice shape *and* a nice name," Jill said.

"Would you like to go swimming?" Constance asked the
girls.

"No thanks," they said.

Ben came in the kitchen door, chewing gum. Since his heart
attack, he had given up smoking and chewed a great deal of
gum. He was tanned and smiling, but he moved a little oddly,
as though he were carrying something awkward. Constance got
a little rush every time she saw Ben.

"Would you like to go swimming with me?" Constance asked.

"Sure," Ben said.

They drove out to the beach and went swimming. On the bluff above the beach was the white silo of a loran station which sent out signals that enabled navigators to determine their position by time displacement. Constance and Ben swam without touching or talking. Then they went home.

Teddy came the next weekend. Patsy's champagne bottle held a browning mum. Teddy was secretive and feminine. She brought two guests of her own, Fred and Miriam. They all lived on a farm in South Woodstock, Vermont, not far from the huge quartz testicle stones there. "There are megalithic erections all over our farm," Teddy told Constance.

A terrible thing had happened to Fred—his wife had just died. A mole on her waist had turned blue and in six weeks she was dead.

Fred told Constance, "The last words she said to me were, 'Life goes on long enough. Not too long, but long enough.' " Fred's eyes would glass up but he did not cry. He had brought a tape of Blind Willie Johnson singing "Dark Was the Night," which he frequently played.

On Saturday they had a large lunch of several dozen ears of fresh corn and a gallon of white wine. Miriam said to Constance, "It wasn't Rose that died, it was Lu-Ellen. Doesn't Fred just wish it was Rose! Lu-Ellen was just a girl in the office he was crazy for."

Miriam whispered this so Fred would not hear. She had corn kernels in her teeth, but apart from that she was the very picture of an exasperated woman. Was she in love with Fred? Constance wondered. Or Steven? Actually, it was Edward she spoke to constantly on the phone. Miriam would say things to Teddy like, "Edward said he got in touch with Jimmy and everything's all right now."

After lunch, there was a long moment of silence while they all listened to the sound of Steven's typewriter. Steven did not eat lunch; he was bringing together the cosmic and the personal, the poetic and the expository. During working hours, he was fueled by grapefruit juice only.

Teddy had brought four quarts of Vermont raspberries to Constance and Ben. The berries had been bruised a little during their passage across the Sound. She had brought Steven a leather-bound book with thick creamy blank pages upon which to record his thoughts.

"Nothing gets past Steven, not a single thing," Teddy said.

"I've never known a cooler intelligence," Miriam said.

"You know," Fred said, "Vermont really has somewhat of a problem. A lot of things that people think are ancient writings on stones are actually just marks left by plows, or the roots of trees. Some of these marks get translated anyway, even though they're not genuine."

Teddy lowered her eyes and giggled.

Later, Teddy and Miriam and Fred took Charlotte and Jill to the cliff which was considered the highest point on the island, and they all jumped off. This was one of the girls' favorite amusements. They loved jumping off the cliff and springing in long leaps down the rosy sand to the beach below, but they hated the climb back up.

The next day it rained. In the afternoon, the girls went with the houseguests to a movie, and Constance went up to their room. The rain had blown in the open window and an acrostic puzzle was sopping on the sill. Constance shut the window and mopped up. She sat on one of the beds and thought of two pet rabbits Charlotte and Jill had had the summer they were eight. Ben would throw his voice into the rabbits and have them speak of the verities in a pompous and irascible tone. Constance had always thought it hilarious. Then the rabbits had died, and the children hadn't wanted another pair. Constance stared out the window. The rain pounded the dark street silver. There was no one out there.

That night, the house was quiet. Constance lay behind Ben on their bed and nuzzled his hair. "Talk to me," Constance said.

"William Gass said that lovers are alike as light bulbs," Ben said.

"That's just alliteration," Constance said. "Talk to me some more." But Ben didn't say much more.

Mercedes arrived. She had fine features and large, grey eyes, but she looked anxious, and her hair was always damp "from visions and insomnia" she told Constance. She entertained Charlotte and Jill by telling them the entire plot line from *General Hospital.* She read the palms of their grubby hands. "Constitutionally, I am more or less doomed to suffer," Mercedes said, pointing to deep lines running down from the ball of her own thumb. But she assured the girls that they would be happy, that they would each have three husbands and be happy with them all. The girls made another list. Jill had William, Daniel and Jean-Paul. Charlotte had Eric, Franklin and Duke.

Constance regarded the lists. She did not want to think of her little girls as wives in love.

"Do you think Mercedes is beautiful?" Constance asked Ben.

"I don't understand what she's talking about," Ben said.

"You don't have to understand what she's talking about to think she's beautiful," Constance said.

"I don't think she's beautiful," Ben said.

"She told me that Steven said that the meanings of her words were not philogistic, but telepathic and cumulative."

"Let's go downtown and get some gum," Ben said.

The two of them walked down to Main Street. Hundreds of people thronged the small town. "Jerry!" a woman screamed from the doorway of a shop. "I need money!" There was slanted parking on the one-way street, the spaces filled with cars that were either extremely rusted or highly waxed and occupied by young men and women playing loud radios.

"What a lot of people," Constance said.

"There's a sphere of radio transmissions about thirty light-years thick expanding outward at the speed of light, informing every star it touches that the world is full of people," Ben said.

Constance stared at him. "I'll be glad when the summer's over," she said.

"I can't remember very many Augusts," Ben said. "I'm really going to remember my Augusts from now on."

Constance started to cry.

"I can't talk to you," Ben said. They were walking back home. A group of girls wearing monogrammed knapsacks pedaled past on bicycles.

"That's not talking," Constance said. "That's shorthand, just a miserable shorthand."

In the kitchen, Mercedes was making the girls popcorn as she waited for Steven. She chattered away. The girls gazed at her raptly. Mercedes said, "I love talking to strangers. As you grow older, you'll find that you enjoy talking to strangers far more than to your friends."

Late that night, Constance woke to hear music from Steven's tape deck in the next room. The night was very hot. Beyond the thin curtains was a fat bluish moon.

"That's the saddest piece of music I've ever heard," Constance said. "What is that music?"

"Beethoven," Ben said. "It's pretty sad all right."

The children came into the room and shook Constance's shoulder. "Mummy," Jill said, "we can't sleep. Mercedes told us that last year she tried to kill herself with a pair of scissors."

"Oh!" cried Constance, disgusted. She took the girls back to their room. They all sat on a bed and looked out the window at the moon.

"Mercedes said that if the astronaut Gus Grissom hadn't died on the ground in the Apollo fire, he would probably have died on the moon of a heart attack," Charlotte told Constance. "Mercedes said that Gus Grissom's arteries were clogged with fatty deposits, and that he carried within himself all the prerequisites for tragedy. Mercedes said that if Gus Grissom had had a heart attack on the moon, nobody in the whole world would be able to look up into the sky with the same awe and wonder as before."

Jill said, "Mercedes said all things happen because they must happen."

"I'd like to sock Mercedes in the teeth," Constance said.

Constance had not seen Steven for days. She had only heard the sound of his typewriter, and sometimes there was a glass in the sink that might have been his. Constance had an image in her mind of the Coke bottle caught in the venetian-blind cord tapping out incoherent messages at the end of *On the Beach*. She finally went up to his room and knocked on the door.

"Yo!" Steven yelled.

Constance was embarrassed about disturbing him, and slipped away without saying anything. She went upstairs to the girls' room and looked out the window. A man stood by the mailbox, scrutinizing the pickup hours posted on the front and shaking his head.

Annie came with her child, Nora. Nora was precocious. She was eight, wore a bra, had red hair down to her kneecaps and knew the genuine and incomprehensible lyrics to most of the New Wave tunes. She sang in a rasping, wasted voice and shook her little body back and forth like a mop. Annie looked at Nora as she danced. It was an irritated look, such as a wife might give a husband. Constance thought of David. She had been so bored with David, but now she wondered what it had been, exactly, that was so boring. It was difficult to remember boring things. David had hated mayonnaise. The first thing he had told Constance's mother when they met was that he had owned forty cars in his life, which was true.

"Do you ever think about Susan?" Constance asked Ben.

"She's on television now," Ben said. "It's a Pepsi-Cola commercial but Susan is waving a piece of fried chicken."

"I've never seen that commercial," Constance said sincerely, wishing she had never asked about Susan.

Annie was an older woman with thick, greying hair. She

seemed more impatient than the others for Steven to knock off and get on with it.

"He's making a miraculous synthesis up there, is he?" Annie said wryly. "Passion, time? Inside, outside?"

"Are you in love with Steven?" Constance asked.

"I've found," Annie said, "that Love seldom serves one's purposes."

Constance thought about this. Perhaps Love was neither the goal nor the answer. Constance loved Ben and what good did that do him? He had just almost died from her absorption in him. Perhaps understanding was more important than Love, and perhaps the highest form of understanding was the understanding of oneself, one's motives and desires and capabilities. Constance thought about this but the idea didn't appeal to her much. She dismissed it.

Annie and Nora were highly skilled at a little parlor game in which vowels, numbers and first letters of names would be used by one person, in a dizzying polygamous travelogue, to clue the other as to whispered identities.

"I went," Annie would say, "to Switzerland with Tim for four days and then I went to Nome with Ernest."

"Mick Jagger!" Nora would yell.

Jill, glaring at Nora, whispered in Annie's ear.

"I went," Annie said, "to India with Ralph for a day before I met Ned."

"The Ayatollah Khomeini!" Nora screamed.

Charlotte and Jill looked at her, offended.

That evening, everyone went out except Constance, who stayed home with Nora.

"You know," Nora told her, "you shouldn't drink quinine. They won't let airline pilots drink quinine in their gin. It affects their judgment."

That afternoon, downtown with Annie, Nora had bought a lot of small candles. Now she placed them all around the house in little saucers and lit them. She and Constance turned off all the lights and walked from room to room enjoying the candles.

"Aren't they pretty!" Nora said. She had large white feet and wore a man's shirt as a nightie. "I think they're so pretty.

I don't like electrical lighting. Electrical lighting just lights the whole place up at once. Everything looks so *dead*, do you know what I mean?"

Constance peered at Nora without answering. Nora said, "It's as though nothing can *happen* when it's all lit up like that. It's as though everything *is.* "

Constance looked at the wavering pools of light cast by the little candles. She had never known a mystic before.

"I enjoy things best that I don't have to think about," Nora said. "I mean, I get awfully sick of using my brain, don't you? When you think of the world or of God, you don't think of this gigantic brain, do you?"

"Certainly not," Constance replied.

"Of course you don't," Nora said nicely.

The candles had different aromas. Finally, more or less in order, one after another, they went out. On Sunday, after Nora left with her mother, Constance missed her.

Constance was having difficulty sleeping. She would go to bed far earlier than anyone else, sometimes right after supper, and lie there and not sleep. Once she slept for a little while and had a dream in which the cart she was wheeling through the aisles of the A&P was a crash cart, a complete mobile cardiopulmonary resuscitation unit, of the kind she had seen in the corridors of the intensive-care wing at the hospital. In the dream, she bit her nails as she pushed the cart down the endless aisles, agonizing over her selections. She reached for a box of Triscuits and placed it in the cart between a box of automatic rotating cuffs and a defibrillator. Constance woke up, her own heart pounding. She listened to Ben's quiet breathing for a moment; then she rolled out of bed, dressed and walked downtown. It was just before dawn and the streets were cool and quiet and empty, but someone, during the night, had pulled all the flowers out of the window boxes in front of the shops. Clumps of earth and broken petals made a ragged trail before her. The wreckage rounded a corner. Constance wished Ben were with her. They could just walk along, they wouldn't have to say anything. Constance returned to the house and went back to bed. She had another dream in which crews of workmen were cutting down all the trees around their home, back on the mainland, in another state.

The weekend that Gloria arrived was extremely foggy. Gloria was from the South. She was unsmiling and honest, a Baptist who had just left her husband for good. She had been in love with Steven since she was thirteen years old.

"My parents are Baptists," Constance told her.

Fog slid through the screens. A voice from the street said, "Some dinner party, she served bluefish again!"

Gloria had little calling cards that showed Jesus knocking on the door of your heart. Jesus wore white robes and he had a neatly trimmed beard. He was rapping thoughtfully at the heavy wooden doors of a snug little vine-covered bungalow.

"I remember that picture!" Constance said. "When I was little, that picture just seemed to be everywhere."

"Have one," Gloria said.

The heart did not appear mean, it simply seemed closed. Constance wondered how long the artist had intended Jesus to have been standing there.

Gloria took Charlotte and Jill out to collect money to save marine mammals. They stood on the street and collected over thirty dollars in a Brim coffee can.

"Our salvation lies in learning to communicate with alien intelligences," Gloria said.

Constance wrote a check.

"Whales and dolphins are highly articulate," Gloria told Constance. "They know fidelity, play and sorrow."

Constance wrote another check, made herself a gin and tonic and went upstairs. That night, from Steven's room, she heard murmurs and moans in repetitive sequence.

The following day, Gloria asked, "Have you enjoyed sharing a house with Steven?"

"I haven't seen much of him," Constance said, "actually, at all."

"Summer can be a difficult time," Gloria said.

* * *

On the last day of August, Ben rented a bright red Jeep with neither top nor sides. Ben and Constance and Charlotte and Jill bounced around in it all morning, and at noon they drove on the beach to the very tip of the island, where the lighthouse was, to have their lunch. Approaching the lighthouse, Constance was filled with an odd excitement. She wanted to climb to the top. The steel door had been chained shut, but about four feet up from the base was a large hole knocked through the cement, and inside, beer cans, a considerable amount of broken glass and a lacy black wrought-iron staircase winding upward could be seen. Charlotte and Jill did not go in because they hadn't brought their shoes, but Constance climbed through the hole and went up the staircase. There was a wonderful expectancy to the tight climb upward through the whitewashed gyre. She was a little breathless when she reached the top. Powering the light, in a maze of cables and connectors, were eighteen black, heavy-duty truck batteries. For a moment, Constance's disappointment concealed her surprise. She saw the Atlantic fanning out without a speck on it, and her little family on the beach below, setting out food on a striped blanket. Constance inched out onto the catwalk encircling the light. "I love you!" she shouted. Ben looked up and waved. She went back inside and began her descent. She did not know, exactly, what it was she had expected, but it had certainly not been eighteen black, heavy-duty truck batteries.

In bed that night, Constance dreamed of people laughing. She opened her eyes. The clock beside her had large bright numbers which changed with an audible *flap* every minute. "Ben," she whispered.

"Hi." He was wide awake.

"I dreamed of laughing," Constance said. "I want to laugh."

"We'll laugh tomorrow," Ben said and grinned at his own joke. He turned her away from him and held her. She felt his mouth still smiling against her ear.

Preparation
for a Collie

*T*HERE is Jane and there is Jackson and there is David. There is the dog.

David is burying a bird. He has a carton in which cans of garbanzos were once packed. It is a large carton, much too large for the baby bird. David is digging a hole beneath the bedroom window. He mutters and cries a little. He is spending Sunday morning doing this. He is five.

Jackson comes outside and says, "It's too bad you didn't find a dead swan. It would have fit better in that hole."

Jackson is going to be an architect. He goes to school all day and he works as a bartender at night. He sees Jane and David on weekends. He is too tired in the morning to have breakfast with them. Jane leaves before nine. She sells imported ornaments in a Christmas shop, and Jackson is gone by the time Jane returns in the afternoon. David is in kindergarten all day. Jackson tends bar until long after midnight. Sometimes he steals a bottle of blended whiskey and brings it home with him. He wears saddle shoes and a wedding ring. His clothes are poor but he has well-shaped hands and nails. Jane is usually asleep when Jackson gets in bed beside her. He goes at her without turning on the light.

"I don't want to wake you up," he says.

Jackson is from Virginia. Once, a photograph of him in period dress appeared in *The New Yorker* for a VISIT WILLIAMS-BURG advertisement. They have saved the magazine. It is in their bookcase with their books.

Jackson packs his hair down hard with water when he leaves
the house. The house is always a mess. It is not swept. There
are crumbs and broken toys beneath all the furniture. There
are cereal bowls everywhere, crusty with soured milk. There is
hair everywhere. The dog sheds. It is a collie, three years older
than David. It is Jane's dog. She brought it with her into this
marriage, along with her Mexican bowls and something blue.

Jane could be pretty but she doesn't know how to arrange
her hair. She has violet eyes. And she prefers that color. She
has three pots of violets in the living room on Jackson's old
chess table. They flourish. This is sometimes mentioned by
Jackson. Nothing else flourishes as well here.

Whenever Jackson becomes really angry with Jane, he takes
off his glasses and breaks them in front of her. They seem
always to be the most valuable thing at hand. And they are
replaceable, although the act causes considerable inconve-
nience.

Jane and David eat supper together every night. Jane eats
like a child. Jane is closest to David in this. They are children
together, eating junk. Jane has never prepared a meal in this
house. She is as though in a seasonal hotel. This is not her life;
she does not have to be this. She refuses to become familiar
with this house, with this town. She is a guest here. She has
no memories. She is waiting. She does not have to make anything of these moments. She is a stranger here.

She is waiting for Jackson to become an architect. His theories of building are realistic but his quest is oneiric, he tells her.
He sometimes talks about "sites."

They are getting rid of the dog. Jackson has been putting ads
in the paper. He is enjoying this. He has been advertising for
weeks. The dog is free and many people call. Jackson refuses
all callers. For three weekends now, he and Jane have talked
about nothing except the dog. They will simplify their life and
they cannot stop thinking about it, this dog, this act, this
choice that lies before them.

The dog has crammed itself behind the pipes beneath the

kitchen sink. David squats before him, blowing gently on his
nose. The dog thumps its tail on the linoleum.

"We're getting rid of you, you know," David says.

It is Saturday evening and someone has stopped at the house
to see the dog.

"Is he a full-blooded collie?" the person asks. "Does he have
papers?"

"He doesn't say," Jackson smiles.

After all these years, six, Jane is a little confused by Jackson.
She sees this as her love for him. What would her love for him
be if it were not this? In turn, she worries about her love for
David. Jane does not think David is nice-looking. He has many
worries, it seems. He weeps, he has rashes, he throws up. He
has pale hair, pale flesh. She does not know how she can go
through all these days, each day, embarrassed for her son.

Jane and Jackson lie in bed.

"I love Sundays," Jane says.

Jackson wears a T-shirt. Jane slips her hand beneath it and
strokes his chest. She is waiting. She sometimes fears that she
is waiting for the waiting to end, fears that she seeks and
requires only that recognition and none other. Jackson holds
her without opening his eyes.

It is Sunday. Jane pours milk into a pancake mix.

Something gummy is stuck in David's hair. Jane gets a pair
of scissors and cuts it out.

Jackson says, "David, I want you to stop crying so much and
I want you to stop pretending to bake in Mommy's cupcake
tins." Jackson is angry, but then he laughs. After a moment,
David laughs too.

That afternoon, a woman and a little girl come to the house
about the dog.

"I told you on the phone, I'd give you some fresh eggs for
him." the woman says, thrusting a child's sand bucket at Jane.
"Even if you decide not to give the dog to us, the eggs, of
course, are still yours." She pauses at Jane's hesitation.
"Adams," the woman says. "We're here for the ad."

Jackson waves her to a chair and says, "Mrs. Adams, we seek

no personal aggrandizement from our pet. Our only desire is that he be given a good home. A great many people have contacted us and now we must make a difficult decision. Where will he inspire the most contentment and where will he find canine fulfillment?"

Jane brings the dog into the room.

"There he is, Dorothy!" Mrs. Adams exclaims to the little girl. "Go over and pet him or something."

"It's a nice dog," Dorothy says. "I like him fine."

"She needs a dog," Mrs. Adams says. "Coming over here, she said, 'Mother, we could bring him home today in the back of the car. I could play with him tonight.' Oh, she sure would like to have this dog. She lost her dog last week. A tragedy. Kicked to death by one of the horses. Must have broken every bone in his fluffy little body."

"What a pity!" Jackson exclaims.

"And then there was the accident," Mrs. Adams goes on. "Show them your arm, Dorothy. Why, I tell you, it almost came right off. Didn't it, darling?"

The girl rolls up the sleeve of her shirt. Her arm is a mess, complexly rearranged, a yellow matted wrinkle of scar tissue.

"Actually," Jackson says, "I'm afraid my wife has promised the dog to someone else."

After they leave, Jackson says, "These farm people have the souls of animals themselves."

The dog walks slowly back to the kitchen, swinging its high foolish hips. David wanders back to the breakfast table and picks up something, some piece of food. He chews it for a moment and then spits it out. He kneels down and spits it into the hot-air register.

"David," Jane says. She looks at his face. It is calm and round, a child's face.

It is evening. On television, a man dressed as a chef, holding six pies, falls down a flight of stairs. The incident is teaching numbers.

SIX, the screen screams.

"Six," David says.

Jane and Jackson are drinking whiskey and apple juice. Jane is wondering what they did for David's last birthday, when he was five. Did they have a little party?

"What did we do on your last birthday, David?" Jane asks.

"We gave him pudding and tea," Jackson says.

"That's not true," Jane says, worried. She looks at David's face.

SIX TOCKING CLOCKS, the television sings.

"Six," David says.

Jane's drink is gone. "May I have another drink?" she asks politely, and then gets up to make it for herself. She knocks the ice cubes out of the tray and smashes them up with a wooden spoon. On the side of the icebox, held in place by magnets, is a fragment from a poem, torn from a book. It says, *The dead must fall silent when one sits down to a meal.* She wonders why she put it there. Perhaps it was to help her diet.

Jane returns to the couch and David sits beside her. He says, "You say 'no' and I say 'yes.' "

"No," Jane says.

"Yes," David yells, delighted.

"No."

"Yes."

"No."

"Yes."

"Yes."

David stops, confused. Then he giggles. They play this game all the time. Jane is willing to play it with him. It is easy enough to play. Jackson and Jane send David to a fine kindergarten and are always buying him chalk and crayons. Nevertheless, Jane feels unsure with David. It is hard to know how to act when one is with the child, alone.

The dog sits by a dented aluminum dish in the bright kitchen. Jackson is opening a can of dog food.

"Jesus," he says, "what a sad, stupid dog."

The dog eats its food stolidly, gagging a little. The fur beneath its tail hangs in dirty beards.

"Jesus," Jackson says.

Jane goes to the cupboard, wobbling slightly. "I'm going to kill that dog," she says. "I'm sick of this." She puts down her drink and takes a can of Drāno out of the cupboard. She takes a pound of hamburger which is thawing in a bowl and rubs off the soft pieces onto a plate. She pours Drāno over it and mixes it in.

"It is my dog," Jane says, "and I'm going to get rid of him for you."

David starts to cry.

"Why don't you have another drink?" Jackson says to Jane. "You're so vivacious when you drink."

David is sobbing. His hands flap in the air. Jackson picks him up. "Stop it," he says. David wraps his legs around his father's chest and pees all over him. Their clothing turns dark as though, together, they'd been shot. "Goddamn it," Jackson shouts. He throws his arms out. He stops holding the child but his son clings to him, then drops to the floor.

Jane grabs Jackson's shoulder. She whispers in his ear, something so crude, in a tone so unfamiliar, that it can only belong to all the time before them. Jackson does not react to it. He says nothing. He unbuttons his shirt. He takes it off and throws it in the sink. Jane has thrown the dog food there. The shirt floats down to it from his open fist.

Jane kneels and kisses her soiled son. David does not look at her. It is as though, however, he is dreaming of looking at her.

The Wedding

*E*LIZABETH always wanted to read fables to her little girl but the child only wanted to hear the story about the little bird who thought a steam shovel was its mother. They would often argue about this. Elizabeth was sick of the story. She particularly disliked the part where the baby bird said, "You are not my mother, you are a *snort,* I want to get out of here!" Elizabeth was thirty and the child was five. At night, at the child's bedtime, Sam would often hear them complaining bitterly to one another. He would preheat the broiler for dinner and freshen his drink and go out and sit on the picnic table. In a little while, the screen door would slam and Elizabeth would come out, shaking her head. The child had frustrated her again. The child would not go to sleep. She was upstairs, wandering around, making "cotton candy" in her bone-china bunny mug. "Cotton candy" was Kleenex sogged in water. Sometimes Elizabeth would tell Sam the story that she had prepared for the child. The people in Elizabeth's fables were always looking for truth or happiness and they were always being given mirrors or lumps of coal. Elizabeth's stories were inhabited by wolves and cart horses and solipsists.

"Please relax," Sam would say.

At eleven o'clock every night, Sam would take a double Scotch on the rocks up to his bedroom.

"Sam," the child called, "have some of my cotton candy. It's delicious."

Elizabeth's child reminded Sam of Hester's little Pearl even though he knew that her father, far from being the "Prince of the Air," was a tax accountant. Elizabeth spoke about him often. He had not shared the 1973 refund with her even though they had filed jointly and half of the year's income had been hers. Apparently the marriage had broken up because she often served hamburgers with baked potatoes instead of French fries. Over the years, astonishment had turned to disapproval and then to true annoyance. The tax accountant told Elizabeth that she didn't know how to do anything right. Elizabeth, in turn, told her accountant that he was always ejaculating prematurely.

"Sam," the child called, "why do you have your hand over your heart?"

"That's my Scotch," Sam said.

Elizabeth was a nervous young woman. She was nervous because she was not married to Sam. This desire to be married again embarrassed her, but she couldn't help it. Sam was married to someone else. Sam was always married to someone.

Sam and Elizabeth met as people usually meet. Suddenly, there was a deceptive light in the darkness. A light that reminded the lonely blackly of the darkness. They met at the wedding dinner of the daughter of a mutual friend. Delicious food was served and many peculiar toasts were given. Sam liked Elizabeth's aura and she liked his too. They danced. Sam had quite a bit to drink. At one point, he thought he saw a red rabbit in the floral centerpiece. It's true, it was Easter week, but he worried about this. They danced again. Sam danced Elizabeth out of the party and into the parking lot. Sam's car was nondescript and tidy except for a bag of melting groceries.

Elizabeth loved the way he kissed. He put his hand on her throat. He lay his tongue deep and quiet inside her mouth. He filled her mouth with the decadent Scotch and cigarette flavor of the tragic middle class. On the other hand, when Sam saw Elizabeth's brightly flowered scanty panties, he thought he'd faint with happiness. He was a sentimentalist.

"I love you," Elizabeth thought she heard him say.

Sam swore that he heard Elizabeth say, "Life is an eccentric privilege."

This worried him but not in time.

They began going out together frequently. Elizabeth promised to always take the babysitter home. At first, Elizabeth and Sam attempted to do vile and imaginative things to one another. This was culminated one afternoon when Sam spooned a mound of pineapple-lime Jell-O between Elizabeth's legs and began to eat. At first, of course, Elizabeth was nervous. Then she stopped being nervous and began watching Sam's sweating, good-looking shoulders with real apprehension. Simultaneously, they both gave up. This seemed a good sign. The battle is always between the pleasure principle and the reality principle is it not? Imagination is not what it's cracked up to be. Sam decided to forget the petty, bourgeois rite of eating food out of one another's orifices for a while. He decided to just love Elizabeth instead.

"Did you know that Charles Dickens wanted to marry Little Red Riding Hood?"

"What!" Sam exclaimed, appalled.

"Well, as a child he wanted to marry her," Elizabeth said.

"Oh," Sam said, curiously relieved.

Elizabeth had a house and her little girl. Sam had a house and a car and a Noank sloop. The houses were thirteen hundred miles apart. They spent the winter in Elizabeth's house in the South and they drove up to Sam's house for the summer. The trip took two and one-half days. They had done it twice now. It seemed about the same each time. They argued on the Baltimore Beltway. They bought peaches and cigarettes and fireworks and a ham. The child would often sit on the floor in the front seat and talk into the air-conditioning vent.

"Emergency," she'd say. "Come in please."

*   *   *

On the most recent trip, Sam had called his lawyer from a Hot
Shoppe on the New Jersey Turnpike. The lawyer told him that
Sam's divorce had become final that morning. This had been
Sam's third marriage. He and Annie had seemed very compatible. They tended to each other realistically, with affection and
common sense. Then Annie decided to go back to school. She
became interested in animal behaviorism. Books accumulated.
She was never at home. She was always on field trips, in thick-
ets or on beaches, or visiting some ornithologist in Barnstable.
She began keeping voluminous notebooks. Sam came across
the most alarming things written in her hand.

Mantids are cannibalistic and males often literally lose their
heads to the females. The result, as far as successful mating
is concerned, is beneficial, since the suboesophageal ganglion
is frequently removed and with it any inhibition on the
copulatory center; the activities of male abdomen are carried
out with more vigor than when the body was intact.

"Annie, Annie," Sam had pleaded. "Let's have some people
over for drinks. Let's prune the apple tree. Let's bake the
orange cake you always made for my birthday."

"I have never made an orange cake in my life," Annie said.

"Annie," Sam said, "don't they have courses in seventeenth-
century romantic verse or something?"

"You drink too much," Annie said. "You get quarrelsome
every night at nine. Your behavior patterns are severely limited."

Sam clutched his head with his hands.

"Plus you are reducing my ability to respond to meaningful
occurrences, Sam."

Sam poured himself another Scotch. He lit a cigarette. He
applied a mustache with a piece of picnic charcoal.

"I am Captain Blood," he said. "I want to kiss you."

"When Errol Flynn died, he had the body of a man of
ninety," Annie said. "His brain was unrealistic from alcohol."

She had already packed the toast rack and the pewter and rolled up the Oriental rug.

"I am just taking this one Wanda Landowska recording," she said. "That's all I'm taking in the way of records."

Sam, with his charcoal mustache, sat very straight at his end of the table.

"The variations in our life have ceased to be significant," Annie said.

Sam's house was on a hill overlooking a cove. The cove was turning into a saltwater marsh. Sam liked marshes but he thought he had bought property on a deep-water cove where he could take his boat in and out. He wished that he were not involved in the process of his cove turning into a marsh. When he had first bought the place, he was so excited about everything that he had a big dinner party at which he served *soupe de poisson* using only the fish he had caught himself from the cove. He could not, it seems, keep himself from doing this each year. Each year, the *soupe de poisson* did not seem as nice as it had the year before. About a year before Annie left him, she suggested that they should probably stop having that particular dinner party. Sam felt flimflammed.

When Sam returned to the table in the Hot Shoppe on the New Jersey Turnpike after learning about his divorce, Elizabeth didn't look at him.

"I have been practicing different expressions, none of which seem appropriate," Elizabeth said.

"Well," Sam said.

"I might as well be honest," Elizabeth said.

Sam bit into his egg. He did not feel lean and young and unencumbered.

"In the following sentence, the same word is used in each of the missing spaces, but pronounced differently." Elizabeth's head was bowed. She was reading off the place mat. "Don't look at yours now, Sam," she said, "the answer's on it." She slid his place mat off the table, spilling coffee on his cuff in the process. *"A prominent and————man came into a restaurant at the height of the rush hour. The waitress was————to serve him immediately as she had————."*

Sam looked at her. She smiled. He looked at the child. The child's eyes were closed and she was moving her thumb around in her mouth as though she were making butter there. Sam paid the bill. The child went to the bathroom. An hour later, just before the Tappan Zee Bridge, Sam said, *"Notable."*

"What?" Elizabeth said.

"Notable. That's the word that belongs in all three spaces."

"You looked," Elizabeth said.

"Goddamn it," Sam yelled. "I did not look!"

"I knew this would happen," Elizabeth said. "I knew it was going to be like this."

It is a very hot night. Elizabeth has poison ivy on her wrists. Her wrists are covered with calamine lotion. She has put Saran Wrap over the lotion and secured it with a rubber band. Sam is in love. He smells the wonderfully clean, sun-and-linen smell of Elizabeth and her calamine lotion.

Elizabeth is going to tell a fairy story to the child. Sam tries to convince her that fables are sanctimonious and dully realistic.

"Tell her any one except the 'Frog King,' " Sam whispers.

"Why can't I tell her that one," Elizabeth says. She is worried.

"The toad stands for male sexuality," Sam whispers.

"Oh Sam," she says. "That's so superficial. That's a very superficial analysis of the animal-bridegroom stories."

"I am an animal," Sam growls, biting her softly on the collarbone.

"Oh Sam," she says.

Sam's first wife was very pretty. She had the flattest stomach he had ever seen and very black, very straight hair. He adored her. He was faithful to her. He wrote both their names on the flyleaves of all his books. They were married for six years. They went to Europe. They went to Mexico. In Mexico they lived in a grand room in a simple hotel opposite a square. The trees in the square were pruned in the shape of perfect boxes. Each night, hundreds of birds would come home to the trees. Beside the hotel was the shop of a man who made coffins. So many of the coffins seemed small, for children. Sam's wife grew depressed. She lay in bed for most of the day. She pretended she was dying. She wanted Sam to make love to her and pretend that she was dying. She wanted a baby. She was all mixed up.

Sam suggested that it was the ions in the Mexican air that made her depressed. He kept loving her but it became more and more difficult for them both. She continued to retreat into a landscape of chaos and warring feelings.

Her depression became general. They had been married for almost six years but they were still only twenty-four years old. Often they would go to amusement parks. They liked the bumper cars best. The last time they had gone to the amusement park, Sam had broken his wife's hand when he crashed head-on into her bumper car. They could probably have gotten over the incident had they not been so bitterly miserable at the time.

In the middle of the night, the child rushes down the hall and into Elizabeth and Sam's bedroom.

"Sam," the child cries, "the baseball game! I'm missing the baseball game."

"There is no baseball game," Sam says.

"What's the matter? What's happening!" Elizabeth cries.

"Yes, yes," the child wails. "I'm late, I'm missing it."

"Oh what is it!" Elizabeth cries.

"The child is having an anxiety attack," Sam says.

The child puts her thumb in her mouth and then takes it out again. "I'm only five years old," she says.

"That's right," Elizabeth says. "She's too young for anxiety attacks. It's only a dream." She takes the child back to her room. When she comes back, Sam is sitting up against the pillows, drinking a glass of Scotch.

"Why do you have your hand over your heart?" Elizabeth asks.

"I think it's because it hurts," Sam says.

Elizabeth is trying to stuff another fable into the child. She is determined this time. Sam has just returned from setting the mooring for his sailboat. He is sprawled in a hot bath, listening to the radio.

Elizabeth says, "There were two men wrecked on a desert island and one of them pretended he was home while the other admitted . . ."

"Oh Mummy," the child says.

"I know that one," Sam says from the tub. "They both died."

"This is not a primitive story," Elizabeth says. "Colorless, anticlimactic endings are typical only of primitive stories."

Sam pulls his knees up and slides underneath the water. The water is really blue. Elizabeth had dyed curtains in the tub and stained the porcelain. Blue is Elizabeth's favorite color. Slowly, Sam's house is turning blue. Sam pulls the plug and gets out of the tub. He towels himself off. He puts on a shirt, a tie and a white summer suit. He laces up his sneakers. He slicks back his soaking hair. He goes into the child's room. The lights are out. Elizabeth and the child are looking at each other in the dark. There are fireflies in the room.

"They come in on her clothes," Elizabeth says.

"Will you marry me?" Sam asks.

"I'd love to," she says.

Sam calls his friends up, beginning with Peter, his oldest friend. While they have been out of touch, Peter has become a soft contact lenses king.

"I am getting married," Sam says.

There is a pause, then Peter finally says, "Once more the boat departs."

* * *

It is harder to get married than one would think. Sam has forgotten this. For example, what is the tone that should be established for the party? Elizabeth's mother believes that a wedding cake is very necessary. Elizabeth is embarrassed about this.

"I can't think about that, Mother," she says. She puts her mother and the child in charge of the wedding cake. At the child's suggestion, it has a jam center and a sailboat on it.

Elizabeth and Sam decide to get married at the home of a justice of the peace. Her name is Mrs. Custer. Then they will come back to their own house for a party. They invite a lot of people to the party.

"I have taken out 'obey,' " Mrs. Custer says, "but I have left in 'love' and 'cherish.' Some people object to the 'obey.' "

"That's all right," Sam says.

"I could start now," Mrs. Custer says. "But my husband will be coming home soon. If we wait a few moments, he will be here and then he won't interrupt the ceremony."

"That's all right," Sam says.

They stand around. Sam whispers to Elizabeth, "I should pay this woman a little something, but I left my wallet at home."

"That's all right," Elizabeth says.

"Everything's going to be fine," Sam says.

They get married. They drive home. Everyone has arrived, and some of the guests have brought their children. The children run around with Elizabeth's child. One little girl has long red hair and painted green nails.

"I remember you," the child says. "You had a kitty. Why didn't you bring your kitty with you?"

"That kitty bought the chops," the little girl says.

Elizabeth overhears this. "Oh my goodness," she says. She takes her daughter into the bathroom and closes the door.

"There is more than the seeming of things," she says to the child.

"Oh Mummy," the child says, "I just want my nails green like that girl's."

"Elizabeth," Sam calls. "Please come out. The house is full

of people. I'm getting drunk. We've been married for one hour and fifteen minutes." He closes his eyes and leans his forehead against the door. Miraculously, he enters. The closed door is not locked. The child escapes by the same entrance, happy to be freed. Sam kisses Elizabeth by the shower stall. He kisses her beside the sink and before the full length mirror. He kisses her as they stand pressed against the windowsill. Together, in their animistic embrace, they float out the window and circle the house, gazing down at all those who have not found true love, below.

Woods

*T*HE trailer was sitting on ten ruined tires in the middle of the woods. There was a river fifty feet away but after what it had done to her, she hardly ever looked at it.

The day after they moved in, she had walked down there and stood on the little dock, looking up and down as though she were waiting for a bus. The woods were thick and purplish and ran right into the water. There wasn't any shore. There was the high land and then a line of ropy contorted trees with all the roots exposed like the tendons in an arm, and then the water. And there wasn't any sun. Although it was noon, the light was second-hand and shabby. The sun was enmeshed in a high tree, tangled in the hanging moss, beating feebly or not at all, like something subject to wind or exhaustion. She looked upstream and there was a gentle wide turn to the river and the woods turned black and flaky. White birds were milling, falling down to the water and then being sucked up again, as though by a draft, with no wingbeat and no cry.

Nothing looked as though it were about to change from one week to the next. She bent slightly at the waist and looked straight down. The river bottom was red and the water was different colors at different depths—saffron, red, black. Fish hung ornamentally above a rusting can. A steering wheel from a car was wedged between two logs. She lay down on her stomach and poked at the water with her hand. Bored, she splashed and patted the surface. Two otters erupted for air a foot beyond her lowered head, sleek and toothy with a sound like escaping gas. She shrieked, and ran back to the trailer.

She flung herself on the bed and wept for an hour, and nothing her husband could do would stop her. Finally, she took a hot bath and drank three martinis. The otters were the same otters which had terrified her as a child when they were in a color plate, swimming in the *Book of Knowledge*. She had never been able to remember what volume they were in and was therefore always coming across them. It became a dangerous thing to do her homework. Even when her father had cut the picture out, she would see other things that resembled the otters and she felt that her entire childhood had been ruined. She told this all to her husband. He didn't know what to say. He kissed her and held her on his lap and covered them both with a quilt.

Her name was Lola and she was young and had a pretty face. Her husband Jim had a pretty face too, which was why he was a television newscaster rather than being just another newsman. He had brown heavy hair, carefully cut and combed, and was tall and thirty years old. He would look thirty for the next two decades, which worried Lola.

Jim worked in the capital. It wasn't much of a town but it was crowded with state office buildings and two colleges and an agricultural school, and when he had started to look for a house late in the summer, there wasn't anything to rent. Each day he drove further and further from the town on some realtor's suggestion, Lola by his side, biting her nails and occasionally giving a little cry as though she had been pinched. All they passed were pines and careless farms and an occasional house with a dirt yard and a sign advertising yard eggs and crickets and rabbits. Lola wouldn't look any more. She put her head on his lap and listened to the radio.

The day he finally found the trailer and paid the rent, she wasn't with him. She had a headache pain and was staying behind in the motel room, calling all their friends in the town they had left behind, remembering good times together. The trailer was thirty miles from the capital on blacktop and then another four down a logging road, and was in the next state. He told her that it didn't have a phone but it had a CB radio and an air-conditioner, washing machine, vacuum cleaner, conversation pit and wall-to-wall carpeting. When she arrived, there was half a watermelon in the refrigerator, two jars of cane syrup beneath the sink, and an unflushed toilet. There was a little lawn, a mangled garden within a square of sticks and string, and then the deep bruised woods, thick as a velvet curtain. The ground all around the trailer was red. Lola felt that it looked idiotic, as though someone had tried to pretty the place up.

There were deer, bear, coon, possum, boar and turkey. Up the river, in the spring, men brought skiffs full of bees to the tupelo trees in the swamp.

"That would be something to watch for, love," Jim said. "Once I saw a man covered with bees. They hung off his clothes and all over his face. He walked by my house, going home. He had lost the queen but had found her again and he was covered with black bees, hardly able to see his way."

Lola looked vacantly at him for a long time and then began to drum her knees with her fists. "I don't want to see anything like that! I want to be out of here before Christmas!"

Down the river, eight or so miles, was the Gulf of Mexico. He assured her it was there, but she went to sleep and dreamed that she followed the river and it ended only in a fourteenth-century European town of freaks and circuses. Everything was violent or deformed. Tattooed children were being sold, and tiny dead songbirds, clustered like grapes. The river was green and full of animals, stopping abruptly at the town and never appearing again, as though it were painted on, an apron of a stage. Ballistas were mounted on the walls and hides were drying in the sun and everyone was calling to her.

Whimpering, she woke him up. In the night, something screamed. She could not tell if it was an animal or a bird or whether the process was of slaughter or slaughtering. She kept plucking at her husband's arm, long after he had awakened and turned on the light. He was a very handsome young man with clear untroubled eyes. People depended upon him to dispense events. Lola saw it simply. Without his telling, it did not exist, and after he had related it, it became harmless verbiage. Everything could be reduced by the mentioning of it. She had married him because he made her feel secure. Sometimes, when he was narrating a television special and the show had been pre-taped, he was both on the screen and by her side, and she was dizzy with relief. Those were the times when she understood best her love for him.

"I hate this place," she said shrilly, releasing his arm now and squeezing the bedclothes around her fingers. "I hate it! I hate the river and this awful trailer. I hate these woods!" She watched him with large indignant eyes, the dream already relaxing its grip on her mind, the reason for waking up and needing him going further and further away, almost lost. She was sleepy again. The bed was so warm where he lay. "Hate," she said. "I'm full of hate." He laughed and kissed her on the mouth. Both knew she could not concentrate on anything for very long.

The next morning, she scrubbed at a pot she had left soaking in the sink. Two mice had fallen into the grey water and drowned. She groped at them, thinking they were loosened noodles, screamed and returned to bed. Jim coaxed her up and took her into town with him, the car lurching toward the paved road in the ruts of the logging trucks. They swam through soft hollows, butterflies caroming softly across the windshield.

"If we had a little rain," Jim said, "it would fix up this road."

In the brown grass were wooden barrels of turpentine gum. They came upon a group of Negroes prying the tin pans off the trees and emptying them into the barrels. They wore wide green trousers and denim jackets and shoveled the gum out of the pans with thick sticks. They all stopped working as the car approached and stared at it expressionlessly as it lumbered past. Lola pressed her foot against the floorboards of the car, beating on an imaginary throttle. The car hung in the space before the men and then left them slowly behind, dusting their boots. In the bullet-shaped mirror on the fender, two wide hands rose in an ambivalent gesture.

"What?" Lola said, patting at her hair, looking at the woods again. "What?"

Jim turned to her, shifting into second. "I didn't say anything, love."

She noticed that he was wearing a bright blue shirt, suitable for color broadcast.

In town they had lunch together and she went shopping while he taped interviews with cabinet members at the statehouse. The day was cloudy and people walked fiercely down the sidewalk, three abreast. In the window of a toy store was a wooden man. There were beggars in the streets, small boys with trays of boiled peanuts, girls behind tables selling cakes. Outside a grocery, a blind man sat crosslegged on a mat, a round brown and white dog leashless by his side gripping a child's plastic bucket in its mouth. The man's eyes looked like clots of boiled grits. The bucket was half full of coins. Lola lingered in front of them, her fingers moving nervously across her throat. The dog glanced mildly at her, the bucket unmoving in the slick, stern jaws. The blind man seemed asleep. Lola patted the dog swiftly on the head and walked away without opening her pocketbook. Later, she thought worriedly that the man might not have been blind at all.

She bought some blouses and a potted plant and returned to the capitol where she waited for Jim in a basement coffee shop. Instead of staircases, there were wide ramps leading to the floor above and the halls smelled damp and peculiar, an odor of disinfectant, airlessness and the rotting canvas of coiled fire hoses. There were machines dispensing tuna sandwiches, combs, coffee and nylon stockings, and over it all was the rattle and rap of the pressmen's Telex machines and typewriters.

She put her packages in a corner booth and ordered a soft drink. A young man with a withered arm brought it cautiously to her in a paper cup. There was a black speck making its way through the ice cubes. Lola put a napkin over the cup and pushed it away, beside her plant. The plant was wrapped in pink foil and had drooping striped leaves, a remote hothouse look. She couldn't believe that she had actually bought it. She might just as well open the two doors of the trailer and let the woods fall in if she started filling up the rooms with growing junk. The forest was so thick it seemed static, but she had seen leaves and lizards fouling the mechanisms of the jalousies and she heard branches falling on the roof and tapping against the aluminum siding. The first week she had watched the woods a great deal but had stopped when she began sensing that the trees were moving closer to the windows every time she turned her eyes away, like something out of *Macbeth.* Now, after Jim left, she closed the curtains and put the lights on.

She picked up the plant and put it on the other side of the table behind the salt and pepper shakers.

Five secretaries came into the coffee shop and sat at a round table in the middle of the floor. They all wore bright short dresses and ash-blond wigs and each looked like the one that sat beside her, except a little less so. Other than the secretaries, there was no one in the place but the help, who were all handicapped in one way or another. The woman behind the orange drink machine polished a glass beatifically and occasionally burst into song. She had the widest, whitest, smoothest face Lola had ever seen. It resembled a custard pie.

Lola chewed on her fingernail. She would have gone to the car and waited there but she did not know where Jim had parked it. Her head began to ache, and to calm herself, she tried to think of the last city where Jim had worked, but this only made her more upset and unhappy. They had had many friends and she had always known where she was and where she was going and she always had someone to accompany her there. With her friends, she had chatted about controllable circumstances and about Jim and herself and everyone had shown great interest in this.

When at last her husband came over to the booth, Lola was so relieved that she grasped his wrist and began to shake it as though she were meeting him for the first time.

"Did you have a nice afternoon?" he asked.

She grimaced. "There's something odd about this town," she said. "There seems to be something wrong with everyone in it."

"Government attracts strange types, love." He stood and picked up her packages. "Is that your plant?"

"No," she said, "it must belong to the table."

They drove out of the city and settled along the dull road home at high speed. Nonetheless, they were passed by trucks and aged sedans. All the men drove ferociously, as though they had left something behind that was close to catching up to them. They were going by cropped flat fields that the paper companies had harvested and not replanted. There were no houses here, but a few trailers were set up on concrete blocks, and cows and ponies grazed over the unfenced land. The road ran straight and simple and at the end of it bubbled the sun.

Up ahead on Lola's side, a trailer was burning. First it was not and then it was. As she looked, it shuddered and a front panel blew out and bounced a few times on the ground like a rubber ball. She rolled down the window and rubbed her eyes. The trailer was definitely on fire. A man and a woman and three children fell out of it and scrambled away, the fire rolling down the length of the trailer and through the blown-out section after them, licking at the ground as though it were a pet lapping up scraps. The family settled down at a good distance and sat in a row, rubbing at their arms and at each other's heads. The sides of the trailer were wrinkling like scorched paper and the windows were popping out.

"My God," Jim said. They shot past and Lola craned her neck to keep the incredible vision in sight. Behind them, cars were pulling off the road and people and dogs were running across the field.

"Stop!" she said. "Look, people are stopping! You should stop."

"Terrible, terrible," Jim said. The sun was down, the sky red and glazed. The flames hung like statues in the air. "Everyone stops for something like that," he went on. "Too many people." He looked at Lola, who was twisted awkwardly in the seat,

staring behind them. There was a jog in the road and then the
woods began again. In a moment, she wouldn't be able to see
it any more. He pressed on the accelerator.

"Now I don't want you to be worrying about this. That was
a very old trailer and we live in a mobile home. Sixty feet long."

Lola shook her head and said weakly, "You're a newscaster.
You should have stopped if only because you're a newscaster."

"Well now, honey, you know I don't do that. I don't gather
it or write it. I know you know that. And besides, it's not even
the same state. I don't want you to think about it any more.
No one was hurt and I want you to forget it." He gathered her
toward him and drove with one hand.

"I'm not going to accept this," she said loudly.

They were nearing their trailer. The Negroes were gone and
the turpentine barrels were lined along the road, brimming, as
though with dirty snow. A hawk settled on a tree branch that
broke beneath his weight, rose again and dipped gracefully into
the woods, banking on broad wings through what seemed an
impenetrable maze.

"The trees don't touch his wings," she said suddenly. "Imagine that."

Lola never went into town with Jim again. She wanted him
to know how unhappy she was. The city seemed the carnival
corrupt town of her dream, a place of soiled air, decadent
architecture and wrongly made people. She was pretty. Aberration made her angry and confused and somewhat threatened.
As a child, she feared that she would catch deafness from a
distant grandmother and on her birthdays she would refuse to
open any letter or gift the old woman sent. She was a clean,
exact child, afraid of a great many things.

Jim brought home the groceries and did all the buying. He
had the six o'clock broadcast every evening and was back before
eight. Lola played the part of an invalid. She took many baths,
listened to the radio and slept in the afternoons. She sometimes
sat on the trailer's deck and looked through the thinning trees.
The woods had become lean and haunted; only the magnolia
trees stayed green and waxy like something into and past death.

Fishermen drifted past on the river, flicking their long cane poles, drawing in panfish no bigger than a fist. They waved to Lola. She moved the pages of a book hastily and went inside. The place smelled of cigarettes and mice that wouldn't be trapped. The paneled walls bent to the touch. She felt vulnerable, weakened, as though she were losing something day by day to the outside. She could be shattered. She could be broken. She tried never to go out there, but felt that there was no safety in the fragile trailer. In a storm, the woods creaked and the rain spun down on the roof like hail. She dressed carefully and watched her husband on television and drank wine until he came home. There was nothing to talk about.

"Driving home tonight," he said, "I saw a dog trotting along the road with a loaf of bread in his mouth."

One night in November, he told her that they were going to move to Atlanta two weeks before Christmas. "A new station, looking for new talent. A great opportunity," he said. He had brought home champagne, shrimp and steak. He would make her happy again.

Lola was pale and her face had become rounder and all her muscles ached as though she had been doing violent exercise. She felt as though she were going to fall, even though she was already sitting down. Jim poured her a glass of champagne and went outside to grill the steaks.

That night, she couldn't sleep. Their bedroom had one small window, useless because blocked by the branches of a sweet gum. It was imprisonment, like living in a cell. Lola heard the animals moving, the earth turning below her until just before dawn and then everything stopped. She walked down the narrow hall and saw the mist moving along the river toward the Gulf and a thin lemon lake of brightness rising from the crimson ground.

Three days later, on Thanksgiving, the hunting season began, with a terrific roar of shotguns throughout the woods around them. It was just after daybreak. Lola trembled and pressed her head beneath the pillow.

"If I go outside," she said, "they'll shoot at me. Just for sport."

Jim was horrified. "Don't be ridiculous. What a terrible thing to say!" He pulled away the pillow and stroked her face. "They're not allowed to shoot across a road," he said.

"They hit pets and automobiles and clothes drying on the line and the women hanging up the clothes," she said calmly. "You hear about it all the time."

"Lola, they are not going to shoot at you!"

She shook her head and watched him, waiting for something else. When he didn't say anything right away, she got up and began to dress. The firing became more insistent and varied, rhythmless and roaming. The woods were foggy and like stone, and she imagined them calm and gaining strength from the hammering, converting it to a black and surly energy of their own that would be deployed someday, against her, against everyone.

Jim said, "It's always bad on opening day. It won't be like this again. The boys get bored or discouraged and the hunting slacks off, you'll see."

Beyond the trees, the river smoked. "I don't care," she shrugged. "It doesn't bother me. I never go outside." The woods had no power and made no sense. One could always cut everything down.

Of course, Jim had told her the truth. In the days that followed there were only scattered shots early in the morning and then a silence so intense that Lola felt she would never recover from it, not even in Atlanta.

Early in December, she began boxing dishes and cleaning out drawers, trying to throw away as much as possible. She wanted to abandon everything that had had anything to do with their life in the trailer but she knew that this was preposterous and that they couldn't afford it. She gathered up an armload of clothes and plates and paperback books and, opening the door with her elbow, stepped out onto the deck. Parked in front of her was a red, sprung pickup truck with a large wooden box in the back for dogs. The box was unlatched and there wasn't anything inside except some dirty straw and a plastic dish. Two boys were sitting on the hood of the truck with their backs to Lola, and when they heard the noise behind them, they jumped to the ground and faced her, crouching, with long grins that turned instantly into disappointed frowns. Their faces then gyrated wildly before collectively settling into detached somnolence. One boy rubbed at his eyelid as though he were shining up an apple. "Yo," he said, nodding to Lola. He was bony, with thin dirty hands and close-cropped tan hair that clung to his head like a cap made out of a pecan shell.

Lola's mouth was cold, as though she had been chewing ice. She kept raising her chin as she moved her tongue around in her mouth, until her head was tipped back so far she could barely see them.

The one that had spoken first said, "Name of Cale Barfield. This here," he flapped his hand at his companion, "J.J. Leape."

J. J. stamped his boots on the ground and moved his head up and down curtly as though he were afraid someone was going to see him do it. He wore a Navy flight jacket and had incredibly clear blue eyes, like a baby's.

"I don't know what you're doing here," Lola said. "I couldn't care less who you are, but I certainly would like to know what you're doing here."

"We lost our dawgs," Cale said serenely, pulling himself back up on the hood of the truck. "Three. One blue," he spread his hand before his face and waggled a finger. "One black 'n' tan and one dawg."

"I couldn't care less what you are doing here," Lola said and then stopped, confused. She still had her arms full of trash and she pressed it closer to her chest. "You've got to leave." Her voice seemed to be coming from somewhere behind her.

"We didn't know no one was here. We thought hit a summer camp all closed up. Curtains all closed up. Nothing here. No cars or gear nor nothing. Looks closed to me, don't hit to you, J.J.?"

The boy with the blue eyes slammed the door of the cab shut and sat down on the running board. Hanging in the rear window were two rifles and a shotgun. J.J.'s eyes looked crayoned in. He looked at Lola so carelessly that she felt she wasn't being looked at at all.

"I live here," she said. "And my husband lives here." She began backing into the trailer. She was afraid to look down at herself or where she was going because she thought that if she did, she would find something dreadfully disarranged.

"If we leave the truck setting in one place, them dawgs will find hit," Cale said.

"No," she said.

"Oh yeah, that's shor right," Cale smiled.

She dropped what she was carrying into a chair and slammed the door shut and locked it. Then she poured herself a drink and walked back to the bathroom and closed and locked that door and sat on the edge of the tub and sipped her drink. She was a nice person! She was clean. She didn't throw things out the car window. Her mouth quivered on the rim of the glass. At her feet was a newspaper. A headline said

MOTHER THINKS SON IN GIANT'S COMPANY

She finished the drink and unlocked the bathroom door and walked down the hallway to the kitchen. Cale and J.J. were standing in the living room. Even before she saw them, she could smell the cold air of the woods and their muddy woolen clothes.

"We thought you'd gone and was trying to find paper to write you a note," Cale said. "We've had some drinks of your water and we wanted to tell you about the hogs that's been running through your yard."

"I locked that door," Lola said faintly.

"Nome."

"I know I did."

"Nome. We could open hit."

Lola sat down on the couch. She thought of going back to the bathroom and getting the can of toilet bowl cleaner and throwing it in their eyes, but there wasn't any place for her to go after she had done that. There wasn't any way for her to escape into the woods. It would be like trying to run off the edge of the world, she knew. "Look," she said severely, "my husband is a newscaster on television."

They looked at her politely. "Whatsis name?" Cale asked.

"Dundey." I have them now, she thought wildly. They'll go now. "On WTVB. Jim Dundey."

J.J. seemed interested for the first time. His mouth rolled back and his eyes glazed as though he'd been hit in the back of the head. He started laughing in short whistling gasps. "Jim Dandy! He's suckering you. Thaters no name for a man. Thaters a name of dawg food!" He laughed carefully and with concentration as though it was something that took talent, and then stopped abruptly and shook his head. On the sleeve of his jacket was a wide crust of red, like a scab. Lola thought that if it fell off and onto her carpet, she would drop to the floor and never move again.

Cale wasn't laughing but his face had squeezed up to two-thirds its regular size and his eyebrows were level with his hairline. Everyone was silent and not looking at each other.

"We don't watch no television ourselfs," Cale said in a hoarse voice. "We had a tee vee onct but we swopped hit for a Walker and before he run away he were a twice better Walker than hit were a tee vee."

Lola felt that J.J.'s blue eyes were sitting in her lap. Inside, she was running and running and almost out of breath.

"I wouldn't worry about that none," Cale went on, "if that's indeed his name. Someone's given names to everything on this earth. There ain't nothing what don't got a name." His cheeks fell in as though he had suddenly lost all his teeth. "Ain't that sad?"

"I think that it's a very good thing," Lola said stiffly.

J.J. took two steps forward and two steps back. He smelled like a storm coming. "Bunch of smartasses went around and cat-a-logued hit all," he muttered.

Cale ducked his head uncomfortably and pushed the curtains back. It was dusk and the trees were darker than the sky.

"Now," he said, "if you would lookitere, you could see where them hogs torn the place up."

Lola rose obediently and walked to the window. The ground was tumbled and stacked as though by several erratic plows. Long muddy nests were everywhere. Water-filled hollows. Small trees had been beaten over. The land looked bombed.

"I haven't seen that before," Lola said. "It always looks like a wreck out there to me."

"You here all day long?" Cale asked.

Lola didn't answer. The three of them were in a semicircle, looking at the woods, with their arms dangling and their faces empty as though they had just finished a long and meaningful conversation.

"What I mean was they make a racket. If you'd of heard em you could of shot em. That meat is just so lean and sweet . . ."

"Make enough noise coming through to wake the dead," J.J. said fiercely, as though he had been insulted.

"Uh-huh," Cale said.

"The quick and the dead," J.J. continued. "You familiar with what is 'quick'?"

Lola went to the kitchen sink and stood there, running water over her hands.

"Naw," Cale said, "I ain't."

"Unborn," J.J. said, shrugging.

"Noise even for that," Cale said. "Hit's probably true."

"I am going to make dinner now for my husband," Lola announced, "who is going to be back any moment. And I am going to make myself a drink." She twisted the water faucets on as far as they would go and said, "Would you like to have a drink?" The running water made so much noise, she couldn't hear herself saying it.

J.J. zipped up his jacket and opened the door. He whistled sharply. Nothing happened. He jumped off the deck, not bothering to shut the door, and they heard him get in the truck and start the motor.

"We'll be going now," Cale sighed. "I guess them hounds

might be waiting on the highway." He started out the door and almost collided with J.J., who was coming back in.

"You'll be watching out for them dawgs and keeping them for us then when they come by?" J.J. said, jerking his eyes over Lola. She tried not to pay attention to him. He wore baggy trousers with rows of flap pockets extending all the way down to the cuff. From one of the pockets, he took out three quarters and laid them on the table. "Jest tie em up and give em a bucket of water and this here is for food. One name Don, the black 'n' tan."

"They won't be coming through here," Lola said. "You'll find them someplace else."

J.J. looked at her with no curiosity at all and, with Cale following, went back out to the truck.

"Bye fer now," Cale said.

The truck tore away recklessly, leaving a smell of oil on the air.

It was six o'clock, the light almost gone, and time for the newscast. Lola turned on the television. She made a drink and drank it, then picked up the quarters from the table. On the television, something was being said. She turned off the sound and went outside, on the deck. The woods were wild at night-fall. She heard dim crashings and splashes and the bark of a dog, and through the gaps in the trees was a mottled sky of fading pink and grey discs, microbes moving toward the west.

She had almost gotten away but not in time and now leaving wouldn't save her. She lay down on the deck with the woods all around her. She lay on her stomach and stretched out her arms. She could see the ground through the spaces between the pine planking. Over the months, things had spilled down there. She saw a cigarette lighter and a pencil. She saw a spoon down there, dully twinkling, offering to her the blurred, quite un-recognizable image of her face.

Shepherd

*I*t had been three weeks since the girl's German shepherd had died. He had drowned. The girl couldn't get over it. She sat on the porch of her boyfriend's beach house and looked at the water.

It was not the same water. The house was on the Gulf of Mexico. The shepherd had drowned in the bay.

The girl's boyfriend had bought his house just the week before. It had been purchased furnished with mismatched plates and glasses, several large oak beds, an assortment of green wicker furniture and an art deco ice bucket with its handles in the shape of penguins.

The girl had a house of her own on the broad seawalled bay. The house had big windows overlooking shaggy bougainvillea bushes. There were hardly any studs in the frame and the whole house had shaken when the dog ran through it.

The girl's boyfriend's last name was Chester and everyone called him that. He was in his mid-thirties. The girl realized she was no kid herself. She was five years younger than he was. Chester favored trousers with legs of different colors and wore sunglasses the color of champagne bottles. He wore them day and night like a blind man. Chester had a catamaran. He loved to cook. "It's just another way to cook eggs," he'd say as he produced staggeringly delicious blintzes on Sunday morning. Chester had a writing dentist who had serviced the Weathermen in college. Chester had wide shoulders, great hands and one broken marriage on which he didn't owe a dime.

"You have fallen into the pie," the girl's friends told her.

Three days before the shepherd had drowned, Chester had asked the girl to marry him. They had known each other almost a year. "I love you," he said, "let's get married." They had taken a Quaalude and gone to bed. That had been three weeks and three days ago. They were going to be married in four days. Time is breath, the girl thought.

The girl sat on a rusted glider with faded cushions and drank bourbon from a glass printed with orange suns and pink flamingos. She wore skimpy flowered shorts and a black T-shirt. Tears ran down her face.

The shepherd was brown and black with a blunt, fabulous face. He had a famous trick. When the girl said, "Do you love me?" he would leap up, all fours, into her arms. And he was light, so light, containing his great weight deep within himself, like a dream of weight.

The shepherd had been five years old when he drowned. The girl had had him since he was two months old. She had bought him from a breeder in Miami, a man who had once been a priest. The girl's shepherd came from a litter of five with excellent bloodlines. The mother was graceful and friendly, the father more solemn and alert. The breeder who had once been a priest made the girl spend several minutes alone with each puppy and asked her a great many questions about herself. The girl didn't know what she was doing actually. She had never thought about herself much. When she had finally selected her puppy, she sat in the kitchen with the breeder and drank a Pepsi. The puppy stumbled around her feet, nibbling at the laces of her sneakers. The breeder smoked and talked to the girl with a great deal of assurance. The girl had been quite in awe of him.

He said, "We are all asleep and dreaming, you know. If we could ever actually comprehend our true position, we would not be able to bear it, we would have to find a way out."

The girl nodded and sipped her warm Pepsi. She was embarrassed. People would sometimes speak to her in this way, in this intimate, alarming way as though she were passionate or thoughtful or well-read. The puppy smelled wonderful. She picked him up and held him.

"We deceive ourselves. All we do is dream. Good dreams, bad dreams . . ."

"The ways that others see us is our life," the girl said.

"Yes!" the breeder exclaimed.

The girl sat slowly moving on the glider. She imagined herself standing laughing, younger and much nicer, the shepherd leaping into her arms. Her head buzzed and rustled. The bourbon bobbed around the flamingo's lowered head on the gaudy glass. She stood up and walked from one end of the porch to the other. The shepherd's drowned weight in her arms had been a terrible thing, a terrible thing. She and Chester were both dressed rather elaborately because they had just returned from dinner with two friends, a stockbroker and his girl friend, an art dealer. The art dealer was very thin and very blond. There were fine blond hairs on her face. The small restaurant where they ate appeared much larger than it was by its use of mirrored walls. The girl watched the four of them eating and drinking in the mirrors. The stockbroker spoke of money, of what he could do for his friends. "I love my work," he said.

"The art I handle," his girl friend said, "is intended as a stimulus for discussion. In no way is it to be taken as an aesthetic product."

As the evening wore on, the girl friend became quite drunk. She had a large repertoire of light-bulb jokes.

The girl had asked the woman for her untouched steak tournedos. The waiter had wrapped it for her in aluminum foil, the foil twisted into the shape of a swan. The girl remembered carrying the meat into the house for the shepherd and seeing the torn window screen. She remembered feeling the stillness in her house as it flowed into her eyes.

The girl looked at the Gulf. It was a dazzling day with no surf. The beach was deserted. The serious tanners were in tanning parlors, bronzing evenly beneath sun lamps, saving time. The girl wished the moment were still to come, that she were there, then, waiting, her empty arms outstretched, saying, "Do you love me?" Dogs hear sounds that we cannot, thought the girl. Dogs hear callings.

Chester had dug a deep square hole beneath the largest of the bougainvillea bushes and the girl had laid her dog down into it.

Their pale clothes became dirty from the drowned dog's coat. The girl had thrown her dress away. Chester had sent his suit to the dry cleaners.

Chester liked the dog, but it was the girl's dog. A dog can only belong to one person. When Chester and the girl made love in her house, or when the girl was out for the evening, she kept the shepherd inside, closed up on a small porch with high screened windows. He had taken to leaping out of his pen, a clearing enclosed with cyclone fencing and equipped with old tires. It was supposed to be his playground, his exercise area and keep away boredom and loneliness when the girl was not with him. It was a tall fence, but the shepherd had found a way over it. He had escaped, again and again, so the girl had begun locking him up in the small porch room. The girl had never witnessed his escape, from either of these places, but she imagined him leaping, gathering himself and plunging upward. He could leap so high—there was such lightness in him, such faith in the leaping.

On the beach, at Chester's, the waves glittered so with light, the girl could not bear to look at them. She finished the bourbon, took the empty glass to the kitchen and put it in the sink.

When the girl and the shepherd had first begun their life together, they had lived around Mile 47 in the Florida Keys. The girl worked in a small marine laboratory there. Her life was purely her own and the dog's. Life seemed slow and joyous and remembering those days, the girl felt that she had been on the brink of something extraordinary. She remembered the shepherd, his exuberance, energy, dignity. She remembered the shepherd and remembered being, herself, good. She had been capable of living another life then. She lived aware of happiness.

The girl pushed her hands through her hair. The Gulf seemed to stick in her throat.

There had been an abundance of holy things then. Once the world had been promising. But there had been a disappearance of holy things.

A friend of Chester's had suggested hypnotism. He had been quite enthusiastic about it. The girl would have a few sessions with this hypnotist that he knew, and she would forget the dog. Not forget exactly, rather, certain connections would not be made. The girl would no longer recall the dog in the context of her grief. The hypnotist had had great success with smokers.

Tonight they were going to have dinner with this man and his wife. The girl couldn't bear the thought of it. They would talk and talk. They would talk about real estate and hypnotism and coke and Cancún. All of Chester's friends loved Cancun. Tonight, they would go to a restaurant which had recently become notorious when an elderly woman had died from burns received when the cherries jubilee she was being served set fire to her dress. They would all order flaming desserts. They would go dancing afterwards.

Animals are closer to God than we, the girl thought, but they are lost to him. Her arms felt heavy. The sun was huge, moving ponderously toward the horizon. People were gathering on the beach to watch it go down. They were playing their radios. When the sun touched the horizon, it took three minutes before it disappeared. An animal can live for three minutes without air. It had taken the shepherd three minutes to die after however long he had been swimming in the deep water off the smooth seawall. The girl remembered walking into the house with the meat wrapped in the foil in the shape of a swan, and seeing the broken screen. The house was full of mosquitoes. Chester put some soft ice in a glass and poured a nightcap. Chester always looked out of place in the girl's house. The house wasn't worth anything, it was the land that was valuable. The girl went outside, calling, past the empty pen, calling, down to the bay, seeing the lights of the better houses along the seawall. A neighbor had called the sheriff's department and the lights from the deputy's car shone on the ground on the dark dog.

A buzzer sounded in the beach house. Chester had had the whole house wired. In the week he had owned it, he had put in central air conditioning, replaced all the windows with one-way glass and installed an elaborate infrared alarm system. The buzzer, however, was just a local signal. It stopped. It had been just the door opening, just Chester coming home. Chester activated the total system when they were out or when they were sleeping. The girl thought of invisible frequencies monitoring undisturbed air. The girl found offensive the notion that she could be spared pain, humiliation, or loss by microwaves. She contemplated for a moment the desire Chester had for a complete home security system. There wasn't anything in the house worth stealing. Chester was protecting space. For a moment, the girl found offensive the touch of Chester's hand on her hair.

"Why aren't you dressed?" he asked.

The girl looked at him, and then down at herself, at the thin T-shirt and hibiscus-flowered shorts. I am getting too old to wear this shit, the girl thought. The porch was cooling down fast in the twilight. She shivered and rubbed her arms.

"Why?" the girl said.

Chester sighed. "We're going out to dinner with the Tynans."

"I don't want to go out to dinner with the Tynans," the girl said.

Chester put his hands in his pockets. "You've got to snap out of this," he said.

"I'm flying," the girl said. "I have flown." She thought of the shepherd leaping, the lightness. He had escaped from her. She hadn't gotten anyplace.

"I've been very sympathetic," Chester said. "I've consoled you the best I can."

"There is no consolation," the girl said. "There is no recovery. There is no happy ending."

"We're the happy ending," Chester said. "Give us a break."

The sky was red, the water a dull silver. "I can't bear to see the Tynans again," the girl said. "I can't bear to go to another restaurant and see the sneeze guard over the salad bar."

"Don't scream at me, darling. Doesn't any of that stuff you take ever calm you down? I'm not the dog that you can scream at."

"What?" the girl said.

Chester sat down on the glider. He put his hand on her knee. "I love you," he said. "I think you're wonderful, but I think a little self-knowledge, a little *realism* is in order here. You would stand and *scream* at that dog, darling."

The girl looked at his hand, patting her knee. It seemed an impossibly large, ruddy hand.

"I wasn't screaming," she said. The dog had a famous trick. The girl would ask, "Do you love me?" and he would leap up, all fours, into her arms. Everyone had been amazed.

"The night it happened, you looked at the screen and you said you'd *kill* him when he got back."

The girl stared at the hand stroking and rubbing her knee. She felt numb. "I never said that."

"It was a justifiable annoyance, darling. You must have repaired that screen half a dozen times. He was becoming a discipline problem. He was adopting ways that made people feel uncomfortable."

"Uncomfortable?" the girl said. She stood up. The hand dropped away.

"We cannot change any of this," Chester said. "God knows if it were in my power, I would. I would do anything for you."

"You didn't stay with me that night, you didn't lie down beside me!" The girl walked in small troubled circles around the room.

"I stayed for *hours,* darling. But nobody could sleep on that bed. The sheets were always sandy and covered with dog hairs. That's why I bought a house, for the beds." Chester smiled and reached out to her. She turned and walked through the house, opening the door, tripping the buzzer. "Oh you've got to stop this!" Chester shouted.

When she reached her own house, she went into the bed-room and lay down there. There was a yawning silence all around her, like an enormous hole. Silence was a thing en-trusted to the animals, the girl thought. Many things that human words have harmed are restored again by the silence of animals.

The girl lay on her side, turned, onto her back. She thought of the bougainvillea, of the leaves turning into flowers over the shepherd's grave. She thought of the shepherd by her bed, against the wall, sleeping quietly, his faith in her at peace.

There was a pop, a small explosion in her head that woke her. She lurched up, gasping, from a dream that the shepherd had died. And for an instant, she hovered between two dreams, twice deceived. She saw herself leaping, only to fall back. The moonlight spilled into the clearing.

"I did love you, didn't I?" the girl said. She saw herself forever leaping, forever falling back. "And didn't you love me?"

Train

I NSIDE, the Auto-Train was violet. Both little girls were pleased because it was their favorite color. Violet was practically the only thing they agreed on. Danica Anderson and Jane Muirhead were both ten years old. They had traveled from Maine to Washington, D.C., by car with Jane's parents and were now on the train with Jane's parents and one hundred nine other people and forty-two automobiles on the way to Florida where they lived. It was September. Danica had been with Jane since June. Danica's mother was getting married again and she had needed the summer months to settle down and have everything nice for Dan when she saw her in September. In August, her mother had written Dan and asked what she could do to make things nice for Dan when she got back. Dan replied that she would like a good wall-hung pencil sharpener and satin sheets. She would like cowboy bread for supper. Dan supposed that she would get none of these things. Her mother hadn't even asked her what cowboy bread was.

The girls explored the entire train, north to south. They saw everyone but the engineer. Then they sat down in their violet seats. Jane made faces at a cute little toddler holding a cloth rabbit until he started to cry. Dan took out her writing materials and began writing to Jim Anderson. She was writing him a postcard.

"Jim," she wrote, "I miss you and I will see you any minute. When I see you we will go swimming right away."

"That is real messy writing," Jane said. "It's all scrunched together. If you were writing to anyone other than a dog, they wouldn't be able to read it at all."

Dan printed her name on the bottom of the card and embellished it all with X's and O's.

"Your writing to Jim Anderson is dumb in about twelve different ways. He's a *golden retriever,* for Godssakes."

Dan looked at her friend mildly. She was used to Jane yelling at her and expressing disgust and impatience. Jane had once lived in Manhattan. She had developed certain attitudes. Jane was a treasure from the city of New York currently on loan to the state of Florida where her father, for the last two years, had been engaged in running down a perfectly good investment in a marina and dinner theater. Jane liked to wear scarves tied around her head. She claimed to enjoy grapes and brown sugar and sour cream for dessert more than ice cream and cookies. She liked artichokes. She *adored* artichokes. She *adored* the part in the New York City Ballet's *Nutcracker Suite* where the Dew Drops and the candied Petals of Roses dance to the "Waltz of the Flowers." Jane had seen the *Nutcracker* four *times,* for Godssakes.

Dan and Jane and Jane's mother and father had all lived with Jane's grandmother in her big house in Maine all summer. The girls hadn't seen that much of the Muirheads. The Muirheads were always "cruising." They were always "gunk-holing," as they called it. Whatever that was, Jane said, for Godssakes. Jane's grandmother had a house on the ocean and knew how to make pizza and candy and sail a canoe. She called pizza 'za. She sang hymns in the shower. She sewed sequins on their jeans and made them say grace before dinner. After they said grace, Jane's grandmother would ask forgiveness for things done and left undone. She would, upon request, lie down and chat with them at night before they went to sleep. Jane was crazy about her grandmother and was quite a nice person in her presence. One night, at the end of summer, Jane had had a dream in which men dressed in black suits and white bathing caps had broken into her grandmother's house and taken all her possessions and put them in the road. In Jane's dream, rain fell on all her grandmother's things. Jane woke up weeping. Dan had wept too. Jane and Dan were friends.

The train had not yet left the station even though it was two hours past the posted departure time. An announcement had just been made that said that a two-hour delay was built into the train's schedule.

"They make up the time at night," Jane said. She plucked the postcard from Dan's hand. "This is a good one," she said. "I think you're sending it to Jim Anderson just so you can save it yourself." She read aloud, "This is a photograph of the Phantom Dream Car crashing through a wall of burning television sets before a cheering crowd at the Cow Palace in San Francisco."

At the beginning of summer, Dan's mother had given her one hundred dollars, four packages of new underwear and three dozen stamped postcards. Most of the cards were plain but there were a few with odd pictures on them. Dan's mother wanted to hear from her twice weekly throughout the summer. She had married a man named Jake, who was a carpenter. Jake had already built Dan three bookcases. This seemed to be the extent of what he knew how to do for Dan.

"I only have three left now," Dan said, "but when I get home, I'm going to start my own collection."

"I've been through that phase," Jane said. "It's just a phase. I don't think you're much of a correspondent. You wrote, 'I got sunburn. Love, Dan' . . . 'I bought a green Frisbee. Love, Dan' . . . 'Mrs. Muirhead has swimmer's ear. Love, Dan' . . . 'Mr. Muirhead went water-skiing and cracked his rib. Love, Dan' . . . When you write to people you should have something to say."

Dan didn't reply. She had been Jane's companion for a long time, and was wearying of what Jane's mother called her "effervescence."

Jane slapped Dan on the back and hollered, "Danica Anderson, for Godsakes! What is a clod like yourself doing on this fabulous journey!"

Together, as the train began to move, the girls made their way to the Starlight Lounge in Car 7 where Mr. and Mrs. Muirhead told them they would be enjoying cocktails. They hesitated in the car where the train's magician was with his audience, watching him while he did the magic silks trick, the cut and restored handkerchief trick, the enchanted salt shaker trick, and the dissolving quarter trick. The audience, primarily retirees, screamed with pleasure.

"I don't mind the tricks," Jane whispered to Dan, "but the junk that gets said drives me crazy."

The magician was a young man with a long spotted face. He did a lot of card forcing. Again and again, he called the card that people chose from a shuffled deck. Each time that the magician was successful, the audience participant yelled and smiled and in general acted thrilled. Jane and Dan passed on through.

"You don't really choose," Jane said. "He just makes you think you choose. He does it all with his pinky." She pushed Dan forward into the Starlight Lounge where Mrs. Muirhead was on a banquette staring out the window at a shed and an unkempt bush which was sliding slowly past. She was drinking a martini. Mr. Muirhead was several tables away talking to a young man wearing jeans and a yellow jacket. Jane did not sit down. "Mummy," she said, "can I have your olive?"

"Of course not," Mrs. Muirhead said, "it's soaked in gin."

Jane, Dan in tow, went to her father's table. "Daddy," Jane demanded, "why aren't you sitting with Mummy? Are you and Mummy having a fight?"

Dan was astonished at this question. Mr. and Mrs. Muirhead fought continuously and as bitterly as vipers. Their arguments were baroque, stately, and although frequently extraordinary, never enlightening. At breakfast, they would be quarreling over an incident at a cocktail party the night before or a dumb remark made fifteen years ago. At dinner, they would be howling over the fate, which they called by many names, which had given them one another. Forgiveness, charity and cooperation were qualities unknown to them. They were opponents *pur sang*. Dan was sure that one morning, Jane would be called from her classroom and told as gently as possible by Mr. Mooney, the school principal, that her parents had splattered one another's brains all over the lanai.

Mr. Muirhead looked at the children sorrowfully and touched Jane's cheek.

"I am not sitting with your mother because I am sitting with this young man here. We are having a fascinating conversation."

"Why are you always talking to young men?" Jane asked.

"Jane, honey," Mr. Muirhead said, "I will answer that." He took a swallow of his drink and sighed. He leaned forward and said earnestly, "I talk to so many young men because your mother won't let me talk to young women." He remained hunched over, patting Jane's cheek for a moment, and then leaned back.

The young man extracted a cigarette from his jacket and hesitated. Mr. Muirhead gave him a book of matches. "He does automobile illustrations," Mr. Muirhead said.

The young man nodded. "Belly bands. Pearls and flakes. Flames. All custom work."

Mr. Muirhead smiled. He seemed happier now. Mr. Muirhead loved conversations. He loved "to bring people out." Dan supposed that Jane had picked up this pleasant trait from her father and distorted it in some perversely personal way.

"I bet you have a Trans Am yourself," Jane said.

"You are so-o-o right," the young man said. "It's ice-blue. You like ice-blue? Maybe you're too young." He extended his hand showing a large gaudy stone in a setting that seemed to be gold. "Same color as this ring," he said.

Dan nodded. She could still be impressed by adults. Their mysterious, unreliable images still had the power to attract and confound her, but Jane was clearly not interested in the young man. She demanded much of life. She had very high standards when she wanted to. Mr. Muirhead ordered the girls ginger ales and the young man and himself another round of drinks. Sometimes the train, in the mysterious way of trains, would stop, or even reverse, and they would pass unfamiliar scenes once more. The same green pasture filled with slanty light, the same row of clapboard houses, each with the shades of their windows drawn against the heat, the same boats on their trailers, waiting on dry land. The moon was rising beneath a spectacular lightning and thunder storm. People around them were commenting on it. Close to the train, a sheen of dark birds flew low across a dirt road.

"Birds are only flying reptiles, I'm sure you're all aware," Jane said suddenly.

"Oh my God, what a horrible thought!" Mr. Muirhead said. His face had become a little slack and his hair had become somewhat disarranged.

"It's true, it's true," Jane sang. "Sad but true."

"You mean like lizards and snakes?" the young man asked. He snorted and shook his head.

"*Glorified* reptiles, certainly," Mr. Muirhead said, recovering a bit of his sense of time and place.

Dan suddenly felt lonely. It was not homesickness, although she would have given anything at that moment to be poking around in her little aluminum boat with Jim Anderson. But she wouldn't be living any longer in the place she thought of as "home." The town was the same but the place was different. The house where she had been a little tiny baby and had lived her whole life belonged to someone else now. Over the summer, her mother and Jake had bought another house which Jake was going to fix up.

"Reptiles have scales," the young man said, "or else they are long and slimy."

Dan felt like bawling. She could feel the back of her eyes swelling up like cupcakes. She was surrounded by strangers saying crazy things. Even her own mother often said crazy things in a reasonable way that made Dan know she was a stranger too. Dan's mother told Dan everything. Her mother told her she wouldn't have to worry about having brothers or sisters. Her mother discussed the particular nature of the problem with her. Half the things Dan's mother told her, Dan didn't want to know. There would be no brothers and sisters. There would be Dan and her mother and Jake, sitting around the house together, caring deeply for one another, sharing a nice life together, not making any mistakes.

Dan excused herself and started toward the lavatory on the level below. Mrs. Muirhead called to her as she approached and handed her a folded piece of paper. "Would you be kind enough to give this to Mr. Muirhead?" she asked. Dan returned to Mr. Muirhead and gave him the note and then went down to the lavatory. She sat on the little toilet as the train rocked along and cried.

After a while, she heard Jane's voice saying, "I hear you in there, Danica Anderson. What's the matter with you?"

Dan didn't say anything.

"I know it's you," Jane said. "I can see your stupid shoes and your stupid socks."

Dan blew her nose, pushed the button on the toilet and said, "What did the note say?"

"I don't know," Jane said. "Daddy ate it."

"He ate it!" Dan exclaimed. She opened the door of the stall and went to the sink. She washed her hands and splashed her face with water. She giggled. "He really ate it?"

"Everybody is looped in that Starlight Lounge," Jane said. Jane patted her hair with a hairbrush. Jane's hair was full of tangles and she never brushed hard enough to get them out. She looked at Dan by looking in the mirror. "Why were you crying?"

"I was thinking about your grandma," Dan said. "She said that one year she left the Christmas tree up until Easter."

"Why were you thinking about my grandma!" Jane yelled.

"I was thinking about her singing," Dan said, startled. "I like her singing."

In her head, Dan could hear Jane's grandmother singing about Death's dark waters and sinking souls, about Mercy Seats and the Great Physician. She could hear the voice rising and falling through the thin walls of the Maine house, borne past the dark screens and into the night.

"I don't want you thinking about my grandma," Jane said, pinching Dan's arm.

Dan tried not to think of Jane's grandma. Once, she had seen her fall coming out of the water. The beach was stony. The stones were round and smooth and slippery. Jane's grandmother had skinned her arm and bloodied her lip.

The girls went into the corridor and saw Mrs. Muirhead standing there. Mrs. Muirhead was deeply tanned. She had put her hair up in a twist and a wad of cotton was noticeable in her left ear. The three of them stood together, bouncing and nudging against one another with the motion of the train.

"My ear is killing me," Mrs. Muirhead said. "I think there's something they're not telling me. It crackles and snaps in there. It's like a bird breaking seeds in there." She touched the bone between cheekbone and ear. "I think that doctor I was seeing should lose his license. He was handsome and competent, certainly, but on my last visit, he was vacuuming my ear and his secretary came in to ask him a question and she put her hand on his neck. She stroked his neck, his secretary! While I was sitting there having my ear vacuumed!" Mrs. Muirhead's cheeks were flushed.

The three of them gazed out the window. The train must have been clipping along, but things outside, although gone in an instant, seemed to be moving slowly. Beneath a street light, a man was kicking his pickup truck.

"I dislike trains," Mrs. Muirhead said. "I find them depressing."

"It's the oxygen deprivation," Jane said, "coming from having to share the air with all these people."

"You're such a snob, dear," Mrs. Muirhead sighed.

"We're going to supper now," Jane said.

"Supper," Mrs. Muirhead said. "Ugh."

The children left her looking out the window, a disconsolate, pretty woman wearing a green dress with a line of frogs dancing around it.

The dining car was almost full. The windows reflected the eaters. The countryside was dim and the train pushed through it.

Jane steered them to a table where a man and woman silently labored over their meal.

"My name is Crystal," Jane offered, "and this is my twin sister, Clara."

"Clara!" Dan exclaimed. Jane was always inventing drab names for her.

"We were triplets," Jane went on, "but the other died at birth. Cord got all twisted around his neck or something."

The woman looked at Jane and smiled.

"What is your line of work?" Jane persisted brightly.

There was silence. The woman kept smiling, then the man said, "I don't do anything, I don't have to do anything. I was injured in Vietnam and they brought me to the base hospital and worked on reviving me for forty-five minutes. Then they gave up. They thought I was dead. Four hours later, I woke up in the mortuary. The Army gives me a good pension." He pushed his chair away from the table and left.

Dan looked after him, astonished, a cold roll raised halfway to her mouth. "Was your husband really dead for all that while?" she asked.

"My husband, ha!" the woman said. "I'd never laid eyes on that man before the six-thirty seating."

"I bet you're a professional woman who doesn't believe in men," Jane said slyly.

"Crystal, how did you guess! It's true, men are a collective hallucination of women. It's like when a group of crackpots get together on a hilltop and see flying saucers." The woman picked at her chicken.

Jane looked surprised, then said, "My father went to a costume party once wrapped from head to foot in aluminum foil."

"A casserole," the woman offered.

"No! A spaceman, an alien astronaut!"

Dan giggled, remembering when Mr. Muirhead had done that. She felt that Jane had met her match with this woman.

"What do you do!" Jane fairly screamed. "You won't tell us!"

"I do drugs," the woman said. The girls shrank back. "Ha," the woman said. "Actually, I test drugs for pharmaceutical companies. And I do research for a perfume manufacturer. I am involved in the search for human pheromones."

Jane looked levelly at the woman.

"I know you don't know what a pheromone is, Crystal. To put it grossly, a pheromone is a smell that a person has that can make another person do or feel a certain thing. It's an irresistible signal."

Dan thought of mangrove roots and orange groves. Of the smell of gas when the pilot light blew out on Jane's grandmother's stove. She liked the smell of the Atlantic Ocean when it dried upon your skin and the smell of Jim Anderson's fur when he had been rained upon. There were smells that could make you follow them, certainly.

Jane stared at the woman, tipping forward slightly in her seat.

"Relax, will you, Crystal, you're just a child. You don't even *have* a smell yet," the woman said. "I test all sorts of things. Sometimes I'm part of a control group and sometimes I'm not. You never know. If you're part of the control group, you're just given a placebo. A placebo, Crystal, is something that is nothing, but you don't know it's nothing. You think you're getting something that will change you or make you feel better or healthier or more attractive or something, but you're not really."

"I know what a placebo is," Jane muttered.

"Well that's terriffic, Crystal, you're a prodigy." The woman removed a book from her handbag and began to read it. The book had a denim jacket on it which concealed its title.

"Ha!" Jane said, rising quickly and attempting to knock over a glass of water. "My name's not Crystal!"

Dan grabbed the glass before it fell and hurried after her. They returned to the Starlight Lounge. Mr. Muirhead was sitting with another young man. This young man had a blond beard and a studious manner.

"Oh, this is a wonderful trip!" Mr. Muirhead said exuberantly. "The wonderful people you meet on a trip like this! This is the most fascinating young man. He's a writer. Been everywhere. He's putting together a book on cemeteries of the world. Isn't that some subject? I told him anytime he's in our town, stop by our restaurant, be my guest for some stone crab claws."

"Hullo," the young man said to the girls.

"We were speaking of Père-Lachaise, the legendary Parisian cemetery," Mr. Muirhead said. "So wistful. So grand and romantic. Your mother and I visited it, Jane, when we were in Paris. We strolled through it on a clear crisp autumn day. The desires of the human heart have no boundaries, girls. The mess of secrets in the human heart are without number. Witnessing Père-Lachaise was a very moving experience. As we strolled, your mother was screaming at me, Jane. Do you know why, honey-bunch? She was screaming at me because back in New York, I had garaged the car at the place on East 84th Street. Your mother said that the people in the place on East 84th Street never turned the ignition all the way off to the left and were always running down the battery. She said that there wasn't a soul in all of New York City who didn't know that the people running the garage on East 84th Street were idiots who were always ruining batteries. Before Père-Lachaise, girls, this young man and I were discussing the Panteón, just outside of Guanajuato in Mexico. It so happens that I am also familiar with the Panteón. Your mother wanted some tiles for the foyer so we went to Mexico. You stayed with Mrs. Murphy, Jane. Remember? It was Mrs. Murphy who taught you how to make egg salad. In any case, the Panteón is a walled cemetery, not unlike the Campo Santo in Genoa, Italy, but the reason everybody goes there is to see the mummies. Something about the exceptionally dry air in the mountains has preserved the bodies and there's a little museum of mummies. It's grotesque of course, and it certainly gave me pause. I mean it's one thing to think we will all gather together in a paradise of fadeless splendor like your grandma thinks, lamby-lettuce, and it's another thing to think as the Buddhists do that latent possibilities withdraw into the heart at death, but do not perish, thereby allowing the being to be reborn, and it's one more thing, even,

to believe like a Goddamn scientist in one of the essential laws
of physics which states that no energy is ever lost. It's one thing
to think any of those things, girls, but it's quite another to be
standing in that little museum looking at those miserable mummies. The horror and indignation were in their faces still. I
almost cried aloud, so vivid was my sense of the fleetingness of
this life. We made our way into the fresh air of the courtyard
and I bought a package of cigarettes at a little stand which sold
postcards and film and such. I reached into my pocket for my
lighter and it appeared that my lighter was not there. It seemed
that I had lost my lighter. The lighter was a very good one that
your mother had bought me the Christmas before, Jane, and
your mother started screaming at me. There was a very gentle,
warm rain falling, and there were bougainvillea petals on the
walks. Your mother grasped my arm and reminded me that the
lighter had been a gift from her. Your mother reminded me
of the blazer she had bought for me. I spilled buttered popcorn
on it at the movies and you can still see the spot. She reminded
me of the hammock she bought for my fortieth birthday,
which I allowed to rot in the rain. She recalled the shoulder
bag she bought me, which I detested, it's true. It was somehow
left out in the yard and I mangled it with the lawnmower.
Descending the cobbled hill into Guanajuato, your mother
recalled every one of her gifts to me, offerings both monetary
and of the heart. She pointed out how I had mishandled and
betrayed every one."

No one said anything. "Then," Mr. Muirhead continued,
"there was the Modena Cemetery in Italy."

"That hasn't been completed yet," the young man said
hurriedly. "It's a visionary design by the architect Aldo Rossi.
In our conversation, I was just trying to describe the project to
you."

"You can be assured," Mr. Muirhead said, "that when the
project is finished and I take my little family on a vacation to
Italy, as we walk, together and afraid, strolling through the
hapless landscape of the Modena Cemetery, Jane's mother will
be screaming at me."

"Well, I must be going," the young man said. He got up.

"So long," Mr. Muirhead said.

"Were they really selling postcards of the mummies in that place?" Dan asked.

"Yes they were, sweetie-pie," Mr. Muirhead said. "In this world there is a postcard of everything. That's the kind of world this is."

The crowd was getting boisterous in the Starlight Lounge. Mrs. Muirhead made her way down the aisle toward them and with a deep sigh, sat beside her husband. Mr. Muirhead gesticulated and formed words silently with his lips as though he was talking to the girls.

"What?" Mrs. Muirhead said.

"I was just telling the girls some of the differences between men and women. Men are more adventurous and aggressive with greater spatial and mechanical abilities. Women are more consistent, nurturent and aesthetic. Men can see better than women, but women have better hearing," Mr. Muirhead said.

"Very funny," Mrs. Muirhead said.

The girls retired from the melancholy regard Mr. and Mrs. Muirhead had fixed upon one another, and wandered through the cars of the train, occasionally returning to their seats to fuss in the cluttered nests they had created there. Around midnight, they decided to revisit the game car where earlier, people had been playing backgammon, Diplomacy, anagrams, crazy eights and Clue. They were still at it, variously throwing down queens of diamonds, moving troops through Asia Minor and accusing Colonel Mustard of doing it in the conservatory with a wrench. Whenever there was a lull in the playing, they talked about the accident.

"What accident?" Jane demanded.

"Train hit a Buick," a man said. "Middle of the night." The man had big ears and a tattoo on his forearm.

"There aren't any good new games," a woman complained. "Haven't been for years and years."

"Did you fall asleep?" Jane said accusingly to Dan.

"When could that have happened?" Dan said.

"We didn't see it," Jane said, disgusted.

"Two teenagers escaped without a scratch," the man said. "Lived to laugh about it. They are young and silly but it's no joke to the engineer. The engineer has a lot of paperwork to do after he hits something. The engineer will be filling out forms for a week." The man's tattoo said MOM AND DAD.

"Rats," Jane said.

The children returned to the darkened dining room where *Superman* was being shown on a small television set. Jane instantly fell asleep. Dan watched Superman spin the earth backward so he could prevent Lois Lane from being smothered in a rock slide. The train shot past a group of old lighted buildings. SEWER KING, a sign said. When the movie ended, Jane woke up.

"When we lived in New York," she said muzzily, "I was sitting in the kitchen one afternoon doing my homework and this girl came in and sat down at the table. Did I ever tell you this? It was the middle of the winter and it was snowing. This person just came in with snow on her coat and sat right down at the table."

"Who was she?" Dan asked.

"It was me, but I was old. I mean I was about thirty years old or something."

"It was a dream," Dan said.

"It was the middle of the afternoon, I tell you! I was doing my homework. She said, 'You've never lifted a finger to help me.' Then she asked me for a glass with some ice in it."

After a moment, Dan said, "It was probably the cleaning lady."

"Cleaning lady! Cleaning lady for Godssakes, what do you know about cleaning ladies!"

Dan felt her hair bristle as though someone were running a comb through it back to front, and realized she was mad, madder than she'd been all summer, for all summer she'd only felt humiliated when Jane was nasty to her.

"Listen up," Dan said, "don't talk to me like that any more."

"Like what," Jane said coolly.

Dan stood up and walked away while Jane was saying, "The thing I don't understand is how she ever got into that apartment. My father had about a dozen locks on the door."

Dan sat in her seat in the quiet, dark coach and looked out at the dark night. She tried to recollect how it seemed dawn happened. Things just sort of rose out, she guessed she knew. There was nothing you could do about it. She thought of Jane's dream in which the men in white bathing caps were pushing all her grandma's things out of the house and into the street. The inside became empty and the outside became full. Dan was beginning to feel sorry for herself. She was alone, with no friends and no parents, sitting on a train between one place and another, scaring herself with someone else's dream in the middle of the night. She got up and walked through the rocking cars to the Starlight Lounge for a glass of water. After four A.M. it was no longer referred to as the Starlight Lounge. They stopped serving drinks and turned off the electric stars. It became just another place to sit. Mr. Muirhead was sitting there, alone. He must have been on excellent terms with the stewards because he was drinking a Bloody Mary.

"Hi, Dan!" he said.

Dan sat opposite him. After a moment she said, "I had a very nice summer. Thank you for inviting me."

"Well, I hope you enjoyed your summer, sweetie," Mr. Muirhead said.

"Do you think Jane and I will be friends forever?" Dan asked.

Mr. Muirhead looked surprised. "Definitely not. Jane will not have friends. Jane will have husbands, enemies and lawyers." He cracked ice noisily with his white teeth. "I'm glad you enjoyed your summer, Dan, and I hope you're enjoying your childhood. When you grow up, a shadow falls. Everything's sunny and then this big Goddamn *wing* or something passes overhead."

"Oh," Dan said.

"Well, I've only heard that's the case actually," Mr. Muirhead said. "Do you know what I want to be when I grow up?"

He waited for her to smile. "When I grow up I want to become an Indian so I can use my Indian name."

"What is your Indian name?" Dan asked, smiling.

"My Indian name is 'He Rides a Slow Enduring Heavy Horse.' "

"That's a nice one," Dan said.

"It is, isn't it?" Mr. Muirhead said, gnawing ice.

Outside, the sky was lightening. Daylight was just beginning to flourish on the city of Jacksonville. It fell without prejudice on the slaughterhouses, Dairy Queens and courthouses, on the car lots, sabal palms and a billboard advertisement for pies.

The train went slowly around a long curve, and looking backward, past Mr. Muirhead, Dan could see the entire length of it moving ahead. The bubble-topped cars were dark and sinister in the first flat and hopeful light of the morning.

Dan took the three postcards she had left out of her bookbag and looked at them. One showed Thomas Edison beneath a banyan tree. One showed a little tar-paper shack out in the middle of the desert in New Mexico where men were supposed to have invented the atomic bomb. One was a "quicky" card showing a porpoise balancing a grapefruit on the top of his head.

"Oh, I remember those," Mr. Muirhead said, picking up the "quicky" card. "You just check off what you want." He read aloud, *"How are you? I am fine ( ) lonesome ( ) happy ( ) sad ( ) broke ( ) flying high( )"* Mr. Muirhead chuckled. He read, *"I have been good ( ) no good ( ). I saw The Gulf of Mexico ( ) The Atlantic Ocean ( ) The Orange Groves ( ) Interesting Attractions ( ) You in My Dreams ( )."*

"I like this one," Mr. Muirhead said, chuckling.

"You can have it," Dan said. "I'd like you to have it."

"You're a nice little girl," Mr. Muirhead said. He looked at his glass and then out the window. "What do you think was on that note Mrs. Muirhead had you give me?" he asked. "Do you think there's something I've missed?"

The Excursion

*J*ENNY lies a little. She is just a little girl, a child with fears. She fears that birds will fly out of the toilet bowl. Starlings with slick black wings. She fears trees and fishes and the bones in meat. She lies a little but it is not considered serious. Sometimes it seems she forgets where she is. She is lost in a place that is not her childhood. Sometimes she will say to someone, Mrs. Coogan at the Capt'n Davy Nursery School, for example, that her mother is dead, her father is dead, even her dog Tonto is dead. She will say that she has no toys, that she lives with machinery she cannot run, that she lives in a house with no windows, no view of the street, that she lives with strangers. She has to understand everything herself.

Poor Mrs. Coogan! She pats Jenny's shoulder. Jenny wears pretty and expensive dresses with blue sneakers. The effect is charming. She has blond hair falling over a rather low brow and an interesting, mobile face. She does everything too fast. She rushes to bathtimes and mealtimes and even to sleep. She sleeps rapidly with deep, heartbreaking sighs. Such hurry is unnecessary. It is as though she rushes forward to meet even her memories.

Jenny does not know how to play games very well. When the others play, she is still. She stands with her stomach thrust out, watching the others with a cool, inward gaze. Sometimes, something interrupts her, some urgent voice, perhaps, or shout, and she makes a startled, curious skip. Her brown eyes brim with confusion. She turns pale or very red. Yes, sometimes Jenny has bad days. The crayons are dead, the swings are dead, even little Johnny Lewis who sits so patiently on his mat at snacktime will be dead. He is thirsty and when he gets the cup of juice which Mrs. Coogan gives him, Jenny is glad for his sake.

"I am so happy Johnny Lewis got his juice!" Jenny cries.

Poor Mrs. Coogan. The child is such a puzzle.

"I don't care for the swimming," Jenny tells her, even though Mrs. Coogan doesn't take her little group swimming. She takes them for a walk. Down to the corner, where the school bus carrying the older children goes by.

"Perhaps you'll like it when you get a little older, when you get a little better at it," Mrs. Coogan says.

Jenny shakes her head. She thinks of all the nakedness, milling and bobbing and bumping against her in the flat, warm, dark water. She says this aloud.

"Oh my dear," Mrs. Coogan says.

"I don't understand about the swimming," Jenny says.

Jenny's father picks her up at four. In the car, he always has a present for her. Today it is a watch. It is only a toy watch, but it has moving parts and the manufacturer states that if it is not abused it will keep fairly reasonable time.

Mrs. Coogan says to Jenny's father, "All children fib a little. It's their nature. Their lives are incompatible with the limits imposed upon their experience."

Jenny feels no real insecurity while Mrs. Coogan speaks, but she is a little anxious. She is with a man. She doesn't smell very good. Outside other men are striking the locked door with sticks.

"Leña," they call. "Leña."

Jenny's father frowns at Mrs. Coogan. He does not wish to be aware that Jenny lies. To him, it is a terrible risk of oneself to lie. It risks control, peace, self-knowledge, even, perhaps, the proper acceptance of love. He is a thoughtful, reasonable man. He loves his only child. He wills her safe passage through the world. He does not wish to acknowledge that lying gives a beat and structure to Jenny's life that the truth has not yet justified. Jenny's imagination depresses him. He senses an ultimatum in it.

Jenny runs to the car. Her father is not with her. He is behind her. Suddenly the child realizes this and whips around to catch him with her eyes. Once again, she succeeds.

Jenny's mother is in the front seat, checking over her grocery list. Jenny kisses her and shows her the big, colorful watch. A tiny girl sits on a swing within the watch's face. When Jenny winds it, the girl starts swinging, the clock starts to run.

Jenny sits in the back. The car moves out into the street. She hears a mother somewhere crying. Some mother, calling, "Oh come back and let me rock you on your little swing!"

Jenny says nothing. She is propelled by sidereal energies. Loving, for her, will not be a free choosing of her destiny. It will be the discovery of the most fateful part of herself. She is with a man. When he kisses her, he covers her throat with his hand. He rubs his fingers lightly down the tendons of her neck. He holds her neck in his big hand as he kisses her over and over again.

"Raisin Bran or Cheerios?" Jenny's mother asks. "Cheddar or Swiss?"

Jenny is just a little girl. She worries that there will not be enough jam, not enough cookies. When she walks with her mother through the supermarket, she nervously pats her mother's arm.

Now, at home, Jenny reads. She is precocious in this. When she first discovered that she could read, she did not tell anyone about it. The words took on the depths of patient, dangerous animals, and Jenny cautiously lived alone with them for awhile. Now, however, everyone realizes that she can read, and they are very proud of her. Jenny reads in the newspaper that that day in San Luis Obispo, California, a seventeen-year-old girl came out of a clothing store, looked around horrified, screamed, and died. The newpaper said that several years previous to this, the girl's sister had woken early, given a piercing scream, and died. The newspaper said that the parents now fear for the welfare of their other two daughters. Women suffer from the loss of a secret once known. Jenny will realize this someday. Now, however, she merely thinks, "What is the dread that women have?"

Jenny gets up and goes to her room. A stuffed bear is propped on her bureau. She takes it to the kitchen and gives it some orange juice. Then she takes it to the bathroom and puts it on the toilet seat for a moment. Then she puts it to bed.

Jenny wakes crying in the night and rushes into her parents' room. She is not sure of the time; she is not sure if they will be there. Of course they are there. Jenny is just a child. On a bedside table are her mother's reading glasses and a little vase of marigolds. Deeply hued, yellow, red and orange. Her parents are very patient. She is a normal little girl with fears, with nightmares. The nightmares do no real harm, that is, they will not alter her life. She is afraid that she is growing, that she will grow too much. She returns to her room after being comforted, holding one of the little flowers.

The man likes flowers, although he dislikes Jenny's childishness. He removes Jenny's skimpy cotton dress. He puts the flowers between her breasts, between her legs. The house is full of flowers. It is Mexico on the Day of the Dead. Millions of marigolds have been woven into carpets and placed on the graves. Jenny's mouth hurts, her stomach hurts. Yes, the man dislikes her childishness. He kneels beside her, his hands on her hips, and forces her to look at his blank, warm face. It is a youthful face, although he is certainly no longer a young man. Jenny had seen him when he was younger, drunk, blue-eyed. It doesn't matter. He doesn't age. He has had other loves and he has behaved similarly with them all. How could it be otherwise? Even so, Jenny knows that she has originated with him, that anything before him was nostalgia for this. Even so, there are letters, variously addressed, interchangeably addressed, it would seem. These letters won't be kept. It isn't the time, but they are here now, in a jumble, littered with the toys. Jenny reads them as though in a dream. This is Jenny! As in a dream too, she is less reasonable but capable of better judgment.

I won't stay here. It is a tomb, this town, and the streets are full of whores, women with live mice or snakes or fish in the clear plastic heels of their shoes. Death and the whores are everywhere, walking in these bright, horrible shoes.

How unhappy Jenny's mother would be if she were to see this letter! She comes into the child's room in the morning and helps her tie her shoes.

"You do it like this," she says, crossing the laces, "and then you do this, you make a bunny ear here, see."

Her mother holds her on her lap while she teaches her to tie her shoes. Jenny is so impatient. She wants to cry as she sees her mother's eager fingers. Jenny's nightie is damp and sweaty. Her mother takes it off and goes to the sink where she washes it with sweet-smelling soap. Then she makes Jenny's breakfast. Jenny is not hungry. She takes the food outside and scatters it on the ground. The grass covers it up. Jenny goes back to her room. Everything is neatly put away. Her mother has made the bed. Jenny takes everything out again, her toy stove and type-writer and phone, her puppets and cars, the costly and minute dollhouse furnishings. Everything is there: a tiny papier-mâché pot roast dinner, lamps, rugs, andirons, fans, everything. The cupboards are full of play bread, the play pool is full of water.

Jenny's face is tense and intimate. She knows everything, but how aimless and arbitrary her knowledge is! For she has only desire; she has always had only the desire for this, her sleek, quiescent lover. He is so cold and so satisfying for there is no discovery in him. She goes to the bed and curls up beside him. He is dark and she is light. There are no shadings in Jenny's world. He is a tall, dark tree rooted in the stubborn night, and she is a flame seeking him—unstable, transparent. They are in Oaxaca. If they opened the shutters they would see the stone town. The town is made of a soft, pale green stone that makes it look as though it has been rained upon for centuries. Shadows in the shape of men fall from the buildings. Everything is cool, almost rotten. In the markets, the fruit beads with water; the fragile feathered skulls of the birds are moist to the touch.

The man sleeks her hair back behind her ears. She is not so pretty now. Her face is uneven, her eyes are closed. "You're asleep," he says. "You're making love to me in your sleep. *Vete a la chingada.*" He says it slangily and softly, scornfully as any Mexican. She is nothing, nowhere. There is something exquisite in this, in the way, now, that he holds her throat. The pressure *is* so familiar. She yearns for this.

But he turns from her. He leaves.

Jenny pretends sleep. She plays that she is sleeping. She is fascinated with her sleep where everything takes place as though it were not so. Nothing is concealed. On stationery from the Hotel Principal there is written:

Nobody to blame. Call 228

She sits at a small desk, drinking beer and reading. She is reading about the Aztecs. She notes the goddess TLAZOLTEOTL, the goddess of filth and fecundity, of human moods, sexual love and confession. Jenny sits very straight in the chair. Her neck is long, full, graceful. But she feels out of breath. The high, clear air here makes her pant. The man pants too while he climbs the steep, stone steps of the town. He smokes too much. At night, when they return from drinking, he coughs flecks of blood onto the bathroom mirror. The blood is on the tiles, in the basin. Jenny closes her own mouth tightly as she hears him gag. Breath is outside her, expelled, not doing her any good. She stands beside the man as he coughs. There is not much blood, but it seems to be everywhere, late at night, after they have been drinking, everywhere except on the man's clothes. He is impeccable about his clothes. He always wears a grey lightweight suit and a white shirt. He has two suits and they are both grey, and he has several shirts and they are all white. He is always the same. Even in his nakedness, his force, he is smooth, furled, closed. He is simple to her. There is no other way offered. He offers her the death of his sterility. His sexuality is the source of life, and his curse is death. He offers her nothing except his dying.

She wets her hands and wipes off the mirror. She cannot imagine him dead really. She is just a child embracing the crisis of a woman. The death she sees is that of herself in his emptiness. And he fills her with it. He floods her with emptiness. She grasps his thick, longish hair. She feels as if she is floating through his hair, falling miraculously away from danger into death. Safe at last.

"Jenny, Jenny, Jenny," her mother calls.

"I want a baby," Jenny says. "Can I have a baby?"

"Of course," her mother says, "when you get to be a big girl and fall in love."

Jenny will write on the stationery of the Hotel Principal:

The claims of love and self-preservation are opposed.

The man looks over her shoulder. He is restless, impatient to get going. They are going to the baths outside of town, in the mountains. A waterfall thuds into a long, stone basin which has been artificially heated. It is a private club, crowded with Americans and wealthy Mexicans. When Jenny and the man arrive at the baths, they first go to a tiny stone cubicle where the man strips. He hangs his clothes carefully from the wooden pegs which are fixed in the stone. Jenny looks outside where a red horse grazes from a long, woven tether. There is water trickling over the face of the hillside. There is very little grass. The water sparkles around the horse's hooves. The man turns Jenny from the window and begins to undress her. She is like a little child with artless limbs. He rolls her pants down slowly. He slips her sweater off. He does everything slowly. Her clothes fall to the floor which is wet with something, which smells sweet. With one hand, the man holds her arms firmly behind her back. He doesn't do anything to her. She cannot smell him or even feel his breath. She can see his face which is a little stern but not frightening. It holds no disappointment for her. She tries to move closer to him, but his grip on her arms

prevents her. She begins to tremble. Her body feels his stroking, his touch, even though he does nothing. Her body starts
to beat, to move in the style of their lovemaking. She becomes
confused, the absence of him in her is so strong.

Later, the man goes out to the pool. Jenny hates the baths,
but they come here several times a week on the man's insis-
tence. She dresses and goes out to the side of the pool and
watches the man swim back and forth. There are many people
here, naked or nearly so, tossing miniature footballs back and
forth. She sees the man grasp the ankles of a woman and begin
to tow her playfully through the water. The woman wears silver
earrings. Her hair is silver, her pubic hair is silver. Her mouth
is a thickly frosted white. The water foams on her skin in tiny
translucent bubbles. The woman laughs and moves her legs up
in a scissors grip around the man's waist. Jenny sees him kiss
her.

Another man, a Mexican, comes up to Jenny. He is bare-
chested and wears white trousers and tall, yellow boots. He
absently plucks at his left nipple while he looks at her.

"Ford Galaxie," he says at last. He takes a ring of car keys
from his pocket and jerks his head toward the mountains.

"No," Jenny says.

"Galaxie," the Mexican says. "Galaxie. *Rojo.*"

Jenny sees the car, its red shell cold in the black mountains,
drawn through the landscape of rock and mutilated maguey.
Drawn through, with her inside, quietly transported.

"No," she says. She hates the baths. The tile in the bottom
of the pool is arranged in the shape of a bird, a heron with thin
legs and a huge, flat head. Her lover stands still in the water
now, looking at her, amused.

"Jenny," her mother laughs. "You're such a dreamer.
Would you like to go out for supper? You and Daddy and I can
go to the restaurant that you like."

For it is just the summer. That is all it is, and Jenny is only
five. In the house which they are renting on Martha's Vine-
yard, there is a dinghy stored in the rafters of the living room.
The landlord is supposed to come for it and take it down, but

he does not. Jenny positions herself beneath the dinghy and scatters her shell collection over her legs and chest. She pretends that she has been cast out of it and floated to the bottom of the sea.

"Jenny-cake, get up now," her mother says. The child rises heavily from the floor. The same sorrow undergone for nothing is concluded. Again and again, nothing.

"Oh Jenny-cake," her mother says sadly, for Jenny is so quiet, so pale. They have come to the island for the sunshine, for play, to offer Jenny her childhood. Her childhood eludes them all. What is the guide which Jenny follows?

"Let's play hairdresser," her mother says. "I'll be the hairdresser and you be the little girl."

Jenny lets her comb and arrange her hair.

"You're so pretty," her mother says.

But she is so melancholy, so careless with herself. She is bruised everywhere. Her mother parts her hair carefully. She brings out a dish of soapy water and brushes and trims Jenny's nails. She is put in order. She is a tidy little girl in a clean dress going out to supper on a summer night.

"Come on Jenny," her mother urges her. "We want to be back home while it's still light." Jenny moves slowly to the door that her father is holding open for them.

"I have an idea," her mother says, "I'll be a parade and you be the little girl following the parade."

Jenny is so far away. She smiles to keep her mother from prattling so. She is what she will be. She has no energy, no talent, not even for love. She lies face down, her face buried in a filthy sheet. The man lies beside her. She can feel his heart beating on her arm. Pounding like something left out of life. A great machine, a desolate engine, taking over for her, moving her. The machine moves her out the door, into the streets of the town.

There is a dance floor in the restaurant. Sometimes Jenny dances with her father. She dances by standing on top of his shoes while he moves around the floor. The restaurant is quite expensive. The menu is written in chalk on a blackboard which is then rolled from table to table. They go to this restaurant mostly because Jenny likes the blackboard. She can pretend that this is school.

There is a candle on each table, and Jenny blows it out at the beginning of each meal. This plunges their table into deep twilight. Sometimes the waitress relights the candle, and Jenny blows it out again. She can pretend that this is her birthday over and over again. Her parents allow her to do this. They allow her to do anything that does not bring distress to others. This usually works out well.

Halfway through their dinner, they become aware of a quarrel at the next table. A man is shouting at the woman who sits beside him. He does not appear angry, but he is saying outrageous things. The woman sits very straight in her chair and cuts into her food. Once, she puts her hand gently on the side of his head. He does not shrug it off nor does it appear that he allows the caress. The woman's hand falls back in her lap.

"Please don't," the woman says. "We're spoiling the others' dinner."

"I don't care about the others," the man says. "I care about you."

The woman's laugh is high and uneasy. Her face is serene, but her hands tremble. The bones glow beneath her taut skin. There is a sense of blood, decay, the smell of love.

"Nothing matters except you," the man says again. He reaches over and picks up the food from her plate. It is some sort of creamed fish. He squeezes it in his hand and lets it drop on the table between them. It knocks over the flowers, the wine. "What do you care what others think?" he says.

"I don't know why people go out if they're not intending to have a nice time," Jenny's mother whispers. Jenny doesn't speak. The man's curses tease her ears. The reality of the couple, now gone, cheats her eyes. She gazes fixedly at the abandoned table, at the garbage there. Everywhere there is disorder. Even in her parents' eyes.

"Tomorrow we're going sailing," her father says. "It's going to be a beautiful day."

"I would say that woman had a problem there," Jenny's mother says.

Outside, the sunset has dispersed the afternoon's fog. The sun makes long paddle strokes through the clouds. At day's end, the day creaks back to brightness like a swinging boom. Jenny walks down the street between her parents. At the curb, as children do, she takes a little leap into space, supported, for the moment, by their hands.

And now gone for good, this moment. It is night again.

"It's been night for a long time," the man says. He is shaving at the basin. His face, to about an inch below his eyes, is a white mask of lather. His mouth is a dark hole in the mask.

Jenny's dizzy from drinking. The sheets are white, the walls are white. One section of the room has a raised ceiling. It rises handsomely to nothing but a single light bulb, shaded by strips of wood. The frame around the light is very substantial. It is as though the light were caged. The light is like a wild thing up there, pressed against the ceiling, a furious bright creature with slanty wings.

In the room there is a chair, a table, a bureau and a bed. There is a milkshake in a glass on a tin tray. On the surface of the milk, green petals of mold reach out from the sides toward the center.

"Clean yourself up and we'll go out," the man says.

Jenny moves obediently to the basin. She hangs her head over the round black drain. She splashes her hands and face with water. The drain seems very complex. Grids, mazes, avenues of descent, lacings, and webs of matter. At the very bottom of the drain she sees a pinpoint of light. She's sure of it. Children lie there in that light, sleeping. She sees them so clearly, their small, sweet mouths open in the light.

"We know too much," Jenny says. "We all know too much almost right away."

"Clean yourself up better than that," the man says.

"You go ahead. I'll meet you there," Jenny says. For she has plans for the future. Jenny has lived in nothing if not the future all her life. Time had moved between herself and the man, but only for years. What does time matter to the inevitability of relations? It is inevitability that matters to lives, not love. For had she not always remembered him? And seen him rising from a kiss? Always.

When she is alone, she unties the rope that ties her luggage together. The bag is empty. She has come to this last place with nothing, really. She has been with this man for a long time. There had always been less of her each time she followed him. She wants to do this right, but her fingers fumble with the rope. It is as though her fingers were cold, the rope knotted and soaked with sea water. It is so difficult to arrange. She stops for a moment and then remembers in a panic that she has to go to the bathroom. That was the most important thing to remember. She feels close to tears because she almost forgot.

"I have to go to the bathroom," she cries.

Her mother leads her there.

"This is not a nice bathroom," her mother says. Water runs here only at certain times of the day. It is not running now. There are rags on the floor. The light falling through the window is dirty.

"Help me Mother," Jenny says.

Her stomach is so upset. She is afraid she will soil herself. She wants to get out in the air for a moment and clear her head. Her head is full of lies. Outside the toilet, out there, she remembers, is the deck of the motor sailer. The green sails which have faded to a style of blue are luffing, pounding like boards in the wind. She closes the door to the toilet. Out here is the Atlantic, rough and blue and cold. Of course there is no danger. The engines are on; they are bringing the people back to the dock. The sails have the weight of wood. There is no danger. She is all right. She is just a little girl. She is with her mother and father. They are on vacation. They are cruising around the island with other tourists. Her father has planned an excursion for each day of their vacation. Now they are almost home. No one is behaving recklessly. People sit quietly on the boat or move about measuredly, collecting tackle or coiling lines or helping children into their sweaters.

Jenny sees the man waiting on the dock. The boat's engines whine higher as the boat is backed up, as it bumps softly against the canvas-wrapped pilings. The horrid machine whines higher and higher. She steps off into his arms.

He kisses her as he might another. She finds him rough, hurtful at first, but then his handling of her becomes more gentle, more sure in the knowledge that she is willing.

His tongue moves deeply, achingly in her mouth. His loving becomes autonomous now. It becomes, at last, complete.

The Yard Boy

*T*HE yard boy was a spiritual materialist. He lived in the Now. He was free from the karmic chain. Being enlightened wasn't easy. It was very hard work. It was manual labor actually.

The enlightened being is free. He feels the sorrows and sadness of those around him but does not necessarily feel his own. The yard boy felt that he had been enlightened for about two months, at the most.

The yard boy had two possessions. One was a pickup truck. The other was a plover he had stuffed and mounted when he thought he wanted to be an ornithologist, in the days before he had become a spiritual materialist. The bird was in the room he rented. The only other thing in the room was a bed. The landlady provided sheets and towels. Sometimes when he came back from work hot and sweaty with little bits of leaves and stuff caught in his hair, the landlady would give him a piece of key lime pie on a blue plate.

The yard boy was content. He had hard muscular arms and a tanned back. He had compassion. He had a girl friend. When he thought about it, he supposed that having a girl friend was a cop-out to the security which he had eschewed. This was a preconception however and a preconception was the worst form of all the forms of security. The yard boy believed he was in balance on this point. He tried to see things the way they were from the midst of nowhere, and he felt that he had worked out this difficulty about the girl friend satisfactorily.

The important thing was to be able to see through the veils of preconception.

The yard boy was a handsome fellow. He seldom spoke. He was appealing. Once he had run over an old lady and had broken her leg, but no one had gotten mad at him about it. Now that he was a yard boy his hands smelled of 6-6-6. His jeans smelled of tangelos. He was honest and truthful, a straightforward person who did not distinguish between this and that. For the girl friend he always had a terrific silky business which was always at the ready.

The yard boy worked for several very wealthy people. In the morning of every day he got into his pickup and drove over the causeways to the Keys where he mowed and clipped and cut and hauled. He talked to the plants. He always told them what he was going to do before he did it so that they would have a chance to prepare themselves. Plants have lived in the Now for a long time but they still have to have some things explained to them.

At the Wilsons' house the yard boy clips a sucker from an orange tree. It is February. Even so, the orange tree doesn't like it much. Mrs. Wilson comes out and watches the yard boy while he works. She has her son with her. He is about three. He doesn't talk yet. His name is Tao. Mrs. Wilson is wealthy and can afford to be wacky. What was she supposed to do after all, she asked the yard boy once, call her kid George? Fred? For Godssakes.

Her obstetrician had told her at the time that he had never seen a more perfectly shaped head.

The Wilsons' surroundings are splendid. Mrs. Wilson has splendid clothes, a splendid figure. She has a wonderful Cuban cook. The house is worth three quarters of a million dollars. The plantings are worth a hundred thousand dollars. Everything has a price. It is fantastic. A precise worth has been ascribed to everything. Every worm and aphid can be counted upon. It costs a certain amount of money to eradicate them. The sod is laid down fresh every year. For weeks after the lawn is installed, the seams are visible and then the squares of grass gather together and it becomes, everywhere, in sun or shade, a smooth, witty and improbable green like the color of a parrot.

Mrs. Wilson follows the yard boy around as he tends to the hibiscus, the bougainvillea, the poinciana, the horse cassia, the Java flower, the flame vine. They stand beneath the mango, looking up.

"Isn't it pagan," Mrs. Wilson says.

Close the mouth, shut the doors, untie the tangles, soften the light, the yard boy thinks.

Mrs. Wilson says, "It's a waste this place, don't you think? I've never understood nature, all this effort. All this will . . ." She flaps her slender arms at the reeking of odors, the rioting colors. Still, she looks up at the mangoes, hanging. Uuuuuh, she thinks.

Tao is standing between the yard boy and Mrs. Wilson with an oleander flower in his mouth. It is pink. Tao's hair is golden. His eyes are blue.

The yard boy removes the flower from the little boy's mouth. "Toxic," the yard boy says.

"What is it!" Mrs. Wilson cries.

"Oleander," the yard boy says.

"Cut it down, dig it out, get rid of it," Mrs. Wilson cries. "My precious child!" She imagines Tao being kidnapped, held for an astronomical ransom by men with acne.

Mrs. Wilson goes into the house and makes herself a drink. The yard boy walks over to the oleander. The oleander shakes a little in the breeze. The yard boy stands in front of it for a few minutes, his clippers by his side.

Mrs. Wilson watches him from the house. She swallows her drink and rubs the glass over her hot nipples. The ice clinks. The yard boy raises the clippers and spreads them wide. The bolt connecting the two shears breaks. The yard boy walks over to the house, over to where Mrs. Wilson stands behind glass doors. The house weighs a ton with the glass. The house's architect was the South's most important architect, Mrs. Wilson once told the yard boy. Everything he made was designed to give a sense of freedom and space. Everything was designed to give the occupants the impression of being outside. His object was to break down definitions, the consciousness of boundaries. Mrs. Wilson told the yard boy the architect was an asshole.

Behind the glass, Mrs. Wilson understands the difficulty. Behind Mrs. Wilson's teeth is a tongue that tastes of bourbon.

"I'll drive you downtown and we can get a new whatever," she says. She is determined.

She and he and Tao get into Mrs. Wilson's Mercedes 350 SL. Mrs. Wilson is a splendid driver. She has taken the Mercedes up to 130, she tells the yard boy. It is 130 that the engine is capable of, nothing more. The engine stroked beautifully at 130, no sound of strain at all.

She drives past the beaches, over the causeways. She darts in and out of traffic with a fine sense of timing. Behind them, occasionally, old men in Gremlins jump the curb in fright. Mrs. Wilson glances at them in the rear-view mirror seeming neither satisfied nor dissatisfied. She puts her hand on the yard boy's knee. She rubs his leg.

Tao scrambles from the back into the front seat. He gets on the other side of the yard boy. He bites him.

I am living in a spiritual junkyard, thinks the yard boy. I must make it into a simple room with one beautiful object.

Sweat runs down the yard boy's spine. Tao is gobbling at his arm as though it is junket.

"What is going on!" yells Mrs. Wilson. She turns the Mercedes around in the middle of the highway. A Good Humor truck scatters a tinkle of music and a carton of Fudgesicles as it grinds to a stop. Mrs. Wilson is cuffing Tao as she speeds back home. She is embarrassed at his rudeness. Her shaven armpit rises and falls before the yard boy's eyes.

"Save the oleander!" she yells at both of them. "What do I care!"

In the driveway she runs around to Tao's side of the car and pinches the child's nose. He opens his mouth. She grabs him by the hair and carries him suspended into the house.

The yard boy walks to his truck, gets in and drives off. The world is neither nest nor playground, the yard boy thinks.

The yard boy lies in his room thinking about his girl friend.
Open up, give in, allow some space, sprinkle and pour, he thinks.
Outside, the garbage men are picking up the trash. They whistle and bang the cans about. The trash from the house where the yard boy lives contains the discards of the righteous. Tea bags, lime rinds, Charmin tubes, wilted flowers. The garbage men whoop to the truck that carries them off as though it were a horse. Sometimes the yard boy has bad dreams in this room. Sometimes he dreams of demons with eyes as big as saucepans and bodies the size of thumbs. But mostly he has good thoughts about his girl friend. He believes that her mind has the same energy, speed and pattern of his mind even though she isn't a spiritual materialist.

The yard boy is mowing the grass around Johnny Dakota's swimming pool. Dakota is into heroin and intangible property. As he is working, the yard boy hears a big splash behind him. He looks into the swimming pool and sees a rock on the bottom of it. He finishes mowing the grass and then he gets a net and fishes the rock out. It is as big as his hand. It is grey with bubbly streaks of iron and metal running through it. The yard boy thinks it is a meteorite. It would probably still be smoldering with heat had it not landed in the swimming pool.
It is interesting but not all that interesting. The possibility of its surviving the earth's atmosphere is one tenth of one percent. Other things are more interesting than this. Nevertheless, the yard boy shows it to Johnny Dakota. Johnny Dakota might want to place it in a taped-up box in his house to prevent the air from corroding it.
Johnny Dakota looks up at the sky, then at the piece of space junk and then at the yard boy. He is a sleek, fit man. Only his eyes and his hands look old. His hands have deep ridges in them and smashed nails. He once told the yard boy that his mother,

whom he loved, had died from plucking a wild hair from her nose while vacationing in Calabria. His father had choked on a bread stick in a Chicago restaurant. Life is ruthless, he had told the yard boy. The darkness is always near.

Johnny Dakota usually takes his swim at this time of the morning. He is wearing his swim trunks and flip-flops. If he had been in the pool he could have been brained. Once his mother had dreamed of losing a tooth and two days later her cousin dropped dead.

Johnny Dakota is angry. Anyone could tell. His face is dark. His mouth is a thin line. He gives the yard boy two twenties and tells him to bury the rock in the back yard. He tells him not to mention this to anyone.

The yard boy takes the rock and buries it beneath a fiddle-leaf fig at the north end of the house. The fig tree is distressed. It's magnetic, that's the only thing known about this rock. The fig tree is almost as upset as Johnny Dakota.

The yard boy lies in his room. His girl friend is giving him a hard time. She used to visit him in his room several nights a week but now she doesn't. He will take her out to dinner. He will spend the two twenties on a fantastic dinner.

The yard boy is disgusted with himself. The spider's web is woven in the wanting, he thinks. He has desire for his girl friend. His mind is shuttling between thoughts of the future and thoughts of the past. He is dissatisfied. He is out of touch with the sharp simplicity and wonderfulness of the moment. He looks around him. He opens his eyes wide. The yard boy's jeans are filthy. A green insect crawls in and out of the scapular feathers of the plover.

The yard boy goes downstairs. He gives the plover to his landlady. She seems delighted. She puts it on a shelf in the pantry, just above the pie plates. The landlady has white hair, a wen, and old legs that end in sneakers. She wants the yard boy to look at a plant she has just bought. It is in a big green plastic pot in the sunshine of her kitchen. Nothing is more obvious than the hidden, the yard boy thinks.

"This plant is insane," the yard boy says.

The landlady is shocked. She backs off a little from the plant which is a rabbit's-foot fern.

"It has seen something terrible," the yard boy says.

"I bought it on sale," the landlady says. "At that place where I always go."

The yard boy shakes his head. The plant waves a wrinkly leaf and drops it.

"Insane?" the landlady asks. She would like to cry. She has no family, no one.

"Mad as a hatter," the yard boy says.

The restaurant that the yard boy's girl friend chooses is not expensive. It is a fish restaurant. The plates are plastic. There is a bottle of tabasco sauce on each table. The girl friend doesn't at all like fancy food, although she doesn't mind accepting a bowl of chowder and a few glasses of wine.

A few booths over, a middle-aged couple are having an argument. They both have sunburns and wear white skirts and Haitian shirts. The argument seems to be about monograms. They are both yelling and one woman picks up a handful of oyster crackers and flings it into the other woman's face. The oyster crackers stick all over the woman's damp, sunburned face. The yard boy knows he should be satisfied with whatever situation arises but he is having a little difficulty with his enlightenment.

The yard boy's girl friend is not talking to him. She has not been talking to him for days actually.

The woman that has been hit with the handful of oyster crackers walks past, an oyster cracker bobbing on her widow's peak.

The yard boy miserably eats his pompano. When they are finished, his girl friend goes to the cashier for some toothpicks. While she is gone, another girl comes up with a baby.

"Would you watch my baby for me while I go to the ladies'?" she asks.

The yard boy holds the baby. The girl leaves. The yard boy's
girl friend returns. They don't talk about the baby or anything.
The girl friend sighs and crosses her legs. An hour passes. The
restaurant is about to close. The yard boy and his girl friend
and the baby are the last patrons. There is no one in the ladies'.
The yard boy calls the manager and the manager calls the
police. The baby chortles and spits up a little, not much. The
police let the girl friend go first, and a few hours later they let
the yard boy go.

The yard boy gets into his truck and drives off.

Life and the world are merely the dance of illusion, the yard
boy thinks. He smells baby on his sweater.

The yard boy's landlady has put her rabbit's-foot fern out by
the garbage cans. The yard boy picks it up and puts it in the
cab of his truck. It goes wherever he goes now.

The yard boy gets a note from his girl friend. It says:

> My ego is too healthy for real involvement with you. I don't
> like you. Good-by.
>
> > Alyce

The yard boy works for Mr. Crown who is an illustrator. Mr.
Crown lives in a fine house on the bay. Across the street,
someone is building an even finer house on the Gulf. Mr.
Crown was once the most renowned illustrator of Western art
in the country. In his studio he has George Custer's jacket.
Sometimes the yard boy poses for Mr. Crown. The year before,
a gentleman in Cody, Wyoming, bought Mr. Crown's painting
of an Indian who was the yard boy for fifty thousand dollars.
This year, however, Mr. Crown is not doing so well. He has
been reduced to illustrating children's books. His star is falling.
Also, the construction across the street infuriates him. The new
house will block off his view of the sun as the sun slides daily
into the water.

Mr. Crown's publishers have told him that they are not

interested in cowboys. There have been too many cowboys for too long.

The yard boy is spraying against scale and sooty mold.

"I don't need the money but I am insulted," Mr. Crown tells the yard boy.

Mr. Crown goes back into the house. The yard boy seeds some rye on the lawn's bare spots and then takes a break to get a drink of water. He sits in the cab of his truck and drinks from a plastic jug. He sprinkles some water on the rabbit's-foot fern. The fern sits there on the seat, dribbling a little vermiculite, crazy as hell.

The fern and the yard boy sit.

It is not a peaceful spot to sit. The racket of the construction on the Gulf is considerable. Nonetheless, the yard boy swallows his water and attempts to dwell upon the dignity and simplicity of the moment.

Then there is the sound of gunfire. The yard boy cranes his neck out of the window of his pickup truck and sees Mr. Crown firing from his studio at the workers across the street. It takes the workers several moments to realize that they are being shot at. The bullets make big mealy holes in the concrete. The bullets whine through the windows that will exhibit the sunset. The workers all give a howl and try to find cover. The yard boy curls up behind the wheel of his truck. The little rushy brown hairs on the fern's stalks stick straight out.

A few minutes later the firing stops. Mr. Crown goes back to the drawing board. No one is hurt. Mr. Crown is arrested and posts twenty-five thousand dollars bond. Charges are later dropped. The house across the street is built. Still, Mr. Crown seems calmer now. He gives up illustrating. When he wants to look at something, he looks at the bay. He tells the yard boy he is putting sunsets behind him.

The yard boy and the rabbit's-foot fern drive from lawn to lawn in the course of their days, the fern tipping forward a little in its green pot, the wind folding back its leaves. In the wind, its leaves curl back like the lips of a Doberman pinscher.

The yard boy sees things in the course of his work that he wouldn't dream of telling the fern even though the fern is his only confidant. The fern has a lot of space around it in which anything can happen but it doesn't have much of an emotional life because it is insane. Therefore, it makes a good confidant.

The yard boy has always been open. He has always let be and disowned. Nevertheless, he has lost the spontaneity of his awakened state. He is sad. He can feel it. The fern can feel it too which makes it gloomier than ever. Even so, the fern has grown quite fond of the yard boy. It wants to help him any way it can.

The yard boy doesn't rent a room any more. He lives in his truck. Then he sells his truck. He and the rabbit's-foot fern sit on the beach. The fern lives in the shade of the yard boy. The yard boy doesn't live in the Now at all any more. He lives in the past. He thinks of his childhood. As a child he had a comic-book-collection high of three hundred and seventy-four with perfect covers. His parents had loved him. His parents had another son whom they loved too. One morning this son had fallen out of a tree onto the driveway and played with nothing but a spoon and saucepan for the next twenty-five years. When the yard boy has lived in the past as much as is reliable, he lives in the future. It is while he is living in the future that his girl friend walks by on the beach. She is walking by in a long wet T-shirt that says I'M NOT A TOURIST I LIVE HERE. The rabbit's-foot fern alerts the yard boy and they both stare at her as she walks by.

It is a beautiful day. The water is a smooth green, broken occasionally by porpoises rising. Between the yard boy and his girl friend is sand a little less white than the clouds. Behind the yard boy are plantings of cabbage palms and succulents and Spanish bayonets. The bayonets are harsh and green with spikes that end in black tips like stilettos.

Act but do not rely upon one's own abilities, thinks the yard boy. He chews upon his nails. The moon can shine in one hundred different bowls, he thinks. What a lot of junk the yard boy thinks. He is as lost in the darkness of his solid thoughts as a yard boy can be. He watches his girl friend angrily as she boogies by.

The rabbit's-foot fern brightens at the yard boy's true annoyance. Its fuzzy long-haired rhizomes clutch its pot tightly. The space around it simmers, it bubbles. Each cell mobilizes its intent of skillful and creative action. It turns its leaves toward the Spanish bayonet. It straightens and sways. Straightens and sways. A moment passes. The message of retribution is received along the heated air. The yard boy sees the Spanish bayonet uproot itself and move out.

Winter Chemistry

*I*T was the middle of January and there was nothing to look forward to. The radio station went off at dusk and dusk came early in the afternoon and then came the dark and nothing to watch but a bleached-out moon lying over fields slick as a frosted cake, and nothing to hear at all.

There was nothing left of Christmas but the cold. The cold slouched and pressed against the people. Their blood was full of it. And their eyes and the food that they ate. The people walked the streets wearing woolen masks as though they were gangsters, or as though they were deformed. Old ladies died of breaks and foolish wounds in houses where no one came, and fish froze in the quiet of their rivers.

The cold didn't invent anything like the summer has a habit of doing and it didn't disclose anything like the spring. It lay powerfully encamped—waiting, altering one's ambitions, encouraging ends. The cold made for an ache, a restlessness and an irritation, and thinking that fell in odd and unemployable directions. The pain would start in your lap, boring up and tearing through like a big-beaked bird, traveling up your spine then to the base of your skull, entering your brain like fever. So it was explained.

Judy Cushman and Julep Lee were the best of friends. Each knew things that the other did not, and each had a different manner of going after the things that they wanted. Each loved the handsome chemistry teacher of the high school. Love had different beginnings but always the same end. Someone was going to get hurt. Julep was too discreet to admit this for she tried not to think of shabby things.

They were fourteen and the only thing that was familiar to them was the town and the way they spent their lives there, which they hated.

They slept a great deal and talked about the same things always and made brownies and popcorn and drank Coca-Cola. Julep always made a great show of drinking Coca-Cola because she claimed that her father had given her three shares of stock in it the day she was born. Judy would laugh about this whenever she thought to. "On the day, I was born," she'd say, "I received the gifts of beauty and luck."

Their schoolbooks lay open and unread, littered with crumbs and nail trimmings. Every night that didn't bring a blizzard, they would spy on the chemistry teacher, for they were fourteen and could only infrequently distinguish what they did from what they merely dreamt about.

The chemistry teacher had enormous trembling eyes like a deer and a name in your mouth sweet as a candy bar. DEBEVOISE. He was tall and languid and unmarried and handsome. He lived alone in a single rented room on the second floor of a large house on the coast. The house was the last one on a street that abruptly became a field of pines and stones. Every night the girls would come to the field and, crouching in a hollow, watch him through a pair of cheap binoculars. For a month they had been watching him move woodenly around the small room and still they did not know what it was they wanted to happen. The walls of the room were painted white and he sat at a white desk with his white shirt rolled down to his wrists. The only thing that was on the desk was a tiny television set with a screen the size of a book. He watched it and drank from a glass. Sometimes he would run his own hands through his own dark hair.

Judy Cushman and Julep Lee felt that loving him was a success in itself.

But still they did not know what they waited for in the snow.

The rocks dug into their skinny shanks. Their ears went deaf with the cold. At times, Judy thought that she wanted him to bring a woman up there. Or perhaps do something embarrassing or dirty all by himself. But she was not sure about this.

As for Julep, she seldom said things that she had not said once, long before, so there was no way of knowing what she thought.

Julep was the thinnest human being in town, all angles and bruises and fierce joinings. Even her lips were hard and spare and bloodless as bone. Her hair was such a pale, parched blond that it looked white and her brows and lashes were the same color, although her eyes, under heavy round lids that worked slowly as a doll's, were brown.

Her parents had moved from the South to the North when she was four years old, and she had lived on the same bitter and benumbed coast ever since. She steered her way through each day incredulously, as though she had been kidnapped and sent to some grim prison yard in another world. She couldn't employ the cold to any advantage so she dreamed of heat, of a sun fierce enough to melt the monstrous town and set her free. She talked about the sun as though it were a personal friend of hers, waiting in the next room for her to get ready and go out with it.

Julep was a Baptist, a clarinetist in the band, a forward on the six-girl basketball team which was famous throughout the state, undefeated, unthreatened, unsmiling. She had scabs upon her knees, a blue silk uniform in her locker, fingernails split and ragged from the gritty leather ball. Julep was an innocent.

Now, Judy Cushman too was an innocent, but had a tendency to see things in a greedy, rutting way. Judy was tiny and tough and wore a garter belt. Almost every one of her eyebrows was plucked from her head and her hair was stacked over a foot high, for her older sister was a hairdresser who taught her half of everything she knew.

Judy was full and sleek and a favorite with the boys and she would tell Julep things that Julep almost died hearing. She would say, "Last night Tommy Saloma exposed himself to my eyes only in the rumpus room of his house," and Julep would almost faint. She would say, "Billy Colter touched my breast in Library," and Julep would gasp and hold her head at an unnaturally high angle for she felt that if she held her head on the slightest cant, everything inside her would stream terribly from her mouth, everything she was made of, falling out of her head and shaking out on the floor in front of them.

Judy always told her friend the most awful things she could think of, true or false, and made promises that she would not keep and insulted and disappointed and teased her as much as possible. Julep allowed this and was always deeply affected and bewildered by this, which flattered Judy enormously. This pleasure compensated for the fact that Julep had white hair that Judy would have given anything in the world to have. It annoyed her that her friend had such strange and devastating hair and didn't know how to cut or curl it properly.

After school, they would often go to Julep's house. They usually went there rather than to Judy's because Julep's room was bigger. Judy's room was just a closet with a bright light bulb and a studio bed and the smell of underwear.

"Look now," Judy said, peeling off a strip of Scotch tape from her bangs, "we've got to broaden our conversational base. Why don't we talk about men or movies? Or even mixed drinks?"

Julep shrugged. "We don't know anything about those things." She looked at the black worn Bible on her bedside table. She had read there that the sun would someday become black as a sackcloth of hair and the moon would turn red as blood. This was because of the evil in people, and Julep worried that this would happen to the sun before she had a chance to get back to where it was again.

"You don't know anything is all." Judy plucked at her sweater and smiled the bittersweet smile she found so crushing on the lips of the girl models of the fashion magazines. Her new breasts rose and fell eerily beneath a sweater of puce.

"I know that someday you're gonna poke someone's eye out with those things," Julep said pointing at her friend's chest. "If I were you, I'd be worried sick."

Judy yawned. Julep stared out the window. The sun was still up but nowhere in sight. The air was blue and the snow falling through it was blue, and the trees were as black as though they had been burned.

"I'm leaving," Judy said abruptly and swept out of Julep's bedroom and downstairs to the kitchen.

Julep rubbed at the frost forming inside the windowpane with a thin grey nail which was bleeding beneath the quick. She felt her head sweating. If she pressed her hands to it, it would pop like a too heavy tick on a dog. If Hell were hot then Heaven must be freezing cold. She backed away from the window and thudded down the stairs.

Judy had drawn on her boots and coat. She waved coyly at Julep.

"Well, aren't we going over there tonight to watch him?" Julep asked nervously, swinging her eyes heavily toward her friend. Looking often cost Julep a great deal of effort as though her eyes were boxes of bricks she had to push around in front of her.

"No," Judy said, for she wanted to punish Julep for her dullness. Her books were lying on the kitchen table beside a small dish that said LET ME HOLD YOUR TEABAG. Judy rolled her eyes and then shook her head at Julep. Julep's father owned a little grocery and variety store down the street, and in the window of it was a hand-lettered sign.

WHY MAKE THE RICH RICHER
PATRONIZE THE POOR
THANK YOU

"How can you stand to live in such a dump?" she asked. "With such dummies?" Julep didn't know. Judy left and walked through the heavy snow to dumb Julep's father's dumb store where she bought a package of gum and lifted a mascara and eyeliner set.

Julep ate supper. Chowder, bread, two glasses of milk and three pieces of cake. She felt that she was feeding something inside her that belonged in a pen in the zoo. A plow traveled up the street, its orange light chopping through the blackness. She went to bed early, for she had tests and a basketball game the next day. She thought of the tropical ocean, of enormous white flowers on yellow stalks motionless in the sun. Things would carry distantly over the water there. Things would start out from ugly places and never reach Julep at all.

Judy Cushman and Julep Lee had become friends the summer before when they were on the beach. It was a bitter, shining Maine day and they were alone except for two people drowning just beyond the breaker line. The two girls sat on the beach, eating potato chips, unable to decide if the people were drowning or if they were just having a good time. Even after they disappeared, the girls could not believe they had really done it. They went home and the next day read about it in the newspapers. From that day on, they spent all their time together, even though they never mentioned the incident again.

Debevoise was thirty-four and took no part in adventure. He didn't care for women and he couldn't care for men. He lived in a corner second-story room of a rambling boarding house. The room had two windows, one of which overlooked the field and the other, the sea. There were no curtains on the windows and he never pulled the shades. He ate breakfast with the elderly owners, lunch every noon at the high school and drove to a hotel in the next town for dinner every night. He was stern and deeply tanned and exceptionally good-looking. As for the teaching, he barely recognized his students as human beings, considering them all mentally bludgeoned by the unremitting landscape. He couldn't imagine chemistry doing any better or worse by them than anything else.

And the girls felt hopeless, stubborn and distraught, for they had come a long way on just a whisper more than nothing.

They could approach the house either by walking up the beach, climbing the metal rungs welded into the rock, which was dangerous and gave them no cover, or they could walk through the little town and across the field. Their post was a small depression beside an enormous pine, the branches of which swept the ground. Further away was a rim of rocks which they had assembled as another hiding place. Every night they could see everything from either one of these locations.

Every night the chemistry teacher was projected brightly behind the square window glass and watching him was like watching a museum. The girls would often close their eyes and even doze off for a time, and the snow would fall on them and freeze in their hair. Sometimes he would take off all his clothes and walk around the room, punching at the wall but never hitting it. Seeing him naked was never as exciting as the girls kept on imagining it would be since no one had ever told them what to feel about this.

Even so, Julep would come back to the house smiling, as though someone had made a very exciting promise to her. No one was there to notice this, for her mother was always locked in her room, powdered and rouged and in a lacy bed jacket like an invalid, watching TV and eating ice cream from the store, and her father had been sleeping for hours, twitching and suicidal, dreaming of meat going bad in faulty freezers.

On the nights when the girls saw the chemistry teacher without his clothes, Judy pretended to swoon with delight but actually felt hostile toward this vision which was both improbable and irresistible. His body was brown all over and did not seem real. The boys she knew were so comprehensible. Of Debevoise, she understood nothing. She could pretend he was a movie star, beside her, naked, about to press his tongue against her teeth. Mr. Debevoise was going to put a bruise on her neck! He was going to take her hand and place it on his belt!! But she could not really believe these things.

*   *   *

The morning after Judy had refused to go spying, Julep woke
with a headache and a terrible thirst. She thought for a moment that she had taken up the watch all by herself and
something awful had happened to her. As soon as she stepped
outside, someone was going to tell her about it.

The sky was grey with pieces of black running through it like
something that had died during the night. Walking to school,
Julep suddenly started to cry. Her throat ached and her head
felt heavy. She pulled savagely at her colorless hair, arranging
it so that it fell more directly into and around her eyes. She
stood in front of the school, her arms dangling, looking at her
feet. She looked and looked, shocked. There she began. There
were her boots, tall scuffed riding boots, her only winter foot-
wear, which let in the damp, staining her feet each day the
color of her socks. Then came her chapped knees, yellow and
grey from spills on the gymnasium floor. Then her frayed and
ugly coat. Her insides, too, were not what she would wish, for
she knew that she was convulsively arranged—a steaming mess
of foods and soft scarlet parts, Bible quotes, chemistry equa-
tions and queer bumpings and pains as though there was something down in her frantic to get out.
    Debevoise, she knew, was pure and warm with not a speck
of debris about him.
    Julep walked to school and moved down the busy halls like
a wraith, meek and bony and awkward, her towhead glowing
like a lamp. The class before chemistry was endless. The cold
seeped past the window sills and over the plastic rosebud on
the teacher's desk.
    The classroom fell away and she was alone with Debevoise
in a rubber raft on a clear green ocean. Small sweet fish nibbled
on each other without rancor and parts of them fell off with
no blood attached. Julep's knees touched his and they both had
cameras and were taking pictures of each other. The sun was
burning a hole in the top of her head. . . .

*   *   *

No one ever played in the snow or used it for anything. It came too often and it stayed too long. In the cafeteria, the windows were even with the ground and criss-crossed with a steel mesh to protect the glass from objects flying through the air and across the ground. The snow was higher than the windows. Judy sat alone at a long wooden table. Old food and bobby pins were lodged in its cracks. The cafeteria was a terrible place which everyone recklessly frequented. When Judy saw her friend's narrow nervous frame move jerkily across the room she decided on the spot that she would forgive her and they would resume watching Debevoise that very night. Afterwards, they would go to Julep's room and drink gin and Coca-Cola. They would have highballs and she would make Julep talk about men whether she wanted to or not. Julep could provide the Coca-Colas since she was making money on drinking them.

Julep sat down and looked at Judy shyly. The chemistry teacher walked past them and sat at the faculty table on the other side of the room. He wore a lemon-colored suit, a dark blue shirt and deep yellow tie and the fixed smirk that was his usual workaday expression.

They watched him respectfully. Julep closed her eyes. With her eyes shut, Julep looked sick and unconscious, beyond the range of instruction.

"What would you have him do if you had your way?" Judy whispered. Julep said nothing. Judy tapped her fingers on the table and whispered more loudly, "The way you're sitting there and the way you're looking, you look for all the world as though you'd just gotten raped."

Julep's eyes fell open, blurred and out of focus for several seconds as though they'd been somewhere other than her head for the last few years. "You could ruin the heavenly city itself," she finally said.

Judy called her "Heavenly City" for the rest of the afternoon. In chemistry laboratory, she muttered at her until she had ruined her titration experiments. Julep poured the chemicals in the trough of running water that flowed down the center of the slate work table, and pressed her hands to her roaring head. She could feel Debevoise standing silently beside her, smell the cologne and the new shirt. His bright clothing rested on the rim of her eye like a giddy tropical bird.

After classes, in the gymnasium, Julep sat on a bench behind the scorer in her shining uniform and the high white sneakers that she had won in a state-wide set-shot contest the year before. She could not remember why she had become obsessed with playing basketball. She taped up her wrists.

Judy was a fan in the bleachers, surrounded by boys. The boys were all running combs through their hair and all wore jeans and hunting boots. "Heavenly City!" Judy shouted. "Heavenly City!"

Julep watched the girls from the other team. They caught the basketball delicately as though it were covered with some dreadful slime.

On the court she played extravagantly, her hard white head cresting above the others clutched beneath the board, her bony elbows shocking the girls in the ribs. Her nostrils filled with dust and the tapping heat of the radiators. Julep's team was far ahead. The cords of the net creaked as the ball floated through. Basketball was serious business and Julep felt no levity. Life was what you figured out for yourself.

"Heavenly City, Heavenly City!" Judy persisted from the stands. "Look to your right!" All the boys around her looked soberly down on the court and chewed great wads of gum. "Look to your right," Judy shrieked.

Julep moved her eyes gingerly along the sidelines. The opposing forwards had the ball and were moving it cautiously around on the other half of the court. She stood panting and slightly bent, looking through the stands until her weary eyes rested on Debevoise. He was smiling kindly and looking at her. His dark handsome face was smooth and empty of habitual boredom and disgust, and his lips, in the instant that she saw him, seemed to be moving toward an expression that she had not known he possessed. It was then that the ball hit her squarely in the head and she fell to her knees. She heard a noise from the bleachers, something corrosive and impersonal, a rush and a hissing bubble as though her head had opened up and a wave was coming through it. A titter and blurred silence. As someone helped her up and off the court, she could see the chemistry teacher, smiling into his hands as though his jaws would crack.

Julep walked home slowly in a freezing dusk, her coat in her arms. Her brain was pumping madly, although her heart was still.

Judy came over at eight o'clock, a bottle of gin zipped up in the lining of her coat. She had found it lodged behind the record player in her house. The bottle was very dusty and about two inches of its contents were gone. Judy didn't know if it was still good or not.

Julep was in the bathroom, pressing a hot washcloth against her left eye. Almost all the white had disappeared into a soak of red. Judy did not speak to her about the embarrassment of the basketball game. She thought Julep was crazy to get so excited about playing a boy's game and she was also suspicious that too much of that sort of thing would change her friend's hormones. Magazines told her terrible things and she believed in most of them.

Judy went to the kitchen for glasses and something to mix with the gin. From behind a closed door, she heard a television going and a woman's voice above it. No, the voice said. No, that bum is up to no good. There was a shot, then a bump and rising music. I told you, the voice said. Judy gathered up a handful of stale cookies and went up to Julep. The cookies were in the shape of stars and burnt at the edges.

"Holiday relics," Julep said, mopping at her eye.

"We could make a batch of obscene cookies for Valentine's Day," Judy giggled, pouring the gin.

They each drank a glass of gin and then walked through the town. The town was all one color with hardly anything moving in it and the night was very cold and clear. Beyond the field, the sea was flat as a highway in the moonlight.

"I feel just amazing," Judy said in a high wet voice.

Julep said nothing. She felt only hot and ponderous, as she had when she woke up that morning. She arranged her head scarf over her injured eye. Every once in a while, the eye seemed to roll backward and study her instead of bearing outward toward the night.

They settled beneath the giant tree and Judy fumblingly took the binoculars from her coat. She dropped them in the snow and giggled as she dug them out. She thought that Julep was just trying to be smart and had no doubt poured her gin into the rug or something when she wasn't watching. She pushed against her rudely and raised the binoculars.

"God," she said loudly. "He's nude again."

Julep sat hunched, her arms around her knees. Her clothes were soaked with sweat and rivulets of perspiration ran from the corners of her mouth.

"You're yelling," Julep said. "Someone will hear you." She tried to think of her own nakedness and what it might mean to somebody, even herself, but she had never paid any attention to her own body. Her eye shuddered and then became a piece of raw meat lying tamely in her head.

Debevoise was clamping a sunlamp above his bed. He turned it on and then lay on his back with his hands beneath his head. The bulb hung over him blankly for a moment and then lit shrilly. Almost at the same instant, the door of the house opened and a flashlight beam bored over the field. Judy gave a small shriek and pushed herself backward against the tree trunk.

"Who's there!" a man demanded. "I know you're there." Behind the voice was a pink hallway, an old woman standing in a shawl, her hand in a fist moving across her mouth. There seemed deadening light everywhere. The sea and snow and sunlamp and now the old man walking toward them. The girls knelt beneath the tree like jacked deer.

"Don't go over there, Ernest," the old woman said.

The man stopped and moved the light in a wide arc. "It ain't the first time you been here. You come out or there's going to be trouble."

"Ernest," the old woman said fretfully, turning the porch light off and on as though she were guiding in a ship. Judy and Julep bolted, stumbling across the field, spinning off tree limbs, their hands over their faces. "Hey!" they heard behind them. "Hey! You get outta here."

Julep was sick for three weeks and never moved from the bed. She could hear children on their horses, cantering in the streets. She could hear the plows. She drank soup and sniffed herself beneath the damp bedclothes. She felt that she was an exceedingly fragile organism lying beneath complex layers of mulch. Her face was shrunken and without structure, as though something were burning it up and coring it out from within. The snow fell eternally out of a withered sky, and inside, Julep, beyond the range of dream or reasoning, continued to burn.

She couldn't decide if it had been coming for a long time and she had just gotten in the way of it or if it had always been there with her and she had just recognized it.

Ever since the afternoon of the basketball game, she could not remember how she had once regarded Debevoise. He was the pain and the heat of her head, and no longer something she could think about.

Judy also could not bear to think about Debevoise. It frightened her to think they might be caught. Everyone would think she was queer. The girls would laugh and the boys would take advantage of her whereas now they fought over her and loved her and were half scared to death of her. She was glad that Julep was sick and they didn't have to sit around in the snow. She would never admit that she was being cautious or afraid, but she would tell Julep after she got well that she was bored and had learned everything she wanted to know about Debevoise.

Judy would come to visit Julep but didn't like to look at her. Once, Judy said, "He asked about you, you know."

Julep smiled politely and studied the hem of her sheet.

"He asked if you had moved and I said no, you were sick and

then he said girls keep themselves too skinny these days as a fashion and they don't eat the right foods and get sick."

When Julep returned to school, everything was tiny, as in a dream, and moving with blinding speed. She could not keep up with it all, her muscles, resting for so long, were useless for anything. In the laboratory, she spilled potassium permanganate, staining her hands a deep brown. She watched her hands accompany her now like a dark disease, like a man's hands, soaked and sordid.

She felt cold.

Julep went out now alone to watch Debevoise. Judy was surprised and she became defensive and intrigued, imagining that Julep was at last succeeding in something they had not been able to accomplish together.

"I can't imagine anything going on that we haven't already seen," she said peevishly. "The only thing that could happen is if one of us got up there in that room right with him and we were looking out of that window instead of looking into it. You're going to get sick out there and freeze and go unconscious."

Julep looked at her wrecked hands and rubbed at them briefly with a piece of flannel she had started to carry around with her.

Judy was suspicious. She worried that something interesting had happened. "You've got to have somebody caring for you all the time," she said. "I'm going to go with you one more time but then I'm never going again and I'm going to stop you from going out too." How she would do this last thing, she didn't know. She could tell on Julep, she supposed. That would stop it all dead. She looked on Julep righteously and Julep looked back.

The night was black, moonless and starless, with only the snow shining dully with its own light, and the ice hanging in webs from the trees. They walked with their hands strung out in front of their faces and their elbows sticking out, shuffling a little so they wouldn't trip.

The ground was ice-buckled and with hollows. Judy's knees dipped and, jaw joggling, she bit her tongue. She had fallen out of practice, out of step with the land and her reason for being on it. Julep walked steadily ahead and Judy followed, somewhere in a movie war, a lusted-after orphan, in full bloom and in danger all the time. If only Julep had imagination, she thought, she wouldn't get so involved in things.

They settled down beside the tree, in a new and deeper ditch, with a stone base and the sides smooth ice, alarmingly, impossibly, like a home.

The second floor was in darkness.

"He's not even here," Judy said accusingly.

Julep's grainy face stuck out of her wool wrappings. "He's here," she said.

"Well, what's he doing in the dark!" Judy shouted. "Have you been watching him do something in the dark?" She was getting angry. They crouched in a cloud of her perfume. She felt like throttling Julep, who was tilted slightly toward her, in a trance and satisfied, dumb and patient. She looked toward the house, feeling Debevoise moving thunderously in the dark and making no sense to her. She was getting so angry she thought she would bust. She gave a little squeal and stamped her feet, then stood up and started to make her way back across the field. She was moving fast, kicking her feet out in front of her, moving so fast that she thought when she felt her boots sliding away that she could still catch up with them before she fell, but her legs kept moving forward while the rest of her slid back and she tipped over with a crack.

She lay there whimpering. Unlike Julep, she had never hurt herself in her life. She had never been bruised or sick or burnt and nothing had ever broken. She remained on her back, prodding herself gently, singing to herself in a little girl's voice. She was suddenly pulled roughly to her feet and shaken hard. Debevoise had grabbed her by the coat front and was pushing her back and forth, pinching her breasts, pushing and pulling at her as though to a music beat, his face riding from side to side only inches in front of her, as though it was his head that

was wagging and not her own. His face was raging. It seemed
on the verge of flying apart. He was saying several simple words
to her but she could not seem to understand them. He would
propel her back as he said each word and then yank her toward
him in the silence between the words and it was as though
someone was turning a radio on and off.

Then she simply stopped rocking and with his hands still on
her coat, he toppled toward her, turning her slightly to the left
as he fell so that they both sank side by side in the snow. His
head settled and then broke slowly through a crust of ice. One
eye filled up with snow while the other continued to stare at
her.

Julep, a rock in each hand, took several steps forward and
knelt beside him. There were two wounds in the back of his
well-shaped head. She raised her hands again, dropping them
with a slow, hard force against his skull. They made almost no
sound. The eye that was still staring at Judy seemed to shake.
His mouth was closed tightly but there was blood coming from
between his lips. Judy pushed herself away. His hands remained on her coat, but then dropped off as she crept backward to a tree which she clung to, whimpering.

Julep had lost her mittens. The backs of her hands were cold
from the snow, but her mottled palms were hot from the man's
broken head. She lay down beside him, feeling white and
glistening, turned inside out, scrubbed down and aired. She ran
her hands over the thin shirt he wore, feeling his collarbone,
his ribs, the tight muscles of his stomach. She unbuttoned his
shirt and felt his nipples, which were hard, withered, much like
her own. She pressed her lips against his chest and tasted salt,
then lay her colorless famished head upon his shoulder, which
was as warm as though he'd lived all his days in the sun.

Shorelines

I want to explain. There are only the two of us, the child and me. I sleep alone. Jace is gone. My hair is wavy, my posture good. I drink a little. Food bores me. It takes so long to eat. Being honest, I must say I drink. I drink, perhaps, more than moderately, but that is why there is so much milk. I have a terrible thirst. Rum and Coke. Grocery wine. Anything that cools. Gin and juices of all sorts. My breasts are always aching, particularly the left, the earnest one, which the baby refuses to favor. First comforts must be learned, I suppose. It's a matter of exposure.

I have tried to be clean about my person since the child. I wash frequently, rinse my breasts before feeding, keep my hands away from my eyes and mouth . . . but it's hard to keep oneself up. I have tried to think only harmonious thoughts since the child, but the sun on the water here, that extravagant white water, the sun brings such dishevelment and confusion.

I am tall. I have a mole by my lip. When I speak, the mole vanishes. I address myself to the child quite frequently. He is an infant, only a few months old. I say things like,

"What would you like for lunch? A marmalade crêpe? A peanut-butter cupcake?"

Naturally, he does not answer. As for myself, I could seldom comply with his agreement. I keep forgetting to buy the ingredients. There was a time when I had everything on hand. I was quite the cook once. Pompano stuffed with pecans.

Quiche Lorraine. And curry! I was wonderful with curries. I had such imaginative accompaniments. The whole thing no bigger than a saucer sometimes, yet perfect!

We live in the sun here, on the beach, in the South. It is so hot here. I will tell you exactly how hot it is. It is too hot for orange trees. People plant them but they do not bear. I sleep alone now. I will be honest. Sometimes I wake in the night and realize that I have called upon my body. I am repelled but I do not become distraught. I remove my hands firmly. I raise and lower them to either side of the bed. It seems a little self-conscious, a little staged, to bring my hands away like that. But hands, what do they have to do with any of us?

The heat is the worst at night. I go damp with fever here at night, and I dream. Once I dreamed of baking a bat in the oven. I can't imagine myself dreaming such a thing. I am a sensitive woman. I might have read about it because there are things I know about bats. I am knowledgeable about their eyes. I know that their retinas have only rods and no vascular system. They can only see moving objects. Unlike us, you know.

I try to keep the child cool at night. I give him ice to play with. He accepts everything I have to offer. He is always with me. He is in my care.

I knew when Jace had started the baby. It's true what you've heard. A woman knows.

It has always been Jace only. We were children together. We lived in the same house. It was a big house on the water. Jace remembers it precisely. I remember it not as well. There were eleven people in that house and a dog beneath it, tied night and day to the pilings. Eleven of us and always a baby. It doesn't seem reasonable now when I think on it, but there were always eleven of us and always a baby. The diapers and the tiny clothes, hanging out to dry, for years!

Jace was older than me by a year and a day and I went everywhere with him. My momma tried to bring me around. She said,

"One day you're going to be a woman. There are ways you'll have to behave."

But we were just children. It was a place for children and we were using it up. The sharks would come up the inlet in the morning rains and they'd roll so it would seem the water was boiling. Our breath was wonderful. Everything was wonderful. We would box. Underneath the house, with the dog's rope tangling around our legs, Jace and I would box, stripped to the waist. Red and yellow seaweed would stream from the rope. The beams above us were soft blue with mold. Even now, I can feel exactly what it felt like to be cool and out of the sun.

Jace's fists were like flowers.

Jace is thin and quick. His jeans are white with my washing. I have always done my part. Wherever we went, I planted. If the soil were muck, I would plant vegetables; if dry, herbs; if sandy, strawberries. We always left before they could be harvested. We were always moving on, down the coast. But we always had bread to eat. I made good crusty bread. I had a sourdough starter that was seventy-one years old.

We have always lived on the water. Jace likes to hear it. We have been on all the kinds of water there are in the South. Once we lived in the swamp. The water there was a creamy pink. Air plants covered the trees like tufts of hair. All the life was in the trees, in the nests swinging from high branches.

I didn't care for the swamp, although it's true the sun was no problem there.

In Momma's house, a lemon tree grew outside the window of the baby's room. The fruit hung there for color mostly. Sometimes Momma made a soup. The tree was quite lovely and it flourished. It had been planted over the grease trap of the sink. I am always honest when I can be. It was swill that made it grow.

Here there is nothing of interest outside the child's room. Just the sand and the dunes. The dunes cast no shadow and offer no relief from the sun. A small piece of the Gulf is visible and it flickers like glass. It's as though the water is signaling some message to my child in his crib.

We do not wait for Jace to come back. We do not wait for anything. We do not want anything. Jace, on the other hand, wants and wants. There is nothing he would not accept. He has many trades. Once he was a deep-sea diver. He dove for sponges out of Tarpon Springs. He dove every day, all of one spring and all of one summer. There was a red tide that year that drove people almost mad. Your eyes would swell, your throat would burn. Everything was choking. The water was like chewing gum. The birds went inland. All the fish and turtles died. I wouldn't hear about it. I was always a sensitive woman. Jace would lie in bed, smoking, his brown arms on the white sheets, his pale hair on the pressed pillowcases. Yes, everything was spotless once, and in order.

He said, "The fastest fish can't swim out of it. Not even the barracuda."

I wouldn't hear it. I did not like suffering.

"The bottom was covered with fish," he said. "I couldn't see the sponges for the acres of fish."

I began to cry.

"Everything is all right," he said. He held me. "No one cares," he said. "Why are you crying?"

There were other jobs Jace had. He built and drove. He would be gone for a few weeks or a few months and then he would come back. There were some things he didn't tell me.

The beach land here belongs to the Navy. It has belonged to them for many years. Their purpose has been forgotten. There are a few trees, near the road, but they have no bark or green branches. I point this out to the child, directing his gaze to the blasted scenery. "The land is unwholesome," I say. He refuses to agree. I insist, although I am not one for words.

"Horsetail beefwood can't be tolerated here," I tell him, "although horsetail beefwood is all the land naturally bears. Now if they had a decorative bent," I tell him, "they would plant palms, but there are no palms."

The baby's head is a white globe beneath my heart. He exhausts me, even though his weight is little more than that of water on my hands. He is a frail child. So many precautions are necessary. My hands grow white from holding him.

I am so relieved that Jace is gone. He has a perfect memory. His mouth was so clean, resting on me, and I was so quiet. But then he'd start talking about Momma's house.

"Wasn't life nice then?" he'd say. "And couldn't we see everything there was to see? And didn't life just make the finest sense?"

Even without Jace, I sometimes feel uneasy. There is something I feel I have not done.

It was the third month I could feel the child best. They move, you know, to face their stars.

There is a small town not far from here. I loathe the town and its people. They are watchful country people. The town's economy is dependent upon the Prison. The Prison is a good neighbor, they say. It is unobtrusive, quiet. When an execution is necessary, the executioner arrives in a white Cadillac and he is unobtrusive too for the Cadillac is an old one and there are a great many white cars here. The cars are white because of the terrible heat. The man in the Cadillac is called the "engineer" and no one claims to know his name.

The townspeople are all very handy. They are all very willing to lend a helping hand. They hire Prison boys to work in their yards. You can always tell the Prison boys. They look so hungry and serene.

Martha is the only one of the townspeople who talks to me. The rest nod or smile. Martha is a comfy woman with a nice complexion, but her hair is the color of pork. She is always touching my arm, directing my attention to things she believes I might have overlooked, a sale on gin, for example, or frozen whipped puddings.

"You might could use a sweet or two," she says. "Fill you out."

Her face is big and friendly and her hands seem clean and

dry. She is always talking to me. She talks about her daughter who has not lived with her for many years. The daughter lives in a special home in the next state. Martha says, "She had a bad fever and she stopped being good."

Martha's hand on my shoulder feels like a nurse's hand, intimate and officious. She invites me to her home and I accept, over and over again. She is inviting me in for tea and conversation and I am always opening the door to her home. I am forever entering her rooms, walking endlessly across the shiny wooden floors of her home.

"I don't want to be rich," Martha says. "I want only enough to have a friend over for a piece of pie or a highball. And I would like a frost-free refrigerator. Even in the winter, I have to defrost ours once a week. I have to take everything out and then spread the newspapers and get the bowl and sponge and then I have to put everything back."

"Yes," I say.

Martha's hands are moving among the cheap teacups. "It seems a little senseless," she says.

There are small table fans in the house, stirring the air. The rooms smell of drain cleaner and mold and mildew preventives. When the fans part the curtains to the west, an empty horse stall and a riding ring are visible. Martha crowns my tea with rum, like a friend.

"This is a fine town," Martha says. "Everyone looks out for his neighbor. Even the Prison boys are good boys, most of them up just for stealing copper wire or beating on their women's fellows."

I hold the child tight. You know a mother's fears. He is fascinated by the chopping blades of the little fans, by the roach tablets behind the sofa cushions. Outside, as well, he puts his hands to everything—the thorns on the grapefruit tree, the poisonous oleander, the mottled dumb cane. . . .

"I imagine the wicked arrive at that Prison only occasionally," I say.

"Hardly ever," Martha agrees.

*   *   *

I am trying to explain to you. I am always inside this woman's house. I am always speaking reasonably with this Martha. I am so tired and so sad and I am lying on a bed drinking tea. It is not Martha's bed. It is, I suppose, a bed for her guests. I am lying on a bedspread which is covered by a large embroidered peacock. Underneath the bed is a single medium-sized mixing bowl. In the light socket is a night-light in the shape of a rose. I feel wonderful in this room in many ways. I feel like a column of air. I would like to audition for something. I am so clean inside.

"My husband worries about you," Martha says. She takes the cup away. "We are all good people here," she says. "We all lead good lives."

"What does your husband do, then?" I say. I smile because I do not want her to think I am confused. Actually, I've met the man. He placed his long hands on my stomach, on my thighs.

"We are not unsubtle here," Martha says, tapping her chest.

I met the man and when I met him in this house he was putting in new pine boards over the cement floors. When I arrived, he stopped, but that was what he was doing. He had a gun which shot nails into the concrete. Each nail cost a quarter. The expense distressed Martha and she mentioned it in my hearing. Men resume things, you know. He went back to it. As I lay on the bed, I could hear the gun being fired and I awoke quickly, frightened the noise might awaken the child. You know a mother's presumptions. There was the smell of sawdust and smoke from the nail gun.

"I wouldn't have thought we'd have to worry about you," Martha says unhappily.

When I returned from Martha's house the first time, I passed a farmer traveling on the beach road in his rusty car. Strapped to the roof of the car was a sandhill crane, one wing raised, pumped full of air and sailing in the moonlight. They kill these birds for their meat. The meat, they say, tastes just like chicken. I have found that almost everything tastes like chicken.

There is a garage not far from town where Jace used to buy gas. I stopped there once. There was a large wire meshed cage outside, by the pumps. A sign on it said BABY FLORIDA RATTLERS. Inside were dozens of blue and pink baby rattles on a dirt floor. It gave me a headache. It was such a large cage.

At night I take the child and walk over the beach to the water's edge where it is cool. The child is at peace here, beside the water, and it is here, most likely, where Jace will find us when he comes back. When Jace comes back it will be at night. He always comes in on the heat, at night.

"Darling," I can hear him say, "even as a little boy, I was all there ever was for you."

I can see it quite clearly. I will be on the shoreline, nursing, and Jace will come back on the heat, all careless and easy and "Darling," he'll shout into the wind, into the white roil of water behind us. "Darling, darling," Jace will shout, "where you been, little girl?"

Building

*R*EMODELING their house is Peter's idea, Katherine likes it the way it is. It is an old sprawling wooden house with small dark rooms. The plantings around it are old too, obvious from their type as well as their size. There are huge travelers'-trees, which aren't popular any more, lining the driveway. This is on a key on the west coast of Florida, a key upon which the population has quadrupled in the last four years. Katherine has lived on the key for eight years and is forever finding herself telling new acquaintances how much everything has changed. These people all live in condos on the beach and are unapologetic, articulate and drink in moderation. Katherine hasn't made a friend out of a new acquaintance in a long time.

Katherine first saw their house, and Peter, with her friend Annie, who was house-hunting. Peter is in real estate. He's very successful now and has his own business, but then he was just getting started, working for someone else, and he was showing this house for sale on a Sunday afternoon. Peter grinned at Katherine as though he had met her before, which he had not. Annie thought the house was too dark, which it was, but Katherine liked it, although she was not in the position to buy anything. The house was a relic of the recent past in a neighborhood that had grown up around it. Peter told Katherine that he was thinking of buying it himself, it was such a good investment. Then he asked her to dinner and three months after that, they got married.

It is Katherine who has prevented Peter from improving their house before this. But the house had dry rot, it needed a new roof, new wiring. Really, remodeling was inevitable. Actually, little of the old house will remain. Now that Peter has convinced Katherine of the need to remodel, he encourages her to debate the decisions he makes.

"I want to lose an argument with you every so often," he says, "that way the house will be more the way we both want it."

But Katherine doesn't have arguments with Peter, Peter never argues with anyone. All their friends are amazed, for example, at how well he gets along with the workmen involved in the remodeling. It's unusual, their friends say, not to get upset with some, if not most, of these people in the long run, but Peter gets along with them all, the carpenter, the electrician, the plumber, the dry-wall and insulation man, the mason, the back-hoe operator, the roofer, whereas Katherine finds it difficult to converse with any of these people. Her jaws ache from projecting the illusion of concern. There is a basic misunderstanding between Katherine and all of them. They think she is interested in what is going to happen and she's not.

"This is a house that will tell your story the way you want your story told," the architect says.

"Heart-side up, heart-side out. Always," the carpenter says. He is referring to boards.

The plumber says, "This is a beautiful tub. You should take good care of this tub."

The dry-wall man says, "You were smart not to make square rooms. A square room is an acoustical prison."

The electrician, a tall gaunt boy, says nothing. He looks like someone Katherine knew once, but she doesn't think she's actually met him before. Once all the young men she knew looked like him.

Peter and Katherine's friends have told them that they "complement" one another by which they mean that Katherine is dark and rather glum and retiring and Peter is pale and energetic and gregarious. They've been married for five years.

Katherine has heard that this is a dangerous time, statistically speaking, however she was married to her first husband for only ten months so she feels she has done her part to make statistics meaningless. Katherine's first husband's name was Peter also, although everyone called him by his middle name which was Travis. Even so, Katherine finds that she doesn't call Peter by his name very often. She sometimes calls him "babe" as in "Here's looking at you, babe," when the first drink of the evening is about to be drunk. She isn't aware that Peter uses her name very often either. Katherine suspects that, more or less, this is the way married people are with one another.

Peter and Katherine have rented a house to live in while the remodeling is going on. Katherine has arranged for this—it is the same beach house on the southernmost end of the key where she lived before she met Peter, after her divorce from Travis. She was thrilled when she learned from the elderly owner of the property, Dewey Dobbs, that the house was still cheap and available. Over the years, Dewey has driven a succession of developers half mad with lust and exasperation by refusing to sell his large unkempt holdings on the Gulf of Mexico. There are condominiums to both the south and east of him, pressed against his boundaries, towering high above the tall pine trees that shade his lowly buildings—the house that Peter and Katherine have rented, Dewey's own, and a converted boat shed that Dewey rents to two surfers.

Katherine is happy about living in the beach house. It is little more than a shack really, small, hot, and gummy with salt spray. On the living room wall is a twenty-pound snook that Dewey's son caught in 1947. There are straw mats on the floor and mildew on the ceiling. The water has a highly sulfurous odor and there is a leak beneath the sink which drains into a 7-Eleven Elvis Presley cup. The plastic cup describes the childhood of The King and must be emptied daily. Katherine takes a few clothes, a few books, a tube of zinc oxide, and moves in.

Peter doesn't share Katherine's enthusiasm for the shack. Actually, he hates it, but it doesn't matter, he's seldom there. He works very hard, and he comes home late. When he has

any spare time, he spends it at their "real" house as he refers
to it, watching the construction. He and Katherine are being
exceptionally nice with one another. It is a difficult time, their
friends say—the disruptions, the decisions—but everything,
thanks to Peter, moves along smoothly. Katherine is not hurt
that he has involved them in something that doesn't engage
her, and Peter is not offended by her non-involvement. Katherine feels that she must have learned something about marriage
from being married before that is now working to her benefit.
However, she doesn't know quite what it is, or how, actually,
it works.

Katherine is currently unemployed. In the past she has made
jewelry or elaborate wooden puzzles that she sold at crafts fairs.
She has made pastry for a catering service. She has taught
classes at a botanical garden in town. She is good at cards and
once she wanted to be a croupier on a cruise ship to the
Bahamas, but she has never done that. When she had been
married to Travis, she had done yard work. The two of them
specialized in cleaning and trimming trees and palms. They
had conscientiously refused those jobs where they were re-
quired to take down trees they thought were beautiful. About
once a month, someone would want them to remove a one-
hundred-year-old live oak on the assumption that a situation
would arise in which a fiercely singular wind would come up
in the night and tear off one of the tree's massive limbs and
send it through the roof of their aluminum gardening shed.
Katherine and Travis would try to convince such people of the
stupidity of what they wanted to do and sometimes they were
successful, but more often they were not. They would drive by
later and the tree would be gone. There would be a small
rosebush in its place and bright sun would be streaming down
everywhere. Then at the dump (this was when the dump was
still small and new arrivals were quickly noted) the tree would
be there, chopped and scattered, its branches still green in the
refuse.

There had been a beautiful live oak in front of the house she
had lived in with Travis in the days of their brief marriage.

Neither the house nor the tree exist now, both having recently been leveled so that a cement-block Rent-a-Closet could be built on the site. People rent their condominiums during the height of the season and store their personal belongings in a Rent-a-Closet. Some of the people that Katherine now knows do that very thing. When she had been married to Travis and they had had one of their frequent quarrels and he had left the house, Katherine would often climb high up into the live oak and stay there until he returned. After he had been in the house for awhile, she would climb back down and saunter through the door, trying to give the impression that she had been someplace else, at a bar or with friends or even with a stranger, talking. She wanted him to think that she had someplace to go, away from him, and had gone there.

After their divorce, Katherine got the job at the botanical garden and rented Dewey's beach shack. The retirees who attended her classes at the garden were primarily interested in plants that took little care and they were crazy about bromeliads which are able to flourish in deficient environments. Katherine told them how to force blooms by placing the plant and an apple in a plastic bag and they seemed to be thrilled with this information. After an hour of classes, Katherine conducted tours through the garden. It was boring work and she didn't make much money, but she hadn't needed much money then, and the job gave her time to think and imagine the kind of life that would be hers, eventually, now that she was free from a marriage she had found disappointing. She thought of taking flying lessons and maybe getting a pilot's license. At night, in the beach shack, she stayed up late, listening to the soft thud and rush of the waves upon the sand. She could have enjoyed that time more if she had not been brooding so about Travis.

Four months after their divorce, Travis had gone camping on Cumberland Island and been bitten by ants and gone into anaphylactic reaction and died. The ranger who found him thought he'd had a heart attack but the doctor at the hospital saw the small red welts on his ankles. "It was only a few ants," Travis's mother had written Katherine. Travis was smart and

sentimental, he had curly hair and often wore suspenders. He
did not seem the kind of person to whom such a weird sad
death would happen. As far as Katherine knew, he had not
even had any allergies. Katherine felt that everyone had a
certain closed circle of happenings that happened to them,
certain kinds of things, and that somehow Travis had ex-
changed circles with someone else. Thinking about Travis troubled and baffled Katherine. Even now, she seems to stumble
on the fact that she would not still be married to him even if
he had not died.

When Travis and Katherine got their divorce, his mother
had been very upset. "Why are you doing this!" she exclaimed
to Katherine in a letter. "I don't understand. Thank goodness
there are no little babies to suffer." Katherine rather wished
there had been a baby. Of course he would not have suffered.
Why would he? Katherine feels that if she had had an earlier
child, it would be easier for her to have one now. She feels that
she doesn't have the instincts now to understand a child, and
Peter doesn't mind this, but if she'd like to have a child, it
would be fine, he'd approve of such an idea, really. But there
is no child that Katherine has with Peter and there was no child
she had with Travis. When she had been with Travis she had
an old black Jaguar XK-150 convertible and a toucan. With
Peter, she has a new Volvo station wagon and a turkey.

Peter and Katherine have a turkey because they went to a
communal feast on Thanksgiving Day and the live turkey was
the grand prize in a dart game. The host, a wealthy man who
has made a fortune in swimming pool construction, is a good
friend of Peter's. He is going to install a caged pool for them
at cost as part of their remodeling project. The host always
gives fabulous parties. On Halloween, he gave a party where he
had an open casket on the lanai filled with Big Macs. On
Thanksgiving, there were large quantities of meat, pies, watermelon and liquor. Neither Katherine nor Peter won at darts,
but the winner didn't want the turkey and the runners-
up didn't want it either, so at the end of the evening, Peter
and Katherine loaded the turkey into the Volvo and took

it home. It seemed an amusing thing to do at the time.

There are three things that Katherine feels are very nice about the turkey. One is the way sunlight falls through his red wattles, making them almost transparent. Two are the sounds he makes which are a cross between an electronic game and a mourning dove. And the third is that Katherine likes his feet very much. They are immense, gruesome, Baba Yaga feet. Fairy-tale feet in a story in which the hero declares at the very beginning—I will go I know not where, I shall bring back I know not what—

It is a bit eccentric to have a turkey. All their friends say this, but Katherine doesn't mind being considered a little eccentric. On Thanksgiving, Katherine walked around the party collecting watermelon rinds to take home and use in a pickling recipe that Travis's mother had once sent to her. Katherine had never had the opportunity to try the recipe before because it called for such large quantities. "Isn't she a little young to be so eccentric?" the hostess asked Peter, laughing, as Katherine dropped half-eaten watermelon in a plastic bag. Katherine took the remark as a compliment.

"What on earth are you going to do with a turkey?" Travis's mother writes. "Julia Child says that Americans should grow their own vegetables and raise rabbits to cut down on their food bills. Is something like that your intention?"

Travis's mother is discreet. For example, she never mentions her son, but if she wasn't always thinking about him, why would she continue to correspond with Katherine? When they were first married, she gave Katherine some photographs of Travis as a little boy, and when they were divorced, Katherine returned them to her. Katherine told her that they were breaking up because they had different dreams. This wasn't exactly true, but the explanation seemed vague enough to be inarguable. When Travis realized that Katherine was serious about wanting a divorce, he accused her of having no conception of the real world. "The real world is hidden by your imagination," he said.

Katherine doesn't think she has much of an imagination.

She had never imagined for instance that she would have stopped loving Travis and that he would have died and that she would spend so much of her time now remembering him.

Katherine has difficulty imagining her life at all, not that she has to, she thinks, after all it is happening to her, her life, she doesn't have to imagine it, and trying to imagine the way her life had been with Travis always makes her feel as though a bone were caught in her throat. The things they possessed together have vanished. The Jag had gone through two transmissions, a gas tank and a brake overhaul and had to be sold, and after they decided upon the divorce, it seemed only sensible to give the toucan up too. Travis used to buy ping-pong balls and baby squeak toys for the toucan to play with. He kept grapes in his shirt pocket for the toucan to pluck out. They had bought the bird in a pet store for forty-five dollars which had been a terrific extravagance for them. Now, Katherine has heard that they cost two thousand dollars. They are smuggled into the country by men wearing panty-hose beneath their trousers. The panty-hose holds the baby birds secure but allows them to breathe. No one that Katherine knows has a toucan, but their image frequently appears on shirts, and hanging from the ceiling in an elegant little shop that her friend Annie runs, there is a larger-than-life silk toucan on a macramé swing.

Times have changed, Katherine thinks, and when she thinks of the words, they appear like one of Peter's realty computer print-outs in her brain—TIMES HAVE CHANGED—and she thinks she is still a little young to be thinking like this.

During the remodeling, Katherine spends all her time on the beach and in the shack there. She goes to the other house only to feed the turkey. Peter could feed it but Katherine feels responsible for this peculiarity in their lives. She tries to avoid looking at the house, but that is difficult. It is becoming larger and is about to make a statement of some sort—an expensive, sleek, convivial statement. Katherine prefers studying the turkey, its amazing feet, its warty naked neck of astonishing cerulean.

Every morning, Katherine visits Dewey. Nothing has

changed in his house. He is old, but he has always been old. Even the plastic rectangle electric "environment" that Katherine remembers from years before still sits on top of the television set. The rectangle is full of colored turquoise water which flows and falls in a simulation of rolling surf. It reminds her of Travis, Katherine doesn't know why. Travis had never seen it.

One day, Katherine notices that there is no longer a pan of water outside Dewey's door.

"Don't you still put out water for the snakes?" Katherine asks.

The old man looks baffled.

"You used to put out water for the snakes and the rabbits and they'd come right up to the door."

"I can't remember that," Dewey says.

Dewey is a cripple who scoots around on crutches. One night, years before, he was walking home from the grocery with a pint of coconut ice cream, when a car struck him down, crushing his legs. The woman kept right on driving. When the police later found her, she told them she had heard a noise but she thought she had just knocked over a garbage can.

"How much of life is like that, am I right?" Dewey says. "I was in the wrong place at the wrong time."

Dewey has immense shoulders and a high-pitched crackling voice, and his house smells of kerosene and flowers. He has a bouquet of flowers delivered to his house every week. He also has the newspaper delivered every morning and after he reads it, he puts it carefully back together again so that it looks like a completely fresh, unexamined paper and gives it to Katherine.

Sometimes, Katherine has a drink with Dewey in the evening, before Peter comes home from work.

"Where's your husband?" Dewey asks. "I wish he'd come over and say hello sometime."

Katherine sips her drink and looks through Dewey's greasy windows at the setting sun. She feels confused. "He's very involved in our house," she finally says, "but I'm sure he will."

"Have you met those boys, those surfer boys?" Dewey asks.

"They're good boys. The only book they own is the Bible. When they're not surfing, they're reading the Bible. They're waiting for the Rapture."

"What's the Rapture?" Katherine asks.

"As I understand it," Dewey says, "that's when things get straightened out at last."

In the living room, Dewey has a large bureau which is full of games and tricks. He has cards in which a picture is concealed. When one first looks at it, it appears merely as a nonrepresentational design, but hidden, at a certain angle, using shadings of light and dark and depth perceptions, is the likeness of a cow or a helicopter or William Holden as he appeared in *Sunset Boulevard.* Once the shape becomes apparent, of course, it remains forever accessible to the eye. Katherine thinks that if she had a child, he would be fascinated with the contents of this bureau.

Peter teases Katherine about the surfers who are muscular and tanned with short blond hair. When the boys see Katherine, they smile and converse with her politely in their surf-veggie language. Katherine doesn't flirt with the surfers. She feels older than them, that's all she feels.

Katherine is startled one morning to see the electrician's name in Dewey's newspaper. The article she notices says that his car was stolen outside a local bar and driven to another bar where it remained locked, its windows rolled up tightly, in the parking lot for several days before it was discovered by police. The electrician's mongrel dog was found dead in the car from asphyxiation. The thought of the dog waiting in the car in the rising heat makes Katherine feel panicky. The bar where the car was found has a package store where Katherine buys their liquor and she wonders why it was that she did not go down for wine or bourbon during those days that the car was there. But if she had driven into the parking lot beside the package store, would she have been aware of the situation? She doesn't know, probably not.

Katherine buys a sympathy card, a card that shows a tree on a riverbank, looks up the electrician's name in the phone book and sends it to him. When Travis died, some of Katherine's friends sent her sympathy cards and some, not knowing the etiquette of the situation, did not. Katherine has never sent a sympathy card in her life before but she does now to the hippie electrician whose dog has died, and weeps as she signs her name. She never knows if he receives it or not. Peter tells her that he never returned to work on the house and it was necessary to hire someone else.

In two weeks, just before Christmas, Katherine will be thirty. Annie's daughter, Genevieve, and Katherine have the same birthdate, eighteen years apart. Katherine is Gen's godmother. The child's godfather is a Yale professor whom Katherine has never met. If something happened to Annie and her husband, if their house blew up, say, while Genevieve was at a slumber party somewhere else, would Katherine and the Yale professor be responsible for raising Gen? Katherine doesn't know how this could be done within the constructs of a family situation, but she never mentions this to Annie.

Katherine visits Annie to ask Gen what she would like for her birthday.

"For my birthday," Gen says, "I would like a pure white cockatoo and my own toaster."

"Ha," her mother says.

"I want a cockatoo because they talk," Gen says, unperturbed. "You can teach them a lot of different words."

"I think a cockatoo is a wonderful idea," Annie says. She is joking. "You could teach it to say, 'Have you brushed your teeth, Gen?', 'Have you put out the bathroom light, Gen?', 'Have you hung up your towel, Gen?' You could teach it to say all those things and then I wouldn't have to. We could talk about more important things."

"What things?" Gen asks.

"We could talk and talk," Annie says.

"About what?" Gen insists.

"We could discuss why you can't cut the end off a piece of string," Annie says.

"Why can't you?" Gen asks.

"It's a philosophical question," Annie says, "we could talk about it forever."

"We wouldn't talk," Gen says.

Her mother looks hurt. She pushes her hair up and off her neck, which makes her look younger and sadder.

"How is your turkey?" Gen asks Katherine. "What does he like to do?"

Katherine tells her that the turkey likes corn and egg shells and bagels and then finds herself telling a long Baba Yaga story. She tells Gen that the turkey reminds her of Baba Yaga, a Russian witch who lived in a house on chicken legs. Whenever anyone came along that Baba Yaga did not want to see, the chicken legs would move the house around so that the visitor couldn't find the front door.

Gen had never heard of Baba Yaga.

"Do you like fairy tales?" Katherine asks her.

"I like science fiction," Gen says and wanders from the room, smelling the way Annie would smell if she ever had the opportunity to use her own perfume.

"Have some wine," Annie urges Katherine, "tell me what you're thinking."

"Actually," Katherine says, "I was thinking about how I used to climb trees so a certain person would think I wasn't home."

Annie thinks Katherine is referring to her childhood. "Children are different today," she sighs. "They're entirely different from the way we used to be."

A week before Katherine's birthday, a long envelope arrives from Travis's mother. Each year she sends a birthday card to Katherine one week ahead of time. She must have put the date down wrong on her calendar years ago and transferred it incorrectly to each succeeding year. Katherine opens the envelope and there is a birthday card and a long red and white automobile bumper sticker inside. I LOVE MY VOLVO the sticker says. Travis's mother has a Volvo too, but an old one, a bulbous sedan painted a cheery Coca-Cola red. Katherine doesn't put the sticker on her car. Actually, Katherine doesn't love her

Volvo. She's surprised that Travis's mother doesn't realize that.

Katherine's birthday finally arrives. She has given Gen a tape recorder. As for herself, she and Peter decide to drink champagne all day. She would like to forget this birthday in a fashionable manner. Peter borrows a friend's sailboat and they sail around in the morning drinking champagne. In the afternoon, they return the boat, change their clothes and go to an art opening at a local gallery where there is lots of champagne being served. The artist says that his paintings, which are mathematical and precise, are based on Gestalt principles of illusion. Katherine likes the paintings which give the impression that they have solved something, that something is settled and finished. They don't remind her of anything. The artist is a fat jolly man dressed in black. His wife is beautiful and a smoker and since smoking is not allowed in the gallery, she stands outside mostly, smoking. Peter is a smoker too and he and the artist's wife stand outside beneath the palms and smoke and drink champagne. She smokes Gauloises and he smokes Camels. They are the last smokers left in the world. When Katherine walks outside to join them, she finds herself telling the woman how much everything has changed, how only a few years ago there were pileated woodpeckers and tarpon and sea turtles, but there aren't any more. Peter begins fiddling with a long silk scarf the artist's wife is wearing. He holds a tasseled end in his hand and runs it through his fingers. He rocks back and forth on his heels and tosses one end of the scarf softly around the woman's neck. Katherine walks away, down the street to the Volvo. Just as she is putting the key in the ignition, Peter runs up. She puts the car in gear and Peter jumps into the back seat as the car moves off.

"I'm sorry," he says, "I was being a little ebullient."

"Ebullient?" Katherine says. "Is that how you pronounce that?"

"Yes," Peter says. "Honk the horn on your birthday." He kisses her and climbs into the front seat. "Just honk the horn like you normally would."

Katherine taps the horn and there is a loud blast which

makes her jump in her seat. It's the sound of an ocean liner.

"I could have bought one that had eighty-one different sounds," Peter says. "It was a synthesizer that mixed tone, bass, treble and frequency. You could make zoo sounds, UFO sounds, animal yelps, ambulance and police siren sounds, everything."

"I love this," Katherine says, and she does, but she will have to get used to hitting the horn. She never uses the horn. She is not that kind of a driver. She taps the horn again.

"Do you love me?" Peter asks.

"Yes," Katherine says.

On New Year's Day, Katherine goes to the house with Peter. He is going to plant four citrus trees and a jacaranda. Katherine is going to poison the ants. She measures everything carefully and pours the poison through a funnel into the hills.

"There goes their breakfast nook!" Peter calls to her encouragingly. "There goes their fandango room!"

Katherine measures and mixes. She moves from one end of the property to the other, pouring the smoky green liquid into the mounds.

"There goes their ball game," Peter says. He sets a lemon tree firmly in a hole, taps the earth down around it, sprays the green leaves lightly with a hose. The jacaranda will grow high above the citrus and losing its leaves in winter, allow the sun to shine through its bare branches and ripen the fruit below. In the springtime, when the citrus is in neither fruit nor flower, the jacaranda will be in full color. Katherine watches Peter as he works. She tries to remember the last words Travis ever said to her, the very last words. She can't. She wraps the empty bottle of poison tightly in newspaper and stuffs it in the trash, then runs water from an outside spigot and washes her hands. She goes over to the turkey's pen. The turkey looks at her with vacant dignity. She feeds it pieces of bread and grass through the wire.

"We'll have a big party when this is all finished," Peter says. "We're going to have a wonderful time in this house."

In the lot next door, behind a fence, someone starts a chain saw. The turkey shrieks wildly in response. The turkey loves the sound of chain saws, motorcycles and sudden laughter.

"That's new," Katherine says, pointing through the trees at the shine of a distant roof. "We were never able to see a house over there before."

"They're building too," Peter says. "They've subdivided the land."

"Everything's changing," Katherine says.

"We won't notice them," Peter says, "we'll plant some more trees." When Katherine doesn't reply, Peter says, "I know things change now and I do not care. It's all been changed for me. Let it all change. We'll be gone before it's changed too much. I found that if you took a drink it got very much the same as it was always."

Katherine looks at him.

"Hemingway," Peter says.

"Yes, let's have a drink," Katherine says.

Katherine sits at the kitchen table in the beach shack and writes out invitations for the party Peter's planned. As she writes addresses on envelopes, she thinks of a T-shirt Travis wore all the time. The T-shirt said THE FAINTING EGG. It had something to do with a vegetarian restaurant where one of their friends worked as a waiter. The shirt was dark blue and had white lettering. She remembers it clearly.

On the table with the invitations is a letter from Travis's mother, who writes that she has just won a black and white television set in a soft drink contest. "I pried this little plastic liner out of the bottle cap and there it was, a little picture of a TV! The first time in my life I have ever won anything! I am donating it to the church, however, as I already have a nice TV."

Katherine and Travis's mother have been keeping in touch now for seven years.

Katherine puts everything down on the invitation except the date which she'll fill in later. She and Peter do not know the date of the party because the house isn't finished yet. There have been delays. The weather has been unusually cold and rainy and the carpenter has a lung infection and hasn't been able to work. But even though the work is not completed, they will have to return to the house. For the last few years, Dewey has rented the beach shack for the month of February to a couple from Canada and they are arriving late tonight. After Katherine finishes the invitations, she will sweep the rooms and go home. She and Peter will live in their unfinished house and in a while it will be finished and they will be there.

Katherine walks out to the beach. It is very cold, the sky is grey, the water white with swells. Freezing temperatures are predicted for the night. Dewey has told her that thirty years ago, there was such a severe freeze that even the mangroves died. Katherine watches the boys surf in their black wet suits. They are waiting for the heavenly shout and the trumpet calls, and while they wait, they surf. Katherine watches them until she begins to shiver. Back in the shack, she calls Peter on the telephone and tells him she's just finishing up. He doesn't have to pick her up in the car, she'll walk home.

"It's too cold," Peter says.

"No, I want to."

"I'll warm you up when you get home," Peter says.

Katherine sweeps the shack carefully. She scours the sinks and takes all the silverware out of the tray and checks it to make sure it's clean. The sun goes down, filling the rooms with red light. When she finally leaves, it's dark. She walks north along the beach for a mile until she reaches a small parcel of land that hasn't been developed yet and is still in cedars and cabbage palms. She passes through this to the harrowing three-lane road that bisects the key, crosses the road and enters their neighborhood, a Venetian labyrinth of streets which hum with the sounds of sprinkler systems and pool filters.

In their lot, Peter has covered the newly planted citrus with plastic sheeting to protect them from the cold. He has covered the elephant ears, the Dieffenbachia, the arecas. Katherine makes her way past the enshrouded plants to the house which is ablaze with lights, virtually held aloft and secure in space by thousands of watts. The house is huge, all angles and pitch, bleached wood and glass. Katherine puts the bag of invitations she has been carrying down on the ground, and chews on her nails which smell of Comet. She knows she is worrying about something that has already happened, something in the past which she should resist worrying about. She stands outside in the cold dark and looks into the house at Peter who is making himself a drink. She watches him as he fills a second glass with ice. It is a plastic insulated glass with a felt pelican roosting between the walls of the vacuum seal. It is Katherine's glass, the one she has indicated a preference for. Peter's glass has a piece of knotted rope. There is a fire burning in the new limestone fireplace and Peter stands before it looking at it while Katherine looks into the room, at Peter. Furniture is pushed against the walls and lumber and rolls of screening are stacked in a corner. Some of the furniture is covered with sheets to protect it from dust.

Peter walks through the lighted rooms toward Katherine but doesn't see her. He goes to the telephone and she can tell by the numbers he dials that he is calling the beach house. They both wait while the phone rings and rings. Katherine moves even further from the house and crouches by the turkey pen which Peter has covered with a piece of plastic which doesn't quite reach to the ground. She remembers how she used to hide from Travis long ago, and wonders when it was exactly when all her dreams and attitudes about herself were reduced to the pervasive memory of a dead boy. She knows she will go into the house soon and be with Peter, on this, the coldest night in many years, but for the moment she waits outside, in the dark. Beside her, in the pen, only the turkey's foolish legs are visible, its impossible feet being hidden in straw.

Traveling to Pridesup

OTILLA cooked up the water for her morning tea and opened a carton of ricotta cheese. She ate standing up, dipping cookies in and out of the cheese, walking around the enormous kitchen in tight figure eights as though she were in a gymkhana. She was eighty-one years old and childishly ravenous and hopeful with a long pigtail and a friendly unreasonable nature.

She lived with her sisters in a big house in the middle of the state of Florida. There were three of them, all older and wiser. They were educated in Northern schools and came back with queer ideas. Lavinia, the eldest, returned after four years, with a rock, off of a mountain, out of some forest. It was covered with lichen and green like a plum. Lavinia put it to the north of the seedlings on the shadowy side of the house. She tore up the grass and burnt out the salamanders and the ants and raked the sand out all around the rock in a pattern like a machine would make. The sisters watched the rock on and off for forty years until one morning when they were all out in their Mercedes automobile, taking the air, a sinkhole opened up and took the rock and half the garage down thirty-seven feet. It didn't seem to matter to Lavinia, who had cared for the thing. Growing rocks, she said, was supposed to bring one serenity and put one on terms with oneself and she had become serene so she didn't care. Otilla believed that such an idea could only come from a foreign religion, but she could only guess at this as no one ever told her anything except her father, and he had died long ago from drink. He was handsome and rich, having made his money in railways and grapefruit. Otilla was his darling. She still had the tumbler he was drinking rum from when he died. None of father's girls had ever married, and Otilla, who was thought to be a little slow, had not even gone off to school.

Otilla ate a deviled egg and some ice cream and drank another cup of tea. She wore sneakers and a brand new dress that still had the cardboard pinned beneath the collar. The dress had come in the mail the day before along with a plastic soap dish and three rubber pedal pads for the Mercedes. The sisters ordered everything through catalogs and seldom went to town. Upstairs, Otilla could hear them moving about.

"Louisa," Marjorie said, "this soap dish works beautifully."

Otilla moved to a wicker chair by the window and sat on her long pigtail. She turned off the light and turned on the fan. It was just after sunrise, the lakes all along the Ridge were smoking with heat. She could see bass shaking the surface of the water and she felt a brief and eager joy at the sight—at the morning and the mist running off the lakes and the birds rising up from the shaggy orange trees. The joy didn't come often any more and it didn't last long and when it passed it seemed more a part of dying than delight. She didn't dwell on this however. For the most part, she found that as long as one commenced to get up in the morning and move one's bowels, everything else moved along without confusing variation.

From the window, she could also see the mailbox. The flag was up and there was a package swinging from it. She couldn't understand why the mailman hadn't put the package inside. It was a large sturdy mailbox and would hold anything.

She got up and walked quickly outside, hoping that Lavinia wouldn't see her, as Lavinia preferred picking up the mail herself. She passed the black Mercedes. The garage had never been rebuilt and the car had been parked for years between two oak trees. There was a quilt over the hood. Every night, Lavinia would pull a wire out of the distributor and bring it into the house. The next morning she would put the wire back in again, warm up the Mercedes and drive it twice around the circular driveway and then down a slope one hundred yards to the mailbox. They only received things that they ordered. The Mercedes was fifteen years old and had eleven thousand miles on it. Lavinia kept the car up. She was clever at it.

"This vehicle will run forever because I've taken good care of it," she'd say.

Otilla stood beside the mailbox looking north up the road and then south. She had good eyesight but there wasn't a thing to be seen. Hanging in a feed bag off the mailbox was a sleeping baby. It wore a little yellow T-shirt with a rabbit on it. The rabbit appeared to be playing a fiddle. The baby had black hair and big ears and was making small grunts and whistles in its sleep. Otilla wiped her hands on the bodice of her dress and picked the baby out of the sack. It smelled faintly of ashes and fruit.

Inside the house, the three sisters, Lavinia, Louisa and Marjorie were setting out the breakfast things. They were ninety-two, ninety and eighty-seven respectively. They were in excellent color and health and didn't look much over seventy. Each morning they'd set up the table as though they were expecting the Governor himself—good silver, best china, egg cups and bun cozy.

They settled themselves. The fan was painted with blue rustproof paint and turned right on around itself like an owl. The soft-boiled eggs wobbled when the breeze ran by them.

"Going to be a hot one," Lavinia said.

The younger sisters nodded yes, chewing on their toast.

"The summer's just begun and it appears it's never going to end," Lavinia said.

The sisters shook their heads yes. The sky was getting brighter and brighter. The three of them, along with Otilla, had lived together forever. They weren't looking at the sky or the empty groves which they had seen before. The light was changing very fast, progressing visibly over the table top. It fell on the butter.

"They've been tampering with the atmosphere," Lavinia

said. "They don't have the sense to leave things alone." Lavinia was a strong-willed, impatient woman. She thought about what she had just said and threw her spoon down irritably at the truth of it. Lavinia was no longer serene about anything. That presumption had been for her youth, when she had time. Now everything was pesky to her and a hindrance.

"Good morning," Otilla said. She walked to the wicker chair and sat down. The baby lay in her arms, short and squat like a loaf of bread.

Lavinia's eyes didn't change, nor her mouth nor the set of her jaw. Outside some mockingbirds were ranting. The day had gotten so bright it was as if someone had just shot it off in her face.

"Put it back where you got it," she said slowly.

"I can't imagine where this baby's from," Otilla said.

The baby's eyes were open now and were locked on the old woman's face. Lavinia spoke in a low, furious voice. "Go on out with it, Otilla." She raised her fingers distractedly, waving at the baby as though greeting an old friend.

Otilla picked the baby up and held it out away from her and looked cheerfully at it. "You're wetting."

"My God," Marjorie said, noticing the affair for the first time.

Otilla shook the baby up and down. Her arms were skinny and pale and they trembled a bit with the weight. The baby opened its mouth and smiled noiselessly. "You're hollow inside," Otilla said. "Hollow as a bamboo. Bam Boo To You Kangaroo." She joggled the baby whose face was static and distant with delight. "Bamboo shampoo. Bamboo cockatoo stew."

"My God," Marjorie said. She and Louisa got up and scraped off their plates and rinsed them in the sink. They went into the front room and sat on the sofa.

Otilla held the baby a little awkwardly. Its head flopped back like a flower in the wind when she got up. She had never touched a baby before and she had never thought about them either. She went to the drainboard and laid the baby down and unpinned its diaper. "Isn't that cute, Lavinia, it's a little boy."

"You are becoming senile," Lavinia said. Her fingers were still twitching in the air. She wrapped them in her napkin.

"I didn't make him up. Someone left him here, hanging off the postbox."

"Senile," Lavinia repeated. "Who knows where this baby has been? You shouldn't even be touching him. Perhaps you are just being 'set up' and we will all be arrested by the sheriff."

Otilla folded a clean dishtowel beneath the baby and pinned it together. She took the dirty diaper and scrubbed it out in the sink with a bar of almond soap and then took it outside and hung it on the clothesline. When she came back into the kitchen, she picked the baby off the drainboard and went back to her chair by the window. "Now isn't that nice, Lavinia?" She didn't want to talk but she was so nervous that she couldn't help herself. "I think they should make diapers in bright colors. Orange and blue and green. . . . Deep bright colors for a little boy. Wouldn't that be nice, Lavinia?"

"The dye would seep into their skin and kill them," Lavinia said brusquely. "They'd suffocate like a painted Easter chick."

Otilla was shocked.

"You accept things too easily, Otilla. You have always been a dope. Even as a child, you took anything anyone chose to give you." She got up and took the distributor wire of the Mercedes out of the silverware tray. She clumped down the steps to the automobile, banging the screen door behind her. A spider dropped from the ceiling and fell with a snap on the stove. Otilla heard the engine turn over and drop into idle. The screen door banged again and Lavinia was shouting into the darkened living room.

"We are going in town to the authorities and will be back directly."

There was a pause in which Otilla couldn't hear a thing. Her arm was going to sleep. She shifted the baby about on her lap, banging his head against her knee bone. The baby opened his mouth but not his eyes and gummed on the sleeve of his shirt. "Excuse me," she whispered.

"No, no," Lavinia shouted at the living room. "I can't imagine how it happened either. Someone on their way somewhere. Long gone now. Pickers, migrants."

She came back into the kitchen, pulling on a pair of black ventilated driving gloves. Lavinia was very serious about the Mercedes. She drove slowly and steadily and not particularly well, looking at the dials and needles for signs of malfunction. The reason for riding was in the traveling, she always said, for the sisters never had the need to be anyplace. Getting there was not the object. Arrival was not the point. The car was elegant and disheartening and suited to this use.

"Where are we going?" Otilla asked meekly.

"Where are we going," Lavinia mimicked in a breathless drawl that was not at all like Otilla's voice. Then she said normally, "We are going to drop this infant off in Pridesup. I am attempting not to become annoyed but you are very annoying and this is a very annoying situation."

"I think I would like to keep this baby," Otilla said. "I figure we might as well." The baby was warm and its heart was beating twice as fast as any heart she had ever heard as though it couldn't wait to get on with its living.

Lavinia walked over to her sister and gave her a yank.

"I could teach him to drink from a cup," Otilla said, close to tears. "They learn how to do that. When he got older he could mow the lawn and spray the midge and club-gall." She was on her feet now and was being pushed outside. She put out her free hand and jammed it against the door frame. "I have to get some things together, then, please Lavinia. It's twenty miles to Pridesup. Just let me get a few little things together so that he won't go off with nothing." Her chin was shaking. She was hanging fiercely onto the door and squinting out into the sunlight, down past the rumbling Mercedes into the pit where the rock had fallen and where the seedlings, still rooted, bloomed in the spring. She felt a little fuddled. It seemed that her head was down in the cool sinkhole while the rest of her wobbled in the heat. She jammed the baby so close to her that he squealed.

"I can't imagine what you're going to equip him with," Lavinia was saying. "He can't be more than a few months old. We don't have anything for that." She had stopped pushing her sister and was looking at the car, trying to remember the route to Pridesup, the county seat. It had been five years since she had driven there. Somewhere, on the left, she recollected a concentrate canning factory. Somewhere, also, there was a gas station in the stomach of a concrete dinosaur. She remembered stopping. Otilla had used the rest room and they had all bought cold barbeque. No one ever bought his gasoline, the owner said. They bought his snacks and bait and bedspreads. Lavinia had not bought his gasoline either. She doubted if the place was there now. It didn't look as though it had five years left in it.

"Oh just a little apple juice and a toy or something."

"Well, get it then," Lavinia snapped. She couldn't remember if she took a right or a left upon leaving the driveway; if she kept Cowpen Slough on her west side or her east side. The countryside looked oddly without depth and she had difficulty imagining herself driving off into it. She went into a small bathroom off the kitchen and took off her gloves and rinsed her face, then she went out to the Mercedes. She sat behind the wheel and removed some old state maps from the car's side pocket. They were confusing, full of blank spaces. Printed on the bottom of the first one were the words *Red And Blue Roads Are Equally Good.* She refolded them, fanned herself with them and put them on the seat.

Otilla got into the car with the baby and a paper bag. The baby's head was very large compared to the rest of him. It looked disabling and vulnerable. Lavinia couldn't understand how anything could start out being that ugly and said so. His ears looked like two Parker rolls. She moved the car down the drive and unhesitatingly off onto the blacktop. They drove in silence for a few minutes. It was hot and green out with a smell of sugar on the air.

"Well," Otilla said, "it doesn't seem as though he wants anything yet."

Lavinia wore a pair of enormous black sunglasses. She drove and didn't say anything.

"Look out the window here at that grey and black horse," Otilla said. She lifted the baby up. He clawed at her chin with his hand. "Look out thataway at those sandhill cranes. They're just like storks. Maybe they're the ones that dropped you off at our house."

"Oh shut up. You'll addle the little bit of brain he has," Lavinia yelled.

"It's just a manner of speaking, Lavinia. We both know it isn't so." She opened the bag and took out a piece of bread and began to eat it. The baby pushed his hand into the bread and Otilla broke off a piece of crust and gave it to him. He gnawed on it intently without diminishing it. In the bag, Otilla had a loaf of bread, a can of Coca-Cola and a jar of milk. "I couldn't find a single toy for him," she said.

"He'll have to do with the scenery," Lavinia said. She herself had never cared for it. It had been there too long and she had been too long in it and now it seemed like an external cataract obstructing her real vision.

"Lookit those water hyacinths," Otilla went on. "Lookit that piece of moon still up there in the sky."

Lavinia gritted her teeth. There had not been a single trip they had taken that Otilla had not spoiled. She talked too much and squirmed too much and always brought along food that she spilled. The last time they had driven down this road, she had had a dish of ice cream that had been squashed against the dashboard when the car had gone over a bump. Lavinia braked suddenly and turned the Mercedes into a dirt side road that dropped like a tunnel through an orange grove. She backed up and reversed her direction.

"Where are we going now, Lavinia?"

"We're going to the same place," she said angrily. "This is simply a more direct route." The baby burped softly. They passed the house again, planted white and well-to-do in the sunlight. Embarrassed, neither of them looked at it or remarked upon it.

"I think," Otilla said formally, "that we are both accepting this very well and that you are handling it OK except that I think we could have kept this baby for at least a little while until we read in the paper perhaps that someone is missing him."

"No one is going to be missing him."

"You're a little darlin'," Otilla said to the baby, who was hunched over his bread crust.

"Please stop handling him. He might very well have worms or meningitis or worse." The Mercedes was rocketing down the middle of the road through hordes of colorful bugs. Lavinia had never driven this fast. She took her foot off the accelerator and the car mannerly slowed. Lavinia was hot all over. Every decision she had made so far today seemed proper but oddly irrelevant. If she had gone down to the mailbox first as she had always done, there would have been no baby to find. She was sure of that. The problem was that the day had started out being Otilla's and not hers at all. She gave a short nervous bark and looked at the baby who was swaying on her sister's lap. "I imagine he hasn't had a single shot."

"He looks fine to me, Lavinia. He has bright eyes and he seems clean and cool enough."

Lavinia tugged at the wheel as though correcting a personal injustice rather than the car's direction. "It's no concern to us what he's got anyway. It's the law's problem. It's for the orphanage to attend to."

"Orphanage? You shouldn't take him there. He's not an orphan, he has us." She looked at the pale brown veins running off the baby's head and faintly down his cheeks.

"He doesn't have us at all," Lavinia shouted. She started to gag and gripped her throat with her left hand, giving it little pinches and tugs to keep the sickness down. There had never been a thing she'd done that hadn't agreed with her and traveling had always been a pleasure, but the baby beside her had a strong pervasive smell that seemed to be the smell of the land as well, and it made her sick. She felt as though she were falling into a pan of bright and bubbling food. She took several breaths and said more calmly, "There is no way we could keep him. You must use your head. We have not had the training and we are all getting on and what would happen is that we would die and he'd be left." She was being generous and conversational and instructive and she hoped that Otilla would appreciate this and benefit from it even though she knew her sister was weakheaded and never benefited from things in the proper way.

"But that's the way it's going to be anyway, Lavinia."

The air paddled in Lavinia's ears. The Mercedes wandered on and off the dusty shoulder. The land was empty and there wasn't anything coming toward them or going away except a bright tin can which they straddled. "Of course it is," she said. "You've missed the point."

Lavinia had never cared for Otilla. She realized that this was due mostly to preconception, as it were, for she had been present at the awful moment of birth and she knew before her sister had taken her first breath that she'd be useless. And she had been. The only thing Otilla ever had was prettiness and she had that still, lacking the sense to let it go, her girlish features still moving around indecently in her old woman's face. Sitting there now in a messy nest of bread crusts and obscure stains with the baby playing with her dress buttons, Otilla looked queerly confident and enthusiastic as though at last she were going off on her wedding day. It disgusted Lavinia. There was something unseasonal about Otilla. If she had been a man, Lavinia thought, they might very well have had a problem on their hands.

Otilla noisily shook out one of the road maps. Down one side of it was a colorful insert with tiny pictures of attractions—fish denoting streams, and women in bathing suits, and llamas representing zoos and clocks marking historical societies. All no bigger than a thumbnail. "Why this is just charming," Otilla said. "Here we have a pictorial guide." The baby looked at it grimly and something fell runny from his mouth onto a minute pink blimp. "This is the first time we have had a real destination, Lavinia. Perhaps we can see these things as well." She rested her chin on the baby's head and read aloud, " 'Route S40 through the Pine Barrens. Be sure to see the *Produce Auction, Elephant House, State Yacht Basin Marine View Old Dutch Parsonage Pacing Racing Oxford Furnace Ruins*.' Why just look at all these things," she said into the infant's hair. "This is *very* helpful."

The two regarded the map carefully. "See this," Otilla said excitedly, pointing to a tiny ancient-looking baby with a gold crown on his head. *"Baby Parade. August.* That's for us!" Then she fell silent and after a few miles she turned to Lavinia and said, "This is not for our region at all. This is for the state of New Jersey."

Lavinia was concentrating on a row of garish signs advertising a pecan shop. She'd been seeing them for the last half hour. *Free Ice Water* one said *Lettus Fill Your Jug. Neat Nuts* one said. *Ham Sandwiches Frozen Custard Live Turtles.* She thought she'd stop and discreetly ask the way to Pridesup. *Pecan Clusters Pecan Logs Pecan Pie Don't Miss Us!*

Otilla was picking through the remaining maps when the baby tipped off her lap and into Lavinia's side. Lavinia stomped on the brakes and beat at him with her hand. "Get away," she shrieked, "You'll break my hip!" She tried to pull her waist in from the weight of his head. His smell was sweet, fertile, like an anesthetic and she felt frightened as though someone had just removed something from her in a swift neat operation. She saw the dust motes settling like balloons upon the leather dashboard and white thread tangled in the baby's fingers. *Slow Down You're Almost There Only 2000 Yds.* The baby's face was wrinkling her linen and his hand was fastened around the bottom of the steering wheel.

"Lavinia, you'll frighten him," Otilla said, pulling the baby back across the seat. She arranged him in her lap again and he instantly fell asleep. The Mercedes was almost at a standstill. Lavinia pressed on the gas and the car labored forward, out of gear, past an empty burnt-out shack. *Six Lbs For $1 Free Slushies For The Kiddies.* The door to the place was lying in the weeds.

"That's all right, that's all right," Lavinia said. She took off her sunglasses and rubbed the bridge of her nose. The fingers of her gloves were wet. The engine was skipping, the tachometer needle fluttered on o. She stopped the car completely, shifted into first and resumed. *You've Gone Too Far!* a sign said. She felt like spitting at it. Otilla had fallen asleep now too, her head slightly out the window, her small mouth shining in the side-view mirror. Lavinia picked up a piece of bread, folded it into an empty sandwich and ate it.

When Otilla woke, it was almost dark. The baby had his fingers jammed into his mouth and sucked on them loudly. Otilla unscrewed the top of the mason jar and pushed the lip toward him. He took it eagerly, sucking. Then he chewed, then he lapped. Enough drops went down his throat for him to think it was worthwhile to continue. He settled down to eating the milk that was slapping his cheeks and sliding down his chin back into the jar.

They were on a narrow soft road just wide enough for the car. Close on either side were rows and rows of orange trees, all different shades of darkness in the twilight.

"It's like riding through the parted waters, Lavinia."

Her sister's voice startled her and Lavinia gave a little jump. Her stylish dress was askew and her large faded eyes were watering.

"You woke up to say an asinine thing like that!" she exclaimed. All the while Otilla and the infant had been sleeping, she had driven with an empty mind and eye. She had truly not been thinking of a thing, and though she was lost and indignant and frustrated she did not feel this. She had driven, and the instructions she had received cautiously from the few people she had seen she wrote down on the back of a pocket calendar. When she left the people, they became bystanders, not to be trusted, and she drove on without reference. And the only sounds she heard were the gentle snappings somewhere in her head of small important truths that she had got along with for years—breaking.

She had not looked at the car's equipment, at its dials and

numbers for a long time because when she had last done so, the odometer showed her that they had driven 157 miles.

"How long have we been traveling, Lavinia?"

"I don't know." She remembered that when she had bought the Mercedes, the engine had shone like her silver service. She remembered that there had been one mile on the odometer then. Sitting in the showroom on a green carpet, her automobile had one mile on it and she had been furious. No one could tell her why this was. No one could explain it to her satisfaction.

"Well," Otilla said, "I suppose Louisa and Marjorie have eaten by now." She looked out the window. A white bird was hurrying off through the groves. "This is an awfully good baby," she said, "waiting so long and being so patient for his meal. And this being not the way he's accustomed to getting it besides." She looked behind her. "My, they certainly make these roads straight. It seems like if we had intended to, we could be halfway to New Jersey by now, on our way to seeing all those interesting things. We could stay in a New Jersey motel, Lavinia, and give the baby a nice bath and send out for supper and I've even heard that some of those motels are connected with drive-in theaters and we could see a film directly from our room."

The soft sand tugged at the car's wheels. The stars came out and Lavinia pulled on the headlights.

"Lavinia," Otilla said softly. "I have twelve hundred dollars sitting in the teeth of my mouth alone. I am a wealthy woman though not as wealthy as you and if you want to get there, I don't understand why we just don't stop as soon as we see someone and hire us a car to Pridesup."

"I have no respect for you at all," Lavinia said.

Otilla paused. She ran her fingers over the baby's head, feeling the slight springy depression in his skull where he was still growing together. She could hear him swallowing. A big moth blundered against her face and then fell back into the night. "If you would just stop for a moment," she said brightly, "I could change the baby and freshen up the air in here a bit."

"You don't seem to realize that I know all about you, Otilla. There is nothing you could ever say to me about anything. I happen to know that you were born too early and mother had you in a chamber pot. So just shut up Otilla." She turned to her sister and smiled. Otilla's head was bowed and Lavinia poked her to make sure that she was paying attention. "I have wanted to let you know about that for a long long time so just don't say another word to me, Otilla."

The Mercedes bottomed out on the sand, swerved and dropped into the ditch, the grille half-submerged in muddy water and the left rear wheel spinning in the air. Lavinia still was steering and smiling and looking at her sister. The engine died and the lights went out and for an instant they all sat speechless and motionless as though they were parts of a profound photograph that was still in the process of being taken. Then the baby gagged and Otilla began thumping him on the back.

Lavinia had loved her car. The engine crackled and hissed as it cooled. The windshield had a long crack in it and there was a smell of gasoline. She turned off the ignition.

Lavinia had loved her car and now it was broken to bits. She didn't know what to think. She opened the door and climbed out onto the road where she lay down in the dust. In the middle of the night, she got back into the car because the mosquitoes were so bad. Otilla and the baby were stretched out in the back so Lavinia sat in the driver's seat once more, where she slept.

In the morning, they ate the rest of the bread and Otilla gave the baby the last of the milk. The milk had gone sour and he spit most of it up. Otilla waded through the ditch and set the baby in a field box beneath an orange tree. The fruit had all been picked a month ago and the groves were thick and overgrown. It was hard for Otilla to clear out a place for them to rest. She tried to fan the mosquitoes away from the baby's face but by noon the swarms had gotten so large and the bugs so fat and lazy that she had to pick them off individually with her fingers. Lavinia stayed in the Mercedes until she felt fried, then

she limped across the road. The sun seemed waxed in the same
position but she knew the day was going by. The baby had cried
hard for an hour or so and then began a fitful wail that went
on into the afternoon.

Every once in awhile, Lavinia saw Otilla rise and move
feverishly through the trees. The baby's weeping mingled with
the rattle of insects and with Otilla's singsong so that it seemed
to Lavinia, when she closed her eyes, that there was a healthy
community working out around her and including her in its
life. But when she looked there was only green bareness and
an armadillo plodding through the dust, swinging its outrageous head.

Lavinia went to the Mercedes and picked up the can of
Coca-Cola, but she couldn't find an opener. The can burnt in
her hand and she dropped it. As she was getting out of the car,
she saw Otilla walk out of the grove. She stopped and watched
her shuffle up the road. She was unfamiliar, a mystery, an
event. There was a small soiled bundle on her shoulder. Lavinia
couldn't place the circumstances. She watched and wrung her
hands. Otilla swerved off into the grove again and disappeared.

Lavinia followed her giddily. She walked hunched, on tip-
toe. When she came upon Otilla, she remained stealthily bent,
her skirt still wadded in her hand for silence. Otilla lay on her
back in the sand with the baby beside her, his bug-bitten
eyelids squeezed against a patch of sky that was shining on
them both. The baby's mouth was moving and his arms and
legs were waving in the air to some mysterious beat but Otilla
lay motionless as a stick. Lavinia was disgusted to see that the
top of Otilla's dress was unbuttoned, exposing her grey stringy
breasts. She picked up a handful of sand and tried to cover up
her chest.

The baby's diaper was heavy with filth. She took it off and
wiped it as best she could on the weeds and then pinned it
around him again. She picked him up, holding him carefully
away from her, and walked to the road. He was ticking from
someplace deep inside himself. The noise was deafening. The
noises that had seemed to be going on in her own head earlier

had stopped. When she got to the car, she laid him under it, where it was cool. She herself stood up straight to get a breath, and down the road saw a yellow ball of dust rolling toward her at great speed. The ball of dust stopped alongside and a young man in faded jeans and shirt, holding a bottle of beer, got out and stared at her. Around his waist he wore a wide belt hanging with pliers and hammers and cords.

"Jeez," he said. He was a telephone lineman going home for dinner, taking a shortcut through the groves. The old lady he saw looked as though she had come out of some Arabian desert. She had cracked lips and puffy eyes and burnt skin. He walked toward her with his hand stretched out, but she turned away and to his astonishment, bent down and scrabbled a baby up from beneath the wrecked car. Then she walked past him and clambered into the cab of his truck by herself and slammed the door.

The young man jumped into the truck and smiled nervously at Lavinia. "I don't have nothing," he said excitedly, "but a chocolate bar, but there's a clinic no more'n ten miles away, if you could just hold on until then. Please," he said desperately. "Do you suppose you want this?" he asked, holding out the bottle of beer.

Lavinia nodded. She took the chocolate and put it in the baby's fist. He cried and pushed it toward his mouth and moved his mouth around it and cried. Lavinia pressed the cool bottle of beer against her face, then rolled it back and forth across her forehead.

The truck roared through the groves and in an instant, it seemed, they were out on the highway, passing a sign that said WORSHIP IN PRIDESUP, 11 MILES. Beyond the sign was a field with a carnival in it. Lavinia could hear the sweet cheap music of the midway and the shrieks of people on the Ferris wheel. Then the carnival fell behind them and there was just field, empty except for a single, immense oak, a sight that so irritated Lavinia that she shut her eyes. The oak somehow seemed to give meaning to the field, a notion she found abhorrent.

She felt a worried tapping at her shoulder. When she looked

at the young man, he just nodded at her, then he said, an afterthought, "What's that baby's name? My wife just had one and his name is Larry T."

Lavinia looked down at the baby who glared blackly back at her, and the recognition that her life and her long, angry journey through it, had been wasteful and deceptive and unnecessary, hit her like a board being smacked against her heart. She had a hurried sensation of being rushed forward but it didn't give her any satisfaction, because at the same time she felt her own dying slowing down some, giving her an instant to think about it.

"It's nameless," she whispered.

The Farm

*I*T was a dark night in August. Sarah and Tommy were going to their third party that night, the party where they would actually sit down to dinner. They were driving down Mixtuxet Avenue, a long black avenue of trees that led out of the village, away from the shore and the coastal homes into the country. Tommy had been drinking only soda that night. Every other weekend, Tommy wouldn't drink. He did it, he said, to keep trim. He did it because he could.

Sarah was telling a long story as she drove. She kept asking Tommy if she had told it to him before, but he was noncommittal. When Tommy didn't drink, Sarah talked and talked. She was telling him a terrible story that she had read in the newspaper about an alligator at a jungle farm attraction in Florida. The alligator had eaten a child who had crawled into its pen. The alligator's name was Cookie. Its owner had shot it immediately. The owner was sad about everything, the child, the parents' grief, Cookie. He was quoted in the paper as saying that shooting Cookie was not an act of revenge.

When Tommy didn't drink, Sarah felt cold. She was shivering in the car. There were goosepimples on her tanned, thin arms. Tommy sat beside her smoking, saying nothing.

There had been words between them earlier. The parties here had an undercurrent of sexuality. Sarah could almost hear it, flowing around them all, carrying them all along. In the car, on the night of the accident, Sarah was at that point in the evening when she felt guilty. She wanted to make things better, make things nice. She had gone through her elated stage, her jealous stage, her stubbornly resigned stage and now she felt guilty. Had they talked about divorce that night, or had that been before, on other evenings? There was a flavor she remembered in their talks about divorce, a scent. It was hot, as Italy had been hot when they had been there. Dust, bread, sun, a burning at the back of the throat from too much drinking.

But no, they hadn't been talking about divorce that night. The parties had been crowded. Sarah had hardly seen Tommy. Then, on her way to the bathroom, she had seen him sitting with a girl on a bed in one of the back rooms. He was telling the girl about condors, about hunting for condors in small, light planes.

"Oh, but you didn't hurt them, did you?" the girl asked. She was someone's daughter, a little overweight but with beautiful skin and large green eyes.

"Oh no," Tommy assured her, "we weren't hunting to hurt."

Condors. Sarah looked at them sitting on the bed. When they noticed her, the girl blushed. Tommy smiled. Sarah imagined what she looked like, standing in the doorway. She wished that they had shut the door.

That had been at the Steadmans'. The first party had been at the Perrys'. The Perrys never served food. Sarah had had two or three drinks there. The bar had been set up beneath the grape arbor and everyone stood outside. It had still been light at the Perrys' but at the Steadmans' it was dark and people drank inside. Everyone spoke about the end of summer as though it were a bewildering and unnatural event.

They had stayed at the Steadmans' longer than they should have and they were going to be late for dinner. Nevertheless, they were driving at a moderate speed, through a familiar landscape, passing houses that they had been entertained in many times. There were the Salts and the Hollands and the Greys and the Dodsons. The Dodsons kept their gin in the freezer and owned two large and dappled crotch-sniffing dogs. The Greys imported Southerners for their parties. The women all had lovely voices and knew how to make spoon bread and pickled tomatoes and artillery punch. The men had smiles when they'd say to Sarah, "Why, let me get you another. You don't have a thing in that glass, ah swear." The Hollands gave the kind of dinner party where the shot was still in the duck and the silver should have been in a vault. Little whiskey was served but there was always excellent wine. The Salts were a high-strung couple who often quarreled. Jenny Salt was on some type of medication for tension and often dropped the canapés she attempted to serve. Jenny and her husband, Pete, had a room in which there was nothing but a large doll house where witty mâché figures carried on assignations beneath tiny clocks and crystal chandeliers. Once, when Sarah was examining the doll house's library where two figures were hunched over a chess game which was just about to be won, Pete had always said, on the twenty-second move, Pete told Sarah that she had pretty eyes. She had moved away from him immediately. She had closed her eyes. In another room, with the other guests, she had talked about the end of summer.

On that night, at the end of summer, the night of the accident, Sarah was still talking as they passed the Salts' house. She was talking about Venice. She and Tommy had been there once. They had drunk in the Plaza and listened to the orchestras. Sarah quoted D. H. Lawrence on Venice . . . "Abhorrent green and slippery city . . ." But she and Tommy had liked Venice. They drank standing up at little bars. Sarah had had a cold and she drank grappa and the cold had disappeared for the rest of her life.

After the Salts' house, the road swerved north and became very dark. There were no lights, no houses for several miles. There were stone walls, an orchard of sickly peach trees, a cider mill. There was St. James Episcopal Church where Tommy took their daughter, Martha, to Sunday school. The Sunday school was highly fundamental. There were many arguments among the children and their teachers as to the correct inter-

pretation of Bible story favorites. For example, when Lazarus
rose from the dead, was he still sick? Martha liked the fervor
at St. James. Each week, her dinner graces were becoming
more impassioned and fantastic. Martha was seven.

Each Sunday, Tommy takes Martha to her little classes at
St. James. Sarah can imagine the child sitting there at a low
table with her jars of colors. Tommy doesn't go to church
himself and Martha's classes are two hours long. Sarah doesn't
know where Tommy goes. She suspects he is seeing someone.
When they come home on Sundays, Tommy is sleek, ex-
hilarated. The three of them sit down to the dinner Sarah has
prepared.

Over the years, Sarah suspects, Tommy has floated to the
surface of her. They are swimmers now, far apart, on the top
of the sea.

Sarah at last fell silent. The road seemed endless as in a
dream. They seemed to be slowing down. She could not feel
her foot on the accelerator. She could not feel her hands on
the wheel. Her mind was an untidy cupboard filled with shining bottles. The road was dark and silvery and straight. In the
space ahead of her, there seemed to be something. It beckoned,
glittering. Sarah's mind cleared a little. She saw Martha with
her hair cut oddly short. Sarah gently nibbled on the inside of
her mouth to keep alert. She saw Tommy choosing a succession
of houses, examining the plaster, the floorboards, the fireplaces,
deciding where windows should be placed, walls knocked
down. She saw herself taking curtains down from a window so
that there would be a better view of the sea. The curtains
knocked her glass from the sill and it shattered. The sea was
white and flat. It did not command her to change her life. It
demanded of her, nothing. She saw Martha sleeping, her paint-
smudged fingers curled. She saw Tommy in the city with a
woman, riding in a cab. The woman wore a short fur jacket and
Tommy stroked it as he spoke. She saw a figure in the road
ahead, its arms raised before its face as though to block out the
sight of her. The figure was a boy who wore dark clothing, but

his hair was bright, his face was shining. She saw her car leap forward and run him down where he stood.

Tommy had taken responsibility for the accident. He had told the police he was driving. The boy apparently had been hitch-hiking and had stepped out into the road. At the autopsy, traces of a hallucinogen were found in the boy's system. The boy was fifteen years old and his name was Stevie Bettencourt. No charges were filed.

"My wife," Tommy told the police, "was not feeling well. My wife," Tommy said, "was in the passenger seat."

Sarah stopped drinking immediately after the accident. She felt nauseated much of the time. She slept poorly. Her hands hurt her. The bones in her hands ached. She remembered that this was the way she felt the last time she had stopped drinking. It had been two years before. She remembered why she had stopped and she remembered why she had started again. She had stopped because she had done a cruel thing to her little Martha. It was spring and she and Tommy were giving a dinner party. Sarah had two martinis in the late afternoon when she was preparing dinner and then she had two more martinis with her guests. Martha had come downstairs to say a polite good-night to everyone as she had been taught. She had put on her nightie and brushed her teeth. Sarah poured a little more gin in her glass and went upstairs with her to brush out her hair and put her to bed. Martha had long, thick blond hair of which she was very proud. On that night she wore it in a pony tail secured by an elasticized holder with two small colored balls on the end. Sarah's fingers were clumsy and she could not get it off without pulling Martha's hair and making her cry. She got a pair of scissors and carefully began snipping at the stubborn elastic. The scissors were large, like shears, and they had been difficult to handle. A foot of Martha's gathered hair had abruptly fallen to the floor. Sarah remembered trying to pat it back into place on the child's head.

So Sarah had stopped drinking the first time. She did not feel renewed. She felt exhausted and wary. She read and cooked.

She realized how little she and Tommy had to talk about.
Tommy drank Scotch when he talked to her at night. Sometimes Sarah would silently count as he spoke to see how long
the words took. When he was away and he telephoned her, she
could hear the ice tinkling in the glass.

Tommy was in the city four days a week. He often changed
hotels. He would bring Martha little bars of soap wrapped in
the different colored papers of the hotels. Martha's drawers
were full of the soaps scenting her clothes. When Tommy
came home on the weekends he would work on the house and
they would give parties at which Tommy was charming.
Tommy had a talent for holding his liquor and for buying old
houses, restoring them and selling them for three times what
he had paid for them. Tommy and Sarah had moved six times
in eleven years. All their homes had been fine old houses in
excellent locations two or three hours from New York. Sarah
would stay in the country while Tommy worked in the city.
Sarah did not know her way around New York.

For three weeks, Sarah did not drink. Then it was her birthday. Tommy gave her a slim gold necklace and fastened it
around her neck. He wanted her to come to New York with
him, to have dinner, see a play, spend the night with him in
the fine suite the company had given him at the hotel. They
had got a babysitter for Martha, a marvelous woman who
polished the silver in the afternoon when Martha napped.
Sarah drove. Tommy had never cared for driving. His hand
rested on her thigh. Occasionally, he would slip his hand beneath her skirt. Sarah was sick with the thought that this was
the way he touched other women.

By the time they were in Manhattan, they were arguing.
They had been married for eleven years. Both had had brief
marriages before. They could argue about anything. In mid-
town, Tommy stormed out of the car as Sarah braked for a
light. He took his suitcase and disappeared.

Sarah drove carefully for many blocks. When she had the
opportunity, she would pull to the curb and ask someone how
to get to Connecticut. No one seemed to know. Sarah thought

she was probably phrasing the question poorly but she didn't know how else to present it. After half an hour, she made her way back to the hotel where Tommy was staying. The doorman parked the car and she went into the lobby. She looked into the hotel bar and saw Tommy in the dimness, sitting at a small table. He jumped up and kissed her passionately. He rubbed his hands up and down her sides. "Darling, darling," he said, "I want you to have a happy birthday."

Tommy ordered drinks for both of them. Sarah sipped hers slowly at first but then she drank it and he ordered others. The bar was subdued. There was a piano player who sang about the lord of the dance. The words seemed like those of a hymn. The hymn made her sad but she laughed. Tommy spoke to her urgently and gaily about little things. They laughed together like they had when they were first married. They had always drunk a lot together then and fallen asleep, comfortably and lovingly entwined on white sheets.

They went to their room to change for the theater. The maid had turned back the beds. There was a fresh rose in a bud vase on the writing desk. They had another drink in the room and got undressed. Sarah awoke the next morning curled up on the floor with the bedspread tangled around her. Her mouth was sore. There was a bruise on her leg. The television set was on with no sound. The room was a mess although Sarah could see that nothing had been really damaged. She stared at the television where black-backed gulls were dive-bombing on terrified and doomed cygnets in a documentary about swans. Sarah crept into the bathroom and turned on the shower. She sat in the tub while the water beat upon her. Pinned to the outside of the shower curtain was a note from Tommy, who had gone to work. "Darling," the note said, "we had a *good* time on your birthday. I can't say I'm sorry we never got out. I'll call you for lunch. Love."

Sarah turned the note inward until the water made the writing illegible. When the phone rang just before noon, she did not answer it.

*   *   *

There is a certain type of conversation one hears only when one is drunk and it is like a dream, full of humor and threat and significance, deep significance. And the way one witnesses things when one is drunk is different as well. It is like putting a face mask against the surface of the sea and looking into things, into their baffled and guileless hearts.

When Sarah had been a drinker, she felt that she had a fundamental and inventive grasp of situations, but now that she drank no longer, she found herself in the midst of a great and impenetrable silence which she could in no way interpret.

It was a small village. Many of the people who lived there did not even own cars. The demands of life were easily met in the village and it was pretty there besides. It was divided between those who always lived there and who owned fishing boats and restaurants and the city people who had more recently discovered the area as a summer place and winter weekend investment. On the weekends, the New Yorkers would come up with their houseguests and their pâté and cheeses and build fires and go cross-country skiing. Tommy came home to Sarah on weekends. They did things together. They agreed on where to go. During the week she was on her own.

Once, alone, she saw a helicopter carrying a tree in a sling across the Sound. The wealthy could afford to leave nothing behind.

Once, with the rest of the town, she saw five boats burning in their storage shrouds. Each summer resort has its winter pyromaniac.

Sarah did not read any more. Her eyes hurt when she read and her hands ached all the time. During the week, she marketed and walked and cared for Martha.

It was three months after Stevie Bettencourt was killed when his mother visited Sarah. She came to the door and knocked on it and Sarah let her in.

Genevieve Bettencourt was a woman Sarah's age although she looked rather younger. She had been divorced almost from the day that Stevie was born. She had another son named Bruce who lived with his father in Nova Scotia. She had an old powder-blue Buick parked on the street before Sarah's house. The Buick had one white door.

The two women sat in Sarah's handsome, sunny living room. It was very calm, very peculiar, almost thrilling. Genevieve looked all around the room. Off the living room were the bedrooms. The door to Sarah's and Tommy's was closed but Martha's door was open. She had a little hanging garden against the window. She had a hamster in a cage. She had an enormous bookcase filled with dolls and books.

Genevieve said to Sarah, "That room wasn't there before. This used to be a lobster pound. I know a great deal about this town. People like you have nothing to do with what I know about this town. Do you remember the way things were, ever?"

"No," Sarah said.

Genevieve sighed. "Does your daughter look like you or your husband?"

"No one's ever told me she looked like me," Sarah said quietly.

On the glass-topped table before them there was a little wooden sculpture cutout that Tommy had bought. A man and woman sat on a park bench. Each wore a startled and ambiguous expression. Each had a terrier on the end of a string. The dogs were a puzzle. One fit on top of the other. Sarah was embarrassed about it being there. Tommy had put it on the table during the weekend and Sarah hadn't moved it. Genevieve didn't touch it.

"I did not want my life to know you," Genevieve said. She removed a hair from the front of her white blouse and dropped it to the floor. She looked out the window at the sun. The floor was of a very light and varnished pine. Sarah could see the hair upon it.

"I'm so sorry," Sarah said. "I'm so very, very sorry." She stretched her neck and put her head back.

"Stevie was a mixed-up boy," Genevieve said. "They threw him off the basketball team. He took pills. He had bad friends. He didn't study and he got a D in geometry and they wouldn't let him play basketball."

She got up and wandered around the room. She wore green rubber boots, dirty jeans and a beautiful, hand-knit sweater. "I once bought all my fish here," she said. "The O'Malleys owned it. There were practically no windows. Just narrow high ones over the tanks. Now it's all windows, isn't it? Don't you feel exposed?"

"No, I . . ." Sarah began. "There are drapes," she said.

"Off to the side, where you have your garden, there are whale bones if you dig deep enough. I can tell you a lot about this town."

"My husband wants to move," Sarah said.

"I can understand that, but you're the real drinker, after all, aren't you, not him."

"I don't drink any more," Sarah said. She looked at the woman dizzily.

Genevieve was not pretty but she had a clear, strong face. She sat down on the opposite side of the room. "I guess I would like something," she said. "A glass of water." Sarah went to the kitchen and poured a glass of Vichy for them both. Her hands shook.

"We are not strangers to one another," Genevieve said. "We could be friends."

"My first husband always wanted to be friends with my second husband," Sarah said after a moment. "I could never understand it." This had somehow seemed analogous when she was saying it but now it did not. "It is not appropriate that we be friends," she said.

Genevieve continued to sit and talk. Sarah found herself concentrating desperately on her articulate, one-sided conversation. She suspected that the words Genevieve was using were codes for other words, terrible words. Genevieve spoke thoughtlessly, dispassionately, with erratic flourishes of language. Sarah couldn't believe that they were chatting about food, men, the red clouds massed above the sea.

"I have a friend who is a designer," Genevieve said. "She hopes to make a great deal of money someday. Her work has completely altered her perceptions. Every time she looks at a view, she thinks of sheets. " 'Take out those mountains,' she will say, 'lighten that cloud a bit and it would make a great sheet.' When she looks at the sky, she thinks of lingerie. Now when I look at the sky, I think of earlier times, happier times when I looked at the sky. I have never been in love, have you?"

"Yes," Sarah said, "I'm in love."

"It's not a lucky thing, you know, to be in love."

There was a soft scuffling at the door and Martha came in. "Hello," she said. "School was good today. I'm hungry."

"Hello, dear," Genevieve said. To Sarah, she said, "Perhaps we can have lunch sometime."

"Who is that?" Martha asked Sarah after Genevieve had left.

"A neighbor," Sarah said, "one of Mommy's friends."

When Sarah told Tommy about Genevieve coming to visit her, he said, "It's harassment. It can be stopped."

It was Sunday morning. They had just finished breakfast and Tommy and Martha were drying the dishes and putting them away. Martha was wearing her church-school clothes and she was singing a song she had learned the Sunday before.

". . . I'm going to the Mansion on the Happy Days' Express . . ." she sang.

Tommy squeezed Martha's shoulders. "Go get your coat, sweetie," he said. When the child had gone, he said to Sarah, "Don't speak to this woman. Don't allow it to happen again."

"We didn't talk about that."

"What else could you talk about? It's weird."

"No one talks about that. No one, ever."

Tommy was wearing a corduroy suit and a tie Sarah had never seen before. Sarah looked at the pattern in the tie. It was random and bright.

"Are you having an affair?" Sarah asked.

"No," he said easily. "I don't understand you, Sarah. I've done everything I could to protect you, to help you straighten yourself out. It was a terrible thing but it's over. You have to get over it. Now, just don't see her again. There's no way that she can cause trouble if you don't speak to her."

Sarah stopped looking at Tommy's tie. She moved her eyes to the potatoes she had peeled and put in a bowl of water.

Martha came into the kitchen and held on to her father's arm. Her hair was long and thick, but it was getting darker. It was as though it had never been cut.

After they left, Sarah put the roast in the oven and went into the living room. The large window was full of the day, a colorless windy day without birds. Sarah sat on the floor and ran her fingers across the smooth, varnished wood. Beneath the expensive flooring was cold cement. Tanks had once lined the walls. Lobsters had crept back and forth across the mossy glass. The phone rang. Sarah didn't look at it, suspecting it was Genevieve. Then she picked it up.

"Hello," said Genevieve, "I thought I might drop by. It's a bleak day, isn't it. Cold. Is your family at home?"

"They go out on Sunday," Sarah said. "It gives me time to think. They go to church."

"What do you think about?" The woman's voice seemed far away. Sarah strained to hear her.

"I'm supposed to cook dinner. When they come back we eat dinner."

"I can prepare clams in forty-three different ways," Genevieve said.

"This is a roast. A roast pork."

"Well, may I come over?"

"All right," Sarah said.

She continued to sit on the floor, waiting for Genevieve, looking at the water beneath the sky. The water on the horizon was a wide, satin ribbon. She wished that she had the courage to swim on such a bitter, winter day. To swim far out and rest, to hesitate and then to return. Her life was dark, unexplored. Her abstinence had drained her. She felt sluggish, robbed. Her body had no freedom.

She sat, seeing nothing, the terrible calm light of the day around her. The things she remembered were so far away, bathed in a different light. Her life seemed so remote to her. She had sought happiness in someone, knowing she could not find it in herself and now her heart was strangely hard. She rubbed her head with her hands.

Her life with Tommy was broken, irreparable. Her life with him was over. His infidelities kept getting mixed up in her mind with the death of the boy, with Tommy's false admission that he had been driving when the boy died. Sarah couldn't understand anything. Her life seemed so random, so needlessly constructed and now threatened in a way which did not interest her.

"Hello," Genevieve called. She had opened the front door and was standing in the hall. "You didn't hear my knock."

Sarah got up. She was to entertain this woman. She felt anxious, adulterous. The cold rose from Genevieve's skin and hair. Sarah took her coat and hung it in the closet. The fresh cold smell lingered on her hands.

Sarah moved into the kitchen. She took a package of rolls out of the freezer.

"Does your little girl like church?" Genevieve asked.

"Yes, very much."

"It's a stage," said Genevieve. "I'm Catholic myself. As a child, I used to be fascinated by the martyrs. I remember a picture of St. Lucy, carrying her eyes like a plate of eggs, and St. Agatha. She carried her breasts on a plate."

Sarah said, "I don't understand what we're talking about. I know you're just using these words, that they mean other words, I . . ."

"Perhaps we could take your little girl to a movie sometime, a matinee, after she gets out of school."

"Her name is Martha," Sarah said. She saw Martha grown up, her hair cut short once more, taking rolls out of the freezer, waiting.

"Martha, yes," Genevieve said. "Have you wanted more children?"

"No," Sarah said. Their conversation was illegal, unspeakable. Sarah couldn't imagine it ever ending. Her fingers tapped against the ice-cube trays. "Would you care for a drink?"

"A very tall glass of vermouth," Genevieve said. She was looking at a little picture Martha had made, that Sarah had tacked to the wall. It was a very badly drawn horse. "I wanted children. I wanted to fulfill myself. One can never fulfill oneself. I think it is an impossibility."

Sarah made Genevieve's drink very slowly. She did not make one for herself.

"When Stevie was Martha's age, he knew everything about whales. He kept notebooks. Once, on his birthday, I took him to the whaling museum in New Bedford." She sipped her drink. "It all goes wrong somewhere," she said. She turned her back on Sarah and went into the other room. Sarah followed her.

"There are so many phrases for 'dead,' you know," Genevieve was saying. "The kids think them up, or they come out of music or wars. Stevie had one that he'd use for dead animals and rock stars. He'd say they'd 'bought the farm.'"

Sarah nodded. She was pulling and peeling at the nails of her hands.

"I think it's pretty creepy. A dark farm, you know. Weedy. Run-down. Broken machinery everywhere. A real job."

Sarah raised her head. "You want us to share Martha, don't you," she said. "It's only right, isn't it?"

". . . the paint blown away, acres and acres of tangled, black land, a broken shutter over the well."

Sarah lowered her head again. Her heart was cold, horrified. The reality of the two women, placed by hazard in this room, this bright functional tasteful room that Tommy had created, was being tested. Reality would resist, for days, perhaps weeks, but then it would yield. It would yield to this guest, this visitor, for whom Sarah had made room.

"Would you join me in another drink?" Genevieve asked. "Then I'll go."

"I mustn't drink," Sarah said.

"You don't forget," Genevieve said, "that's just an old saw." She went into the kitchen and poured more vermouth for herself. Sarah could smell the meat cooking. From another room, the clock chimed.

"You must come to my home soon," Genevieve said. She did not sit down. Sarah looked at the pale green liquid in the glass.

"Yes," Sarah said, "soon."

"We must not greet one another on the street, however. People are quick to gossip."

"Yes," Sarah said. "They would condemn us." She looked heavily at Genevieve, full of misery and submission.

There was knocking on the door. "Sarah," Tommy's voice called, "why is the door locked?" She could see his dark head at the window.

"I must have thrown the bolt," Genevieve said. "It's best to lock your house in the winter, you know. It's the kids mostly. They get bored. Stevie was a robber once or twice, I'm sure." She put down her glass, took her coat from the closet and went out. Sarah heard Martha say, "That's Mommy's friend."

Tommy stood in the doorway and stared at Sarah. "Why did you lock the door?" he asked again.

Sarah imagined seeing herself, naked. She said, "There are robbers."

Tommy said, "If you don't feel safe here, we'll move. I've been looking at a wonderful place about twenty miles from here, on a cove. It only needs a little work. It will give us more room. There's a barn, some fence. Martha could have a horse."

Sarah looked at him with an intent, halted expression, as though she were listening to a dialogue no one present was engaged in. Finally, she said, "There are robbers. Everything has changed."

Breakfast

*T*HE phone rang at five in the morning. Clem woke with a grunt. Liberty rolled away from Willie's arms and went into the kitchen and picked up the phone.

"Hello, Mother," she mumbled. Clem, a large white Alsatian with one blind eye, took a long noisy drink from his water dish.

"I want to explain some of the incidents in my life," her mother said. Her voice was clear and determined.

"Everything is all right, Mother. I love you. Daddy loves you."

"I had a terrible dream about penguins tonight, Liberty."

"Penguins are nice, Mother. They don't do anyone any harm."

"There were hundreds of penguins on this beautiful beach and they were all standing so straight, like they do, like children wearing little aprons."

What can she do about her mother? Liberty thinks. Drive up and take her out to lunch? Send her tulips by wire?

"That sounds nice, Mother. It sounds sort of cheerful."

"They were being clubbed to death, Liberty. They were all being murdered by an unseen hand."

"You're all right, Mother. It was just a dream and it's gone now. It's left you and I've got it." Liberty rubbed Clem's hard skull.

"Liberty, I have to tell you that I had another child, a child before you, a child before Daddy. She was two years old. I lost her, Liberty. I lost her on purpose."

"Oh Mother," begged Liberty, "I don't want to know."

"Can you remember yourself as a child, Liberty? You used to limp for no reason and sprinkle water on your forehead to give the appearance of fevers. You used to squeeze the skin beneath your eyes to make bruises."

"Mother, I didn't."

"You were suicidal. You were always asking me suicide riddles like, 'What would happen if a girl was tied up in a rug and thrown off the roof?' 'What would happen if you put a girl in a refrigerator alongside the eggs and the cheese?' "

"None of those things are true," Liberty said uncertainly.

"I believe that one can outwit Time if one pretends to be what one is not. I think I read that."

Clem took a few disinterested laps from his water bowl. He drank to keep Liberty company.

"It's almost Thanksgiving, Liberty. What are you and Willie going to do for Thanksgiving? I think it would be nice if you had turkey and made oyster stuffing and cranberry sauce. It broke my heart when you said you ate mullet last year. I don't think you can do things like that, Liberty. Life doesn't go on forever, you know. Your sister was born on Thanksgiving Day. She weighed almost nine pounds."

Liberty was getting confused. The fluorescent light in the kitchen dimmed and brightened, dimmed and brightened. She turned it off.

"I fell so in love with Daddy, I just couldn't think," Liberty's mother said. "He was so free and handsome and I just wanted to be with him and have a love that would defy the humdrum. He didn't know anything about Brouilly. I had kept Brouilly a secret from him."

"Brouilly?" Liberty asked, not without interest. "That was my sister's name?"

"It's a wine. A very good wine actually. She was cute as the dickens. I was living in New York then and when I fell in love with Daddy, I drove Brouilly eighty-seven miles into the state of Connecticut, enrolled her in an Episcopalian day-care center under an assumed name and left her forever. Daddy and I sailed for Europe the next day. Love, I thought it was! For the love of your father, I abandoned my first-born! Time has a way, Liberty, of thumping a person right back into the basement."

"You've never mentioned this before, Mother."

"Do you know what your father says when I tell him I'm going to tell you? He says, 'Don't start trouble.' "

Liberty didn't say anything. She could hear a distant conversation murmuring across the wires.

"I chose the Episcopalians," her mother was saying tiredly, "because they are aristocrats. Do you know, for instance, that they are thinner than any other religious group?"

"I don't know what to say, Mother. Do you want to try and find her?"

"What could I possibly do for her now, Liberty? She probably races Lasers and has dinner parties for twenty-five or something. Her husband probably has a tax haven in Campione."

"Who was her father?" Liberty asked.

"He made crêpes," her mother said vaguely. "I've got to go now, honey. I've got to go to the bathroom. Bye-bye."

Liberty hung up. The room's light was now grey and Clem glowed whitely in it. A particularly inappropriate image crept open in her mind like a waxy cereus bloom: little groups of Hindus sitting around a dying man or woman or child on the river bank, waiting for death to come, chatting, eating, behaving in fact as though life were a picnic.

Liberty opened the refrigerator door. There was a jug of water aerating there, and a half-empty can of Strongheart. She poured herself a glass of water and spooned the Strongheart, a horse's most paranoid imaginings, into Clem's food bowl.

The phone rang. "I just want you to know," her mother said, "that I'm leaving your father."

"Don't pay any attention to this, Liberty," her father said on another extension. "As you must know by now, she says once a month that she's going to leave me. Once a month for twenty-nine years. Even in the good years when we had friends and ate well and made love a dozen times a week she'd still say it."

Liberty could hear her mother breathing heavily. They were both over five hundred miles away. The miracle of modern communication made them seem as close to Liberty as the kitchen sink.

"Once," Daddy said, "why it couldn't have been more than six months ago, she threw her wedding ring out into the pecan grove and it took a week and a half to find it. Once she tore up every single photograph in which we appeared together. Often, she gathers up all her clothes, goes down to the A&P for cartons, or worse, goes into Savannah and buys costly luggage, boxes her books and our French copper, makes a big bitch of a stew which is supposed to last me the rest of my days and cleans the whole damn place with a vacuum cleaner."

"It's obviously a cry for help, wouldn't you say, Liberty?" her mother said.

"I don't know why you'd want to call Liberty up and pester her and worry her sick," Daddy said. "She has her own life."

"That's right," her mother said, "excuse me, everything's fine here. I made some peach ice cream yesterday."

"Damn *good* peach ice cream," Daddy said. "So, Liberty, how's your own life. How's that Willie treating you?"

"Fine," Liberty said.

"Never could get anything out of Liberty," her mother chuckled.

"You're getting to be old married folks yourselves," Daddy said. "What is it now, going on almost four years?"

"That's right," Liberty said.

"She's a girl who keeps her own witness, that's a fact," her mother said.

"I want you to be happy, honey," Daddy said.

"Thank you," Liberty said.

"But honey, what is it you two do exactly all the time with no babies or jobs or whatever? I'm just curious, understand."

"They adore one another," Liberty's mother said. " 'Adore' is not in Daddy's vocabulary, but what Daddy is trying to say is that a grandson might give meaning and significance to the fact that Daddy ever drew breath."

"That's not what I'm trying to say at all," Daddy said.

"They're keeping their options open. They live in a more complex time. Keep your options open, Liberty! Never give anything up!" Her mother began to sob.

"We'd better be signing off now, honey," Daddy said.

Liberty went into the living room and looked out the window at the light beginning its slow foggy wash over God's visible kingdom, the kingdom being, in this case, an immense banyan tree which had extinguished all other vegetative life in its vicinity. The banyan was so beautiful it looked as though it belonged in heaven or hell, but certainly not on this earth in a seedy failed subdivision in the state of Florida.

She didn't know about the 'adore.' 'Adore' didn't seem to be in Willie's vocabulary either. She supposed she could have told her Daddy about Willie saving people, making complete his incomprehension of his son-in-law. "He's going through a crisis," Daddy would say. "I wouldn't rule out an affair either." Once one got started saying things, Liberty knew, there were certain things that were going to get said back.

In the last six months, Willie had saved three individuals, literally snatched them from Death's Big Grab. It was curious circumstance, certainly, but it had the feel of a calling to it. Willie was becoming a little occult in his attitudes. He was beginning to believe that there was more to life than love. Liberty didn't blame him, but wished she had his vision.

The first person Willie had saved was a young man struck by lightning on the beach. Liberty had been there and seen the spidery lines the hit had made on the young man's chest. Willie had administered cardiopulmonary resuscitation. A few weeks later, the man's parents had come over to the house and given Willie a five-pound box of chocolate-covered cherries. The man's mother had talked to Liberty and cried.

The next two people Willie had saved were an elderly couple in a pink Mercedes who had taken a wrong turn and driven briskly down a boat ramp into eight feet of water. The old woman wore a low-cut evening gown which showed off her pacemaker to good advantage.

"You've always been a fool, Herbert," she said to the old man.

"A wrong turn in a strange city is not impossible, my dear," Herbert said.

To Willie, he said, "Once I was a young man like you. I was an innocent, a rain-washed star, then I married this bat."

" 'A rain-washed star' is nice," Liberty said when Willie told her.

Willie smiled and shook his head.

"Well, I guess I've missed the point again," Liberty said.

"I guess," Willie agreed.

Willie was making connections which Liberty was finding harder and harder to bypass. She believed in love and life's hallucinations, and that every day was judgment day. It wasn't enough anymore. Willie was getting restless with her, she knew. He felt she was bringing him down. His thoughts included her less and less, his coordinates were elsewhere, his possibilities without her becoming more actualized. This was marriage.

Liberty turned on the television without sound and picked up a piece of paper. She sat on the sofa and drew a line down the center of the paper and on the left side wrote *things i would like* and on the right *things i would never do*. She looked at the television where there was a picture of a plate with a large steak and a plump baked potato and some asparagus on it. The potato got up between the steak and the vegetable and a little slit appeared in it which was apparently its mouth and it apparently began talking. Liberty turned on the sound. It was a commercial for potatoes and the potato was complaining about the fact that everyone says steak and potatoes instead of the other way around. It nestled down against the steak again after making its point. The piece of meat didn't say anything. Liberty turned off the television and regarded her list. She was sweating. She had closed all the windows late last night when she had heard the rain, now she cranked them open again.

Deep inside the banyan, it still dripped rain. On one of its trunks, Teddy had carved I LOVE LIBERTY with his jackknife. Teddy was seven years old and fervently wished that Liberty were his mother. He often pointed out that they both had grey eyes and dark hair and a scar on one knee. She could easily be his mother, Teddy reasoned. He and Liberty had been friends for several years now. In the beginning, she had been paid by his mother for taking care of him, but now such an arrangement seemed unseemly. Teddy lived nearby in a large sunny house in a far more refined area of swimming pools and backyard citrus, but he preferred Liberty's more gloomy locus. It was also his mother's preference that he spend as much time as possible away from his own home. Janiella was a diabetic who did not allow her disability to get her down. She was a slender, well-read and passionate, if not nymphomaniacal, woman who enjoyed entertaining while her husband was away, which he frequently was. With Teddy she enforced a rigorous mental and physical schedule and was not very nice to him when he wet the bed.

When Teddy first began to wet the bed, Janiella had long discussions with him about the need for him to accept responsibility for his own bladder. When Teddy continued to refuse responsibility, Janiella began smacking him with a Whiffle bat every time she had to change the sheets. Then she decided on an alarm that would awaken him every three hours throughout the night. All the alarm has managed to do so far is to increase the number of Teddy's dreams. Teddy dreams more frequently than anyone Liberty knows, he dreams and dreams. He dreams that he steals the single candy bar Janiella keeps in the house in the event she has an attack and has to have sugar. He dreams of Janiella crawling through their huge house, not being able to find her Payday.

When the phone rang again, Liberty walked quickly past it into the bathroom where she turned the water on in the shower. She stood in the small stall beneath the spray until the water turned cool. She turned off the water and stared uneasily at the shower curtain, which portrayed mildewed birds rising.

"Hey," Willie said. He pushed the curtain back. His lean jaws moved tightly, chewing gum. Willie made chewing gum look like a prerequisite to good health. He was wearing faded jeans and a snug, faded polo shirt. His eyes were a faded blue. They passed over her lightly. Communication had indeed broken down considerably. Signals were intermittent and could easily be misread. Liberty didn't know anything about him anymore, what he did when he wasn't with her, what he thought. They had been together for six years. They had a little money and a lot of friends. There didn't seem to be a plan.

"That was Charlie," Willie said. "We're going to have breakfast with him."

They could never refuse Charlie when he wanted to eat. Charlie was an alcoholic who seldom ate. He was currently sleeping with Teddy's mother and between his drinking and this unlikely affair, Charlie was a busy man. Liberty thought that Janiella was shallow and selfish and chic. She felt that it was ridiculous for her to be jealous of this woman.

As Liberty was dressing the phone rang again. It was Teddy, whispering.

"Is that tree still outside your house?" Teddy whispered. "Because I'm sure it was here last night. It was waving its arms outside my window, then it flopped away on its white roots. It goes anywhere it feels like going, that tree."

"Trees aren't like people," Liberty said. "They can't move around." She felt her logic was somewhat insincere. "Dreams sometimes make you feel you can understand everything," she said. Liberty herself never dreamed at night, an indication, she believed, of her spiritual torpor.

"Can I come over today, Liberty? Our pool is broken. It has a leak."

"Certainly, baby, a little later, OK? Bring your snorkel and mask and we'll go to the beach."

"Oh, that's fine, Liberty," Teddy said.

Liberty can see him sitting in his small square room, a room in which everything is put neatly away. He jiggles a loose tooth and watches his speckled goldfish swimming in a bowl, swimming over green pebbles through a small plastic arch. Once, he had two goldfish and the bowl was in the living room, but his mother gave a party and one of her friends swallowed one. It was just a joke, his mother said.

Willie and Liberty got into their truck and drove to a little restaurant nearby called The Blue Gate. Clem sat on the seat between them and from the back he could pass for another person, with long pale hair, sitting there. At the restaurant, they all got out and Clem lay down beneath a cabbage palm growing in the dirt parking lot. The Blue Gate was a Mennonite restaurant in a little community of frame houses with tin roofs. Little living petunia crosses grew on some of the lawns. The Blue Gate was popular because the food was delicious and cheap and served in large quantities. Sometimes Liberty and Teddy would go there and eat crullers.

Inside, Charlie was waiting for them at a table by the pie display. He wore a rumpled suit a size too large for him and a clean shirt. His hair was combed wetly back, his face was swollen and his hands shook, nevertheless he seemed in excellent spirits. The last time Liberty had had the pleasure of Charlie's company at table, he had eaten three peas separately in the course of an hour. He had told her fortune in a glass of water and then taken a bite out of the glass.

"Been too long, man," Charlie said to Willie, shaking his hand. "Hi, doll," he said to Liberty.

Charlie ordered eggs, ham, fried mush, orange juice, milk and coffee cake. "I love this place, man," he said. "These are good people, these are *religious* people. You know what's on the bottom of the pie pans? There are *messages* on the bottoms of the pie pans, embossed in the aluminum. Janiella got a pineapple cream cheese pie here last week and it said *Wise men shall seek Him,* man. Isn't that something? The last crumbs expose a Christian message! You should bring a sweet potato pie home, Liberty, get yourself a message."

"There are too many messages in Liberty's life already," Willie said. "Liberty is on some terrible mailing lists."

"Yeah," Charlie nodded. "Yesterday, I got a letter from Greenpeace. They're the ones who want to stop the slaughter of the harp seals, right? Envelope had a picture of a cuddly little white seal and the words *Kiss This Baby Good-Bye.* You get that one, Liberty?"

"Yes," Liberty said.

"You know what those Greenpeace guys did one year? They sprayed green dye all over the seals. Fashion fuckers don't want any *green* baby seal coats, right!" Charlie laughed his high cackling laugh. The Mennonites glanced up from their biscuits and thin pink gravy.

Liberty ordered only coffee and looked at Charlie, at his handsome ruined face. He was a Cajun. His mother still lived in Lafayette, Louisiana. She was a "treater" whose specialty was curing warts over the phone.

"Janiella has a fur coat," Charlie said. "She has lots of lousy habits. She never shuts doors for example. I have to tell you what happened. I was there yesterday, right? I'm beneath the sheets truffling away and her kid comes in. He's forgotten his spelling book. His spelling book! 'Mommy,' he says, 'have you seen my spelling book?' I'm crouched beneath the rosy sheets. My ears are ringing! I try to be very still, but I'm *gagging,* man, and Janiella says sweetly, 'I saw your spelling book in the wastebasket,' and the kid says, 'It must have fallen in there by accident,' and Janiella says, 'You are always saying that, Ted. You are always placing things you don't like in the wastebasket. I found that lovely Dunnsmoor sweater I gave you in the wastebasket. That lovely coloring book on knights and armor from the Metropolitan Museum was in the wastebasket also.' 'I'm too old for coloring books,' the kid says. Picture it, man, they are having a *discussion.* They are arguing fine points."

Liberty did not want to picture it. Breakfast had been placed before them on the table. Charlie looked at the food in surprise.

"Well?" Willie said.

Charlie seemed to be losing his drift. He kept looking at his food as though he were trying to read it.

"So what happened?" Willie insisted. "Finally."

"Well, I don't know, man. The future is not altogether scrutable."

"Janiella and Teddy," Willie said, glancing at Liberty. "The spelling book."

Charlie giggled. "I fell asleep. The last thing I heard was the kid saying, 'I thought Daddy was playing in Kansas City.' I passed out from the heat, man."

"Playing in Kansas City?" Willie asked. He poured syrup on his fried mush. Liberty reached over and scooped up a bit for herself with her coffee spoon.

"He's a baseball player. He catches fly balls and wears a handlebar mustache and spits a lot. I think he suspects something. They've got this immense swimming pool wherein Janiella and I often fool around and there was this little rubber frog that drifted around in it, trailing chlorine from his bottom. Cute little frog with a happy smile, his rubber legs crossed and his rubber eyes happy? Well Mr. Mean came home last weekend and took his twelve-gauge and blasted that poor little froggy to smithereens."

Liberty grimaced. Willie asked Charlie, "Who does Teddy think you are, a visiting uncle?"

"We've never met. I've only laid eyes on him in a photo cube. Janiella wants to keep him out of the house and she's got him busy every minute. He has soccer practice, swim team, safe boating instruction. He's hardly ever at home. After school, he takes special courses in computer language, calligraphy, backgammon. Poor little squirt comes staggering home, his brain on *fire*. I think of myself as a fantastic impetus to his learning."

"Liberty's not happy with this situation at all," Willie said.

"Liberty's all right," Charlie grinned, showing his pale gums. "Liberty's a great girl." The waitress arrived and warily placed a pint carton of milk by Charlie's right hand. The carton of milk had a straw sticking out of it. "Oh look at that!" Charlie exclaimed. "I love this place. You gotta get a pie, Liberty. Bring it home to Clem. He'd scarf it down and get some words. *Be zealous and repent.* Dog'd go wild!"

Liberty reached across to Willie's plate and spooned up another small piece of mush.

"That's extremely irritating," Willie said. "You never order anything and then you eat what I order."

Liberty blushed.

"Liberty!" Charlie cried, "eat off my plate, I beseech you! Let's mix a little yin and yang!" He speared a piece of coffee cake with his fork and fed it to her.

"It's just one of those things," Willie said, "that has been going on for years." He looked unhappily at his plate.

"Really, man, you're losing energy with these negative emotions. You're just going dim on us, man," Charlie said.

"All right," Willie said to Liberty, "let's talk about you for awhile. Tell me something you've never told me before."

"She's going to say 'David,' " Charlie said. He brushed his fingers lightly across the veins in Liberty's wrist.

"David?" Liberty asked. "Who is David?"

"David is the boy you never slept with," Willie said. "David is your lost opportunity."

"I think we're talking too loud," Charlie yelled. "These are polite, God-fearing people. Their babies come by UPS. Big brown Turtle-Waxed trucks turn into their little lanes. They have to sign for them, the babies. The babies grow up to be just like these old geezers here. Nevertheless, it's better to get babies by UPS. The sound of two bodies yattering together to produce a baby is a terrible thing really."

"With David you would be another kind of woman," Willie said. "At this very moment, you could be with David, cuddling David. After you cuddled, you could arise, dress identically in your scarlet union suits, chino pants, ragg socks, Bass boots, British seaman pullovers and down cruiser vests and go out and remodel old churches for use as private residences in fashionable New England coastal towns."

"But David," sighed Charlie, "is missing and presumed at rest."

"Change the present," Willie said. "Through the present, change the future and through the future, the past. Today is the result of some past. If we change today, we change the past."

Charlie shook his head. "Too much to put on a pie plate, man. Besides, it doesn't sound Christian."

"If you were another kind of woman," Willie said, "you could be married to Clay, the lawyer, dealing in torts. You'd have two little ones, Rocky and Sandy. They'd have red hair and be hyperactive. They'd be the terror of the car pool. Clay would have his nuts tied."

"Oh please, man," Charlie exclaimed.

"You and Clay would fly to your vacations in your very own private plane. You'd know French. You'd gain a small reputation as a photographer of wildflowers, really bringing out the stamens and pistils in a studious but quite improper way. Women would flock to the better department stores in order to buy the address books in which your photos appeared. With menopause would come a change in faith, however. You'd get bored with your recipes and your BMW. You'd stop taking dirty pictures. You'd divorce Clay."

"I knew it, I knew it!" shouted Charlie. "There he'd be with his useless nuts!"

"You'd become a believer in past lives. You'd become fascinated with other forms of intelligent life. You'd see that Christ had returned as a humpback whale. You'd become involved in the study of whale language."

"Oh, I love whales too, man," Charlie said, spilling coffee down the front of his pink button-down shirt. "They are poets in tune with every aspect of their world. They sing these songs, man."

"You'd curse the house in Nantucket that Rocky and Sandy had spent so many happy summers in."

"Ahhh, Nantucket, built on blood. Let's abandon this subject," Charlie said. He looked sadly at his shirt. "I've got to throw up, man, the happy vomiter has got to leave you now." He sighed and remained seated. "God is unrelenting and bitchier than a woman, I swear. What do you say, Liberty?"

"Liberty's song is a little garbled," Willie said.

"Aren't ours all," Charlie said graciously. "Ubble-gubble."
He smiled at Liberty, who tried to meet his thoughtful, thick-
ened gaze. She wished that she could watch him without being
seen. The considerable fact that she was attracted to him made
her feel morbid. *things i would like,* she thought, *things i would
never do.* She had to get started on that list.

"Except for Clem's song," Charlie was saying. The dog was
visible from their table, lying beneath the palm tree, his paws
crossed, yawning. A sheriff's deputy sat nearby in his cruiser,
looking at him as though he'd like to write out a ticket. "Clem's
song is serene. How'd you get such a great dog, Liberty?"

"He came in on the night air and settled on her head as she
slept," Willie said.

"Gubble-ubble," Charlie said.

"He was in the envelope with the marriage license," Willie
said. "We sprinkled a little water on him and he puffed up and
was made soul."

"Leave this creep and come away with me," Charlie said.

Willie said, "We got him from the Humane Society. He ate
a child. The police impounded him but what could they do,
after all, this isn't the Middle Ages, we don't hang animals for
crimes. And he was an innocent, a victim himself, belonging
to a schizophrenic, anorectic unwed mother who kept leaving
her infant son alone with him, unfed, in her fleabag apartment."

Charlie said, "I mean it. I love married women. I treat them
right. Your blood will race, I'm telling you. I'm also a cook. I
make great meat loaf, no, forget meat loaf, I'll make gumbo.
I'm third in line for two acres of land in St. Landry Parish. Only
two people have to die and it's all mine. It's got a chinaberry
tree on it. We'll go to cockfights and pole the bayous and drink
beer and eat gumbo."

"Actually," Willie said, "she found him sitting in the road.
He'd been hit by a car. His eye was in a ditch of water hya-
cinths, being examined by two ducks. Blood all over the place.
What a mess."

"Everything's so relative with you, man. I don't know how

you make it through the day," Charlie said. He gazed at Liberty, absorbed.

"A linear life is a tedious life," Willie said. "Man wasn't born to suffer leading his life from moment to moment."

"I love quiet married women," Charlie said. "Their lack of fidelity thrills me. But I am coming to the conclusion that Janiella talks too much. Even *in situ,* she's gabbing away. And she's into very experimental stuff. There are not as many ways of making love as people seem to believe. Janiella may not be for me, actually."

"I'm splitting," Willie announced.

"I think you're making a fetish out of the real world," Charlie said, looking at Willie glumly. He rubbed his face hard with his hands. He wanted a drink, Liberty knew. He had that look in his dark eyes. "And seriously, man, about these people you've been saving, I don't know, I mean about those *old* people particularly. I would allow them to go under if I were you. They might buy another Mercedes and take a wrong turn this time right into school recess. See them! Barreling through shrieking groups of shepherd's-pie-stained Bubble-Yum T-shirts, hand-tooled pointy-toed cowboy boots and small rucksacks stickered with hearts, flattening little hands holding baby bunnies, little sunburned arms . . ." He shook his head. "And that bugger you saved . . ."

"Bugger?" Willie looked rattled.

"You saved a bugger," Charlie said morosely.

"He saved someone who had called his mother a 'bugger' is what I said," Liberty said. "That's what the mother told me."

"You're so literal," Willie said to Liberty. "What the young man said to me was that getting struck by lightning didn't feel like getting laid."

"Well, now *that's* expected," Charlie said. "It's well known that people say mechanical things under certain circumstances."

"Liberty prefers not to read between the lines," Willie said. "The clearly visible is exhausting enough, she feels."

"Liberty's a great girl," Charlie said. "A girl of romantic sensibility, a girl who cares."

"Liberty is a highly depressed individual," Willie said.

"Whatever," Charlie said cheerfully. "Building, building."

Willie stood up and leaned slightly toward Liberty, his hands on the table. His hands were tanned and strong and clean. His wedding band was slender. Liberty remembered the wedding clearly. It had taken place in a lush green tropical forest in the time of the dinosaurs. "I've got to shake myself a little loose," he said, "do you want the truck?"

"No," Liberty said.

"Just a few days," Willie said. "Later," he said to Charlie. He left.

"A butterfly vanishes from the world of caterpillars," Charlie said.

Liberty saw Clem get up and look after the truck as it drove away. He trotted over to the restaurant and peered in, resting his muzzle on a window box of geraniums. Liberty waved to him.

"He can't see that," Charlie said. "Animals live in a two-dimensional world. For example, like with roads? To a dog, each road is a separate phenomenon which has nothing in common with another road."

"That sounds about right," Liberty said. She watched Clem nibble on a pink geranium. His bad eye was like a smooth stone.

"There are lots of roads," Charlie said. He picked up her hand and kissed her palm. "I love you," he said.

Liberty smiled. "Janiella's your married woman."

He shook his head and blew softly on her palm. "There's only you," he said.

"You're a bottle man," Liberty said.

"Liberty!" a child's voice called. It was Teddy, standing by the bakery counter. He hurried over, shoelaces flapping, holding a waxed bag. "Mommy sent me here for rolls because Daddy's home and they're fighting." He sat on Liberty's lap while she tied the laces.

Charlie closed his eyes.

"Who is that?" Teddy demanded.

"My man," Charlie said, "we were just discussing running away together."

"I want to go too," Teddy said. "You won't make me memorize poetry, will you?"

"What kind of monsters do you think we are?" Charlie said.

"My mother makes me do a lot of memorizing. I'm going to go to boarding school next year. 'Marriage needs room,' she says." Teddy pointed to a shelf on the far wall of items for sale —palm canes, dolls, cream pitchers in the shape of cows. "I bought my mother one of those for her birthday," Teddy said, pointing at a cow.

Charlie's long face looked sad. "That touches me," he said. "I have been touched. I have been reached now for sure and I suddenly see things clearly. This is us," he said, touching their arms. "We should do something about us."

"Did this ever happen before?" Teddy asked, his arms lightly encircling Liberty's neck. "It all seems a little familiar."

"A very common feeling in childhood," Charlie said. "Stuff that should have happened but didn't has to keep trying to happen until it does."

Liberty shook her head and smiled.

"Look at this pretty lady smile," Charlie said to Teddy. "I love this lady. I've loved her for a long time. It's been a secret just between us but now you know too."

"I want to run away with you and Liberty and Clem," Teddy said.

"A beautiful woman, a smart dog, a little kid and yours truly," Charlie said. "We can do it! We will become myths in the minds of others. They will say about us," he leaned forward and lowered his voice, "that we all went out for breakfast and never returned."

"Good," Teddy said.

"So where shall we go?" Charlie said. He kissed Liberty's face. The line of people waiting to be seated, old women in bonnets, holding one another's hands, looked at them in alarm.

"There's no place to go," Liberty said.

"There are many places to go," Charlie said. "Hundreds."

"Let's make a list, I love lists!" Teddy said.

"We're the nuclear unit scrambling out, the improbable family whose salvation is at hand," Charlie said. "We'll go to Idaho, British Columbia, New Zealand, the Costa del Sol. We'll go to Nepal. No, forget Nepal, all those tinkly little bells would drive us crazy. What do you say, we'll go to Paraguay. That's where Jesse James went."

"That's where the Germans went," Liberty said. "Jesse James just died."

"You're right," Charlie said. "It wasn't Paraguay. It was Patagonia where Butch Cassidy and the Sundance Kid went." He was fidgeting now. His dark eyes glittered.

"They were outlaws," Teddy said.

"They were outlaws," Charlie said. "Successful outlaws."

"Why are you crying?" Teddy asked Liberty. "Are you crying?"

"We've got to move along, it's later than we think," Charlie said. "How about some lunch?"

Taking Care

*J*ONES, the preacher, has been in love all his life. He is baffled by this because as far as he can see, it has never helped anyone, even when they have acknowledged it, which is not often. Jones's love is much too apparent and arouses neglect. He is like an animal in a traveling show who, through some aberration, wears a vital organ outside the skin, awkward and unfortunate, something that shouldn't be seen, certainly something that shouldn't be watched working. Now he sits on a bed beside his wife in the self-care unit of a hospital fifteen miles from their home. She has been committed here for tests. She is so weak, so tired. There is something wrong with her blood. Her arms are covered with bruises where they have gone into the veins. Her hip, too, is blue and swollen where they have drawn out samples of bone marrow. All of this is frightening. The doctors are severe and wise, answering Jones's questions in a way that makes him feel hopelessly deaf. They have told him that there really is no such thing as a disease of the blood, for the blood is not a living tissue but a passive vehicle for the transportation of food, oxygen and waste. They have told him that abnormalities in the blood corpuscles, which his wife seems to have, must be regarded as symptoms of disease elsewhere in the body. They have shown him, upon request, slides and charts of normal and pathological blood cells which look to Jones like canapés. They speak (for he insists) of leukocytosis, myelocytes and megaloblasts. None of this takes into ac-

count the love he has for his wife! Jones sits beside her in this
dim pleasant room, wearing a grey suit and his clerical collar,
for when he leaves her he must visit other parishioners who are
patients here. This part of the hospital is like a motel. One may
wear one's regular clothes. The rooms have ice-buckets, rugs
and colorful bedspreads. How he wishes that they were traveling and staying overnight, this night, in a motel. A nurse comes
in with a tiny paper cup full of pills. There are three pills, or
rather, capsules, and they are not for his wife but for her blood.
The cup is the smallest of its type that Jones has ever seen. All
perspective, all sense of time and scale seem abandoned in this
hospital. For example, when Jones turns to kiss his wife's hair,
he nicks the air instead.

Jones and his wife have one child, a daughter, who, in turn, has
a single child, a girl, born one-half year ago. Jones's daughter
has fallen in with the stars and is using the heavens, as Jones
would be the first to admit, more than he ever has. It has,
however, brought her only grief and confusion. She has left her
husband and brought the baby to Jones. She has also given him
her dog. She is going to Mexico where soon, in the mountains,
she will have a nervous breakdown. Jones does not know this,
but his daughter has seen it in the stars and is going out to meet
it. Jones quickly agrees to care for both the baby and the dog,
as this seems to be the only thing his daughter needs from him.
The day of the baby's birth is secondary to the position of the
planets and the terms of houses, quadrants and gradients. Her
symbol is a bareback rider. To Jones, this is a graceful thought.
It signifies audacity. It also means luck. Jones slips a twenty
dollar bill in the pocket of his daughter's suitcase and drives her
to the airport. The plane taxis down the runway and Jones
waves, holding all their luck in his arms.

One afternoon, Jones had come home and found his wife
sitting in the garden, weeping. She had been transplanting
flowers, putting them in pots before the first frost came. There
was dirt on her forehead and around her mouth. Her light

clothes felt so heavy. Their weight made her body ache. Each breath was a stone she had to swallow. She cried and cried in the weak autumn sunshine. Jones could see the veins throbbing in her neck. "I'm dying," she said. "It's taking me months to die." But after he had brought her inside, she insisted that she felt better and made them both a cup of tea while Jones potted the rest of the plants and carried them down cellar. She lay on the sofa and Jones sat beside her. They talked quietly with one another. Indeed, they were almost whispering, as though they were in a public place surrounded by strangers instead of in their own house with no one present but themselves. "It's the season," Jones said. "In fall everything slows down, retreats. I'm feeling tired myself. We need iron. I'll go to the druggist right now and buy some iron tablets." His wife agreed. She wanted to go with him, for the ride. Together they ride, through the towns, for miles and miles, even into the next state. She does not want to stop driving. They buy sandwiches and milkshakes and eat in the car. Jones drives. They have to buy more gasoline. His wife sits close to him, her eyes closed, her head tipped back against the seat. He can see the veins beating on in her neck. Somewhere there is a dreadful sound, almost audible. "First I thought it was my imagination," his wife said. "I couldn't sleep. All night I would stay awake, dreaming. But it's not in my head. It's in my ears, my eyes. They ache. Everything. My tongue. My hair. The tips of my fingers are dead." Jones pressed her cold hand to his lips. He thinks of something mad and loving better than he—running out of control, deeply in the darkness of his wife. "Just don't make me go to the hospital," she pleaded. Of course she will go there. The moment has already occurred.

Jones is writing to his daughter. He received a brief letter from her this morning, telling him where she could be reached. The foreign postmark was so large that it almost obliterated Jones's address. She did not mention either her mother or the baby, which makes Jones feel peculiar. His life seems increate as his God's life, perhaps even imaginary. His daughter tells him about the town in which she lives. She does not plan to stay there long. She wants to travel. She will find out exactly what she wants to do and then she will come home again. The town is poor but interesting and there are many Americans there her own age. There is a zoo right on the beach. Almost all the towns, no matter how small, have little zoos. There are primarily eagles and hawks in the cages. And what can Jones reply to that? He writes *Every thing is fine here. We are burning wood from the old apple tree in the fire place and it smells wonderful. Has the baby had her full series of polio shots? Take care.* Jones uses this expression constantly, usually in totally unwarranted situations, as when he purchases pipe cleaners or drives through toll booths. Distracted, Jones writes off the edge of the paper and onto the blotter. He must begin again. He will mail this on the way to the hospital. They have been taking X-rays for three days now but the pictures are cloudy. They cannot read them. His wife is now in a real sickbed with high metal sides. He sits with her while she eats her dinner. She asks him to take her good nightgown home and wash it with a bar of Ivory. They won't let her do anything now, not even wash out a few things. *You must take care.*

Jones is driving down a country road. It is the first snowfall of the season and he wants to show it to the baby who rides beside him in a small cushioned car seat all her own. Her head is almost on a level with his and she looks earnestly at the landscape, sometimes smiling. They follow the road that winds tightly between fields and deep pine woods. Everything is white and clean. It has been snowing all afternoon and is doing so still, but very very lightly. Fat snowflakes fall solitary against the windshield. Sometimes the baby reaches out for them. Sometimes she gives a brief kick and cry of joy. They have done their errands. Jones has bought milk and groceries and two yellow roses which lie wrapped in tissue and newspaper in the trunk, in the cold. He must buy two on Saturday as the florist is closed on Sunday. He does not like to do this but there is no alternative. The roses do not keep well. Tonight he will give one to his wife. The other he will pack in sugar water and store in the refrigerator. He can only hope that the bud will remain tight until Sunday when he brings it into the terrible heat of the hospital. The baby rocks against the straps of her small carrier. Her lips are pursed as she watches intently the fields, the grey stalks of crops growing out of the snow, the trees. She is warmly dressed and she wears a knitted orange cap. The cap is twenty-three years old, the age of her mother. Jones found it just the other day. It has faded almost to pink on one side. At one time, it must have been stored in the sun. Jones, driving, feels almost gay. The snow is so beautiful. Everything is white. Jones is an educated man. He has read Melville, who says that white is the colorless all-color of atheism from which we shrink. Jones does not believe this. He sees a holiness in snow, a promise. He hopes that his wife will know that it is snowing even though she is separated from the window by a curtain. Jones sees something moving across the snow, a part of the snow itself, running. Although he is going slowly, he takes his foot completely off the accelerator. "Look, darling, a snowshoe rabbit." At the sound of his voice, the baby stretches open her mouth and narrows her eyes in soundless glee. The hare is splendid. So fast! It flows around invisible obstructions, something out of a kind dream. It flies across the ditch, its paws like paddles, faintly yellow, the color of raw wood. "Look, sweet," cries Jones, "how big he is!" But suddenly the hare is curved and falling, round as a ball, its feet and head tucked closely against its body. It strikes the road and skids upside down for several yards. The car passes around it, avoids it. Jones brakes and stops, amazed. He opens the door and trots back to the animal. The baby twists about in her seat as well as she can and peers after him. It is as though the animal had never been alive at all. Its head is broken in several places. Jones bends to touch its fur, but straightens again, not doing so. A man emerges from the woods, swinging a shotgun. He nods at Jones and picks the hare up by the ears. As he walks away, the hare's legs rub across the ground. There are small crystal stains on the snow. Jones returns to the car. He wants to apologize but he does not know to whom or for what. His life has been devoted to apologetics. It is his profession. He is concerned with both justification and remorse. He has always acted rightly, but nothing has ever come of it. He gets in the car, starts the engine. "Oh, sweet," he says to the baby. She smiles at him, exposing her tooth. At home that night, after the baby's supper, Jones reads a story to her. She is asleep, panting in her sleep, but Jones tells her the story of al-Boraq, the milk-white steed of Mohammed, who could stride out of the sight of mankind with a single step.

Jones sorts through a collection of records, none of which have been opened. They are still wrapped in cellophane. The jacket designs are subdued, epic. Names, instruments and orchestras are mentioned confidently. He would like to agree with their importance, for he knows that they have worth, but he is not familiar with the references. His daughter brought these records with her. They had been given to her by an older man, a professor she had been having an affair with. Naturally, this pains Jones. His daughter speaks about the men she has been involved with but no longer cares about. Where did these men come from? Where were they waiting and why have they gone? Jones remembers his daughter when she was a little girl, helping him rake leaves. What can he say? For years on April Fool's Day, she would take tobacco out of his humidor and fill it with corn flakes. Jones is full of remorse and astonishment. When he saw his daughter only a few weeks ago, she was thin and nervous. She had torn out almost all her eyebrows with her fingers from this nervousness. And her lashes. The roots of her eyes were white, like the bulbs of flowers. Her fingernails were crudely bitten, some bleeding below the quick. She was tough and remote, wanting only to go on a trip for which she had a ticket. What can he do? He seeks her in the face of the baby but she is not there. All is being both continued and resumed, but the dream is different. The dream cannot be revived. Jones breaks into one of the albums, blows the dust from the needle, plays a record. Outside it is dark. The parsonage is remote and the only buildings nearby are barns. The river cannot be seen. The music is Bruckner's *Te Deum.* Very nice. Dedicated to God. He plays the other side. A woman, Kathleen Ferrier, is singing in German. Jones cannot understand the words but the music stuns him. *Kindertotenlieder.* It is devastating. In college he had studied only scientific German, the vocabulary of submarines, dirigibles and steam engines. Jones plays the record again and again, searching for his old grammar. At last he finds it. The wings of insects are between some of the pages. There are notes in pencil, written in his own young hand.

RENDER:

A. WAS THE TEACHER SATISFIED WITH YOU TODAY?

B. NO, HE WAS NOT. MY ESSAY WAS GOOD BUT IT WAS NOT COPIED WELL.

C. I AM SORRY YOU WERE NOT INDUSTRIOUS THIS TIME FOR YOU GENERALLY ARE.

These lessons are neither of life or death. Why was he instructed in them? In the hospital, his wife waits to be translated, no longer a woman, the woman whom he loves, but a situation. Her blood moves mysteriously as constellations. She is under scrutiny and attack and she has abandoned Jones. She is a swimmer waiting to get on with the drowning. Jones is on the shore. In Mexico, his daughter walks along the beach with two men. She is acting out a play that has become her life. Jones is on the mountaintop. The baby cries and Jones takes her from the crib to change her. The dog paws the door. Jones lets him out. He settles down with the baby and listens to the record. He still cannot make out many of the words. The baby wiggles restlessly on his lap. Her eyes are a foal's eyes, navy-blue. She has grown in a few weeks to expect everything from Jones. He props her on one edge of the couch and goes to her small toy box where he keeps a bear, a few rattles and balls. On the way, he opens the door and the dog immediately enters. His heavy coat is cold, fragrant with ice. He noses the baby and she squeals.

Oft denk'ich, sie sind nur ausgegangen
Bald werden sie wieder nach Hause gelangen

Jones selects a bright ball and pushes it gently in her direction.

It is Sunday morning and Jones is in the pulpit. The church is very old but the walls of the sanctuary have recently been painted a pale blue. In the cemetery adjoining, some of the graves are three hundred years old. It has become a historical landmark and no one has been buried there since World War I. There is a new place, not far away, which the families now use. Plots are marked not with stones but with small tablets, and immediately after any burial, workmen roll grassed sod over the new graves so that there is no blemish on the grounds, not even for a little while. Present for today's service are seventy-eight adults, eleven children and the junior choir. Jones counts them as the offertory is received. The church rolls say that there are three hundred fifty members but as far as Jones can see, everyone is here today. This is the day he baptizes the baby. He has made arrangements with one of the ladies to hold her and bring her up to the font at the end of the first hymn. The baby looks charming in a lacy white dress. Jones has combed her fine hair carefully, slicking it in a curl with water, but now it has dried and it sticks up awkwardly like the crest of a kingfisher. Jones bought the dress in Mammoth Mart, an enormous store which has a large metal elephant dressed in overalls dancing on the roof. He feels foolish at buying it there but he had gone to several stores and that is where he saw the prettiest dress. He blesses the baby with water from the silver bowl. He says, *We are saved not because we are worthy. We are saved because we are loved.* It is a brief ceremony. The baby, looking curiously at Jones, is taken out to the nursery. Jones begins his sermon. He can't remember when he wrote it, but here it is, typed, in front of him. *There is nothing wrong in what one does but there is something wrong in what one becomes.* He finds this questionable but goes on speaking. He has been preaching for thirty-four years. He is gaunt with belief. But his wife has a red cell count of only 2.3 millions. It is not enough! She is not getting enough oxygen! Jones is giving his sermon. Somewhere he has lost what he was looking for. He must have known once, surely. The congregation sways, like the wings of a ray in water. It is Sunday and for patients it is a holiday. The doctors don't visit. There are no tests or diagnoses. Jones would like to leave, to walk down the aisle and out into the winter, where he would read his words into the ground. Why can't he remember his life! He finishes, sits down, stands up to present communion. Tiny cubes of bread lie in a slumped pyramid. They are offered and received. Jones takes his morsel, hacked earlier from a sliced enriched loaf with his own hand. It is so dry, almost wicked. The very thought now sickens him. He chews it over and over again, but it lies unconsumed, like a muscle in his mouth.

Jones is waiting in the lobby for the results of his wife's operation. Has there ever been a time before dread? He would be grateful even to have dread back, but it has been lost, for a long time, in rapid possibility, probability and fact. The baby sits on his knees and plays with his tie. She woke very early this morning for her orange juice and then gravely, immediately, spit it all up. She seems fine now, however, her fingers exploring Jones's tie. Whenever he looks at her, she gives him a dazzling smile. He has spent most of the day fiercely cleaning the house, changing the bed-sheets and the pages of the many calendars that hang in the rooms, things he should have done a week ago. He has dusted and vacuumed and pressed all his shirts. He has laundered all the baby's clothes, soft small sacks and gowns and sleepers which froze in his hands the moment he stepped outside. And now he is waiting and watching his wristwatch. The tumor is precisely this size, they tell him, the size of his clock's face.

Jones has the baby on his lap and he is feeding her. The evening meal is lengthy and complex. First he must give her vitamins, then, because she has a cold, a dropper of liquid

aspirin. This is followed by a bottle of milk, eight ounces, and
a portion of strained vegetables. He gives her a rest now so that
the food can settle. On his hip, she rides through the rooms
of the huge house as Jones turns lights off and on. He comes
back to the table and gives her a little more milk, a half jar of
strained chicken and a few spoonfuls of dessert, usually cobbler,
buckle or pudding. The baby enjoys all equally. She is good.
She eats rapidly and neatly. Sometimes she grasps the spoon,
turns it around and thrusts the wrong end into her mouth. Of
course there is nothing that cannot be done incorrectly. Jones
adores the baby. He sniffs her warm head. Her birth is a deep
error, an abstraction. Born in wedlock but out of love. He puts
her in the playpen and tends to the dog. He fills one dish with
water and one with horsemeat. He rinses out the empty can
before putting it in the wastebasket. The dog eats with great
civility. He eats a little meat and then takes some water, then
meat, then water. When the dog has finished, the dishes are
as clean as though they'd been washed. Jones now thinks about
his own dinner. He opens the refrigerator. The ladies of the
church have brought brownies, venison, cheese and apple
sauce. There are turkey pies, pork chops, steak, haddock and
sausage patties. A brilliant light exposes all this food. There is
so much of it. It must be used. A crust has formed around the
punctures in a can of Pet. There is a clear bag of chicken livers
stapled shut. There are large brown eggs in a bowl. Jones stares
unhappily at the beads of moisture on cartons and bottles, at
the pearls of fat on the cold cooked stew. He sits down. The
room is full of lamps and cords. He thinks of his wife, her
breathing body deranged in tubes, and begins to shake. All
objects here are perplexed by such grief.

Now it is almost Christmas and Jones is walking down by the
river, around an abandoned house. The dog wades heavily
through the snow, biting it. There are petals of ice on the tree
limbs and when Jones lingers under them, the baby puts out
her hand and her mouth starts working because she would like
to have it, the ice, the branch, everything. His wife will be

coming home in a few days, in time for Christmas. Jones has already put up the tree and brought the ornaments down from the attic. He will not trim it until she comes home. He wants very much to make a fine occasion out of opening the boxes of old decorations. The two of them have always enjoyed this greatly in the past. Jones will doubtlessly drop and smash a bauble, for he does every year. He tramps through the snow with his small voyager. She dangles in a shoulder sling, her legs wedged around his hip. They regard the rotting house seriously. Once it was a doctor's home and offices but long before Jones's time, the doctor, who was very respected, had been driven away because a town girl accused him of fathering her child. The story goes that all the doctor said was, "Is that so?" This incensed the town and the girl's parents, who insisted that he take the child as soon as it was born. He did and he cared for the child very well even though his practice was ruined and no one had anything to do with him. A year later the girl told the truth—that the actual father was a young college boy whom she was now going to marry. They wanted the child back, and the doctor willingly returned the infant to them. Of course it is a very old, important story. Jones has always appreciated it, but now he is annoyed at the man's passivity. His wife's sickness has changed everything for Jones. He will continue to accept but he will no longer surrender. Surely things are different for Jones now.

For insurance purposes, Jones's wife is brought out to the car in a wheelchair. She is thin and beautiful. Jones is grateful and confused. He has a mad wish to tip the orderly. Have so many years really passed? Is this not his wife, his love, fresh from giving birth? Isn't everything about to begin? In Mexico, his daughter wanders disinterestedly through a jewelry shop where she picks up a small silver egg. It opens on a hinge and inside are two figures, a bride and groom. Jones puts the baby in his wife's arms. At first the baby is alarmed because she cannot remember this person very well and she reaches for Jones, whimpering. But soon she is soothed by his wife's soft voice and she falls asleep in her arms as they drive. Jones has readied everything carefully for his wife's homecoming. The house is clean and orderly. For days he has restricted himself to only one part of the house so that his clutter will be minimal. Jones helps his wife up the steps to the door. Together they enter the shining rooms.

JOY WILLIAMS is the author of four novels, including *The Quick and the Dead,* which was a finalist for the Pulitzer Prize in 2001, and three collections of stories including *Honored Guest,* as well as *Ill Nature,* a book of essays that was a finalist for the National Book Critics Circle Award for criticism. Among her many honors are the Rea Award for the short story and the Strauss Living Award from the American Academy of Arts and Letters. She lives in Key West, Florida, and Tucson, Arizona.

Printed in the United States
by Baker & Taylor Publisher Services